# TURN UP THE
# LIGHT

Published by Intend® Publishing
P.O. Box 331042 / Murfreesboro TN 37133-1042
intendministries.org

Printed in the United States of America

# TURN UP THE
# LIGHT

FACING EACH DAY
WITH THE STRENGTH OF GOD'S WORD

# G. ALLEN JACKSON

# A Message from Pastor Allen Jackson

This book is intended to add a little positive momentum to each day. Few things bring strength like God's Word and a moment of prayer. Your perspective on God's Word will shape the trajectory of your life. Each day arrives with opportunities and challenges. We can be hindered by the darkness or we can turn up the light! The redemptive work of Jesus and His life-giving words will bring strength and hope to every situation. He is faithful.

My prayer is that this devotional is a tool for you, helping you say yes to the Lord, whether you're on the mountaintop of life, or in the valley. I pray your heart is opened to the scriptures in a new way, and they are a source of freedom and wisdom for you and your family.

May God bless you on your journey.

## G. Allen Jackson
Pastor, World Outreach Church

## GOD DESIGNED FAMILY

*The LORD God said, "It is not good for the man to be alone. I will make a helper suitable for him." . . . So the LORD God caused the man to fall into a deep sleep; and while he was sleeping, he took one of the man's ribs and closed up the place with flesh. Then the LORD God made a woman from the rib he had taken out of the man, and he brought her to the man. The man said, "This is now bone of my bones and flesh of my flesh; she shall be called 'woman,' for she was taken out of man." For this reason a man will leave his father and mother and be united to his wife, and they will become one flesh.*

GENESIS 2:18, 21-24

God designed family. It's His idea. We didn't dream it up or develop it as a survival mechanism. It's a fundamental principle, and it is so important that God introduced it to us in the first chapters of the Bible—before His covenants with Noah and Abraham and before He gave the Ten Commandments. Let's work hard to strengthen our own families and defend God's design for the family in the marketplace of ideas.

## PRAYER

Heavenly Father, thank You for the idea of family. Thank You that You created us to live in relationship with one another in this way. We ask Your blessings and protection on our own families. Help us to keep our marriages and our families strong. Give us wisdom to know how to strengthen our families. In Jesus' name, amen.

# DAY 2

## LEARNING WITH HUMILITY

*And he said to them: "You have a fine way of setting aside the commands of God in order to observe your own traditions! For Moses said, 'Honor your father and your mother,' and, 'Anyone who curses his father or mother must be put to death.'"*

MARK 7:9-10

If you imagine yourself to be on the "younger" side of the age spectrum, I want to encourage you to have the humility and the willingness to respect and learn from those who are ahead of you. We have an amazing ability to observe our own traditions and set aside the instruction of God. We live in an age of pride, and our culture is one of almost unmitigated rebellion. And without God's help, pride and rebellion will keep us from learning—no matter our age.

## PRAYER

Heavenly Father, give me an attitude of humility and respect toward my elders. Help me appreciate their life experiences and the lessons I can learn from them. Renew in me the willingness to learn, for there is much about You I still need to understand. Thank You for the wisdom You promise. In Jesus' name, amen.

# DAY 3

## GOD AS CREATOR

*In the beginning God created the heavens and the earth.*

GENESIS 1:1

I believe there is a rationale for the way truth is presented in Scripture. I believe it is very purposeful that Genesis chapter 1, verse 1 tells us that in the beginning God created the heavens and the earth. The Bible is not a complete history of our universe, but if you will accept the truth of Genesis 1:1 as it is revealed to us, the rest of the Bible will open up and make sense. If you reject that truth, the rest of the Bible will be shrouded in mystery and will remain unknowable.

## PRAYER

Heavenly Father, open my eyes to Your Word. Give me understanding of its unchanging nature. Help me appreciate its majesty and trust in its unchanging truth even as the world scoffs at its claims. I am resting in Your truth. In Jesus' name, amen.

## UNWAVERING FAITH

*Against all hope, Abraham in hope believed and so became the father of many nations, just as it had been said to him, "So shall your offspring be."*

ROMANS 4:18

When Abraham was a young man, God invited him to leave his home and travel to the land God said He would show him. Inexplicably, Abraham packed up and moved. Decades came and went, and Abraham and Sarah still had not had the children God had promised them. God said, "I will see that My promise is worked out in your life," and Abraham believed Him. It's one thing to talk about faith when your life seems to be heading toward the conclusion you want. But to trust God when your life seems to be headed in the other direction is a difficult place. Unwavering faith does not just happen. It is built up in us as we consistently exercise faith in God's promises.

## PRAYER

Heavenly Father, I want to be absolutely unwavering in my belief in Your power to accomplish Your purposes in my life. Help me to stand firmly on the fact that You do not move, that Your love for me is constant, that You have the power to do everything You have promised. In the name of Jesus, amen.

# DAY 5

## GOD USES FAMILY

*This is how the birth of Jesus Christ came about: His mother Mary was pledged to be married to Joseph, but before they came together, she was found to be with child through the Holy Spirit. Because Joseph her husband was a righteous man and did not want to expose her to public disgrace, he had in mind to divorce her quietly. But after he had considered this, an angel of the Lord appeared to him in a dream and said, "Joseph son of David, do not be afraid to take Mary home as your wife, because what is conceived in her is from the Holy Spirit. She will give birth to a son, and you are to give him the name Jesus, because he will save his people from their sins."*

MATTHEW 1:18-21

The redemptive purposes of God were delivered to us through a family. God certainly didn't need a family to care for Jesus. He could have done it another way. If God could feed the Israelites in the desert and bring water from a rock He could have cared for an infant. He put Jesus in a family as a way of validating the system He put in place in Genesis 1-2, a system He wants us to abide by today.

## PRAYER

Thank You, Heavenly Father, for showing us so clearly the importance of family. Thank You that Mary and Joseph were willing to believe the impossible and fulfill the purposes You had for them. Thank You for being our Father and showing us love beyond measure. Thank You for sending Your Son to us as the ultimate gift of love. In His name I pray, amen.

# DAY 6

## GOD IS GLORIFIED IN OUR WEAKNESS

*God chose the foolish things of the world to shame the wise; God chose the weak things of the world to shame the strong. God chose the lowly things of this world and the despised things—and the things that are not—to nullify the things that are, so that no one may boast before him.*

1 CORINTHIANS 1:27-29

How does God make His glory evident in us? It's when His power and His strength and His grace are made evident in the places where our strength is insufficient and incomplete. God is saying, "I'm going to stand you on the stage of all eternity and do remarkable things. Everybody will watch, and when they look at you they will have to know I helped." That's my story. That's your story too. God intends for His Son to receive glory—for all eternity—for what is accomplished through your life and mine.

## PRAYER

Heavenly Father, thank You that Your strength is sufficient for me. Thank You that when I am weak You are strong. Thank You that Your grace is sufficient. Help me to give You all honor and glory for the good things that happen in my life, for it all comes from You. In the name of Jesus, amen.

G. ALLEN JACKSON

## INFLUENCING OUR FAMILY

*He decreed statutes for Jacob and established the law in Israel, which he commanded our forefathers to teach their children, so the next generation would know them, even the children yet to be born, and they in turn would tell their children. Then they would put their trust in God and would not forget his deeds but would keep his commands.*

PSALM 78:5-7

Parents are life trainers. That's the task commanded by God. The capacity of children to learn is staggering, and parents are to shape their character and their thinking. I meet parents who say, "Pastor, I don't want to influence my child's opinions. I want them to form their own." Who do you want to influence them? Advertisers? TV? The neighbor's kids? I'm all for teaching kids how to think for themselves, but God gave us the responsibility to influence that process for Him. Let's give our best efforts to training our young people and pray that we will have a generation of godly adults rising up around us.

## PRAYER

Heavenly Father, forgive us for turning our backs on Your truth. Give us perseverance to be godly parents and teachers. Grant us understanding hearts that we may walk in Your ways and influence our families for You. Through our lives may Your Kingdom come and Your will be done on earth. In Jesus' name, amen.

# DAY 8

## GOD IS OUR REFUGE

*And the God of all grace, who called you to his eternal glory in Christ, after you have suffered a little while, will himself restore you and make you strong, firm and steadfast.*

### 1 PETER 5:10

There is a myth in Christianity that goes like this: If you ever truly yielded your life to God, all your challenges and pain and difficulties would go away. And if you have challenges or pain or difficulties, it's because you haven't fully yielded or there is some dark corner you haven't swept clean. That is not a biblical idea. Jesus told a parable about two people who built two houses—one on sand and one on stone. When the same storm battered both houses, the house on stone stood while the house on sand collapsed. Being a Christ-follower does not remove us from the arena of human suffering, but we have a different set of resources. We have an Almighty God Who gives us strength and shelter in times of trouble and then restores us, all for His glory.

## PRAYER

Heavenly Father, how good You are to me! How faithful You are in times of trouble! Thank You for Your hedge of protection that keeps me from trouble—even trouble I never know about. Thank You for holding me close when the troubles of life are threatening to overwhelm me. Help me to be always grateful for Your watchful care over me. With a grateful heart, and in the name of Jesus. Amen.

# DAY 9

## IMAGE-BEARERS OF GOD

*God created man in his own image, in the image of God he created him;*
*male and female he created them.*

GENESIS 1:27

Human beings are the image-bearers of Almighty God. We are not simply the highest rung on the evolutionary ladder or the mammal with the most fully developed cognitive power. There is something that separates human beings from the rest of creation: We are created in the image of God. That single fact gives us an inherent dignity regardless of gender, race, assets, or IQ. Our fallen nature tempts us to categorize and label others and assign them relative worth, but God sees each of us as unique and valuable because we bear His image.

## PRAYER

Heavenly Father, thank You for creating us in Your image. Thank You for giving humans worth above anything else in Your created order. Give me discernment to see others through Your eyes and to love others as You love them. In Jesus' name, amen.

# DAY 10

## SALT AND LIGHT

*"You are the salt of the earth. But if the salt loses its saltiness, how can it be made salty again? It is no longer good for anything, except to be thrown out and trampled underfoot. You are the light of the world. A town built on a hill cannot be hidden. Neither do people light a lamp and put it under a bowl. Instead they put it on its stand, and it gives light to everyone in the house. In the same way, let your light shine before others, that they may see your good deeds and glorify your Father in heaven."*

MATTHEW 5:13-16

Being salt and light is our God-given assignment. And if we fail in that, Jesus said we will be cast out. Why is that assignment non-negotiable for us? Salt slows down corruption. It can't stop it completely, but it impedes its progress. And light dispels or at least diminishes the darkness. Without salt and light, corruption and darkness will cover the earth. The clear counsel of Scripture is that your life and mine should make a difference. Planet Earth is depending on the people of God. Jesus said so.

## PRAYER

Our Heavenly Father, thank You that Your Word makes Your expectations clear to me. Thank You for giving me examples that I can understand, such as salt and light. Help me to be salt and light not only in my church but in my family, my community, and the world. I trust You for the strength to do that. In Jesus' name, amen.

# DAY 11

## LION OF THE TRIBE OF JUDAH

*The lion has roared—who will not fear? The Sovereign LORD has spoken—who can but prophesy?*

AMOS 3:8

Jesus is identified in Scripture as the Lion of the Tribe of Judah. When we meet Him in the New Testament, He comes as a servant. We typically think of Jesus as a rather passive, soft-spoken gentleman who gathered in the corner with a few friends and shared with them pearls of wisdom and Kingdom instruction—until He was executed by the Romans. But the prophet Amos says, "The lion is going to roar." Jesus is coming back, and this time as a roaring lion.

## PRAYER

Heavenly Father, how I long for Jesus' return! I choose Him as Lord and King every day of my life as I await that day. Help me to live as if I will see You today, face to face. Thank You for the promise of eternity in Your glorious presence. In Jesus' holy name, amen.

# DAY 12

## IMITATORS OF GOD

*Be imitators of God, therefore, as dearly loved children.*

EPHESIANS 5:1

The most valuable lessons in our lives are caught; they come through observation. God designed children to be world-class imitators. The children in your house are learning from you how to live in the world. And one of the most constructive lessons you can teach by example is to speak positively about Christians and the Church. If all they hear is discontent with Christians and churches, when they are old enough to vote with their feet they'll vote no. You're training them what to love—don't fail to show them your passion for the things of the Living God.

## PRAYER

Heavenly Father, show us how to teach our children to thrive in life—not only physically but spiritually. Grant us the wisdom to make You our first priority so that our children will make You their first priority. Help us to be more like You so that we will be worthy of their imitation. Thank You for hearing my prayer. In Jesus' name, amen.

# DAY 13

## GOD'S WILL BE DONE

*Justice is driven back, and righteousness stands at a distance; truth has stumbled in the streets, honesty cannot enter. Truth is nowhere to be found, and whoever shuns evil becomes a prey. The LORD looked and was displeased that there was no justice. He saw that there was no one, he was appalled that there was no one to intervene.*

ISAIAH 59:14-16

God was displeased. He had looked for people to accomplish His purposes in the earth, and none of His people stepped forward. There is a perversion of the Gospel that is so rampant it's about to overwhelm the Church. It says, "God, may Your power be made evident in my life for my purposes. God, may all the resources of Heaven be put at my disposal for my satisfaction and my contentment." Jesus taught us to pray, "YOUR Kingdom come, YOUR will be done." Let us recommit ourselves to knowing and accomplishing the purposes of God.

## PRAYER

Heavenly Father, I come before You asking for a renewed passion to pursue Your purposes. Give me strength to recognize the detractors for what they are and push past them. Give me hope in the face of discouragement. I choose You in all things. In the name of Your Son, amen.

## UNSHAKEABLE TRUST

*Now he has promised, "Once more I will shake not only the earth but also the heavens."*

HEBREWS 12:26

If you haven't noticed, there's a whole lot of shaking going on in the world. The words "once more" indicate the removing of what can be shaken so that what cannot be shaken may remain. In a stable, secure environment it's hard to tell what is temporary and what is eternal. But when things begin to shake, it's obvious what is temporary and what is permanent. These shaking times are not reasons to be overwhelmed with fear and anxiety—they are invitations to put your trust in God's unshakeable Kingdom.

## PRAYER

Heavenly Father, thank You that You are eternal, unchanging, unshakeable. Give me discernment to see the difference between the temporary things of this world and the unshakeable things of Your Kingdom. Give me a greater desire for those unshakeable things than for the temporary things that tempt me away. And even amidst the shaking, help me trust in You. In Jesus' holy name, amen.

## HE IS ABOVE ALL THINGS

*God is our refuge and strength, an ever-present help in trouble. Therefore we will not fear, though the earth give way and the mountains fall into the heart of the sea, though its waters roar and foam and the mountains quake with their surging..."Be still, and know that I am God; I will be exalted among the nations, I will be exalted in the earth." The LORD Almighty is with us; the God of Jacob is our fortress.*

PSALM 46:1-11

Wherever we look in Scripture there is a declaration that the God we worship is Almighty, over and above all things. Too often we imagine God in the context of church, or doctrinal position, or church leadership, or even kindness. Those things are not wrong, but they paint an incomplete picture. Let us not forget that we worship the Living God, the God Almighty.

## PRAYER

Heavenly Father, I come before You in worship, acknowledging that You alone are God. There is none to confront You or challenge Your power. You are unmatched and unequaled in all things. I recognize that You are not like me, and I choose to put my trust and hope in You. Thank You that You are my refuge and strength, my ever-present help in trouble. In Jesus' name, amen.

# DAY 16

## THE LITTLE ONES

*"If anyone causes one of these little ones who believe in me to sin, it would be better for him to have a large millstone hung around his neck and to be drowned in the depths of the sea."*

MATTHEW 18:6

You'd need a preacher to mess that up! Jesus couldn't have made it any clearer: Do not cause trouble for one of these little people! No doubt the crowd that day struggled with what He was saying because they lived in a culture where children were considered laborers and were traded like cattle. Jesus introduced a dramatic shift in an ancient worldview when He said that children are valuable and deserve to be treated with dignity.

## PRAYER

Heavenly Father, thank You for the children You have placed in our care. Thank You for the pure love they have for You. Help me to love You like they do. Thank You for the privilege of showing them what it means to be a Christ-follower, and help me to do well with that task. I ask it in the name of Jesus, amen.

# DAY 17

## WE STILL BELIEVE

*I am not ashamed of the gospel, because it is the power of God for the salvation of everyone who believes: first for the Jew, then for the Gentile.*

ROMANS 1:16

When Paul wrote this to the church at Rome at the end of the first century, you can be assured it's because they were being pressured to doubt or deny the Gospel. Fast-forward to the 21st century, and that hasn't changed. If you have the audacity to say you believe that Jesus was the Son of God, He was born of a virgin, He died on a cross and was raised to life again, He ascended to Heaven, and He is coming back as the judge of all the earth, there are many who say, "You don't really believe that, do you?" Absolutely, I believe it! And I smile when I realize that we face some of the challenges that the earliest Christ-followers faced.

## PRAYER

Heavenly Father, thank You that Paul's words from so many centuries ago are just as relevant to me today. Help me to live every day so that others will see that I am not ashamed of the Gospel of Jesus Christ. Help me to be bold in the face of opposition. Thank You for Your free gift of salvation in Jesus Christ. In His name, amen.

# DAY 18

## CONFIDENCE IN GOD'S PLAN

*This is the word of the LORD concerning Israel . . . "I am going to make Jerusalem a cup that sends all the surrounding peoples reeling. Judah will be besieged as well as Jerusalem. On that day, when all the nations of the earth are gathered against her, I will make Jerusalem an immovable rock for all the nations. All who try to move it will injure themselves."*

### ZECHARIAH 12:1-3

We see this statement by God played out on the news every night—Jerusalem and Judah, the region that surrounds it, are literally encircled by hostility. Don't cringe when you see this happening. God is doing that. And if He creates the contention, He can protect His city and work out His purposes. What God said is coming to pass, and that adds credibility to the other things that He said.

## PRAYER

Heavenly Father, thank You that Your every word is true. Thank You for the confidence we can have in Your plan for the world. I pray for the peace of Jerusalem. I long for the day when Your purposes will be accomplished there and in the Middle East and in all the earth. May the name of Jesus be lifted up. In His name I pray, amen.

# DAY 19

## HUMILITY'S PROMISE

*"God opposes the proud but gives grace to the humble."*

JAMES 4:6

Humble is a fuzzy word, and I'm not sure we know what to do with it. I don't believe being humble means degrading or demeaning yourself. It's not a denial of the strengths and abilities and opportunities that God has given you. I think being humble is recognizing both what God created you to be and the reality of what you are not. But humility comes with a promise. Imagine that people are lining up in two lines. Get in one line, and you know God will oppose you. Get in the other line, and you know God will give you grace. Which line do you want to get in?

## PRAYER

Heavenly Father, thank You for the clear direction You give me in James 4:6. I thank you for the gifts and strengths you give me, acknowledging they come only by your grace and mercy. Let me share these abilities to your glory and service. Help me to always keep Your holiness and perfection in mind and to judge myself by it. In Jesus' name, amen.

# TRUST THROUGH THE STORM

*I urge you to keep up your courage, because not one of you will be lost; only the ship will be destroyed. Last night an angel of the God to whom I belong and whom I serve stood beside me and said, "Do not be afraid, Paul. You must stand trial before Caesar; and God has graciously given you the lives of all who sail with you."*

ACTS 27:22-24

Paul had been arrested in Jerusalem and subjected to a fixed trial. We find him chained to a Roman soldier on a ship bound for Rome, where he will appeal his case to Caesar. And that's when the storms begin. They've been battered for days. The sailors have thrown the cargo overboard. All hope is lost, and they are waiting to die. And then an angel shows up. I object a bit to God's timing. He could have sent Paul this message before he left Jerusalem and given the weary apostle a few more peaceful days of sailing. But God needed to tell Paul—and those who sailed with him—that because He had more work for Paul to do, He would spare the lives of everyone on the ship. And Paul, as always, took the opportunity to remind them that he belonged to a great God.

## PRAYER

Heavenly Father, You know that I sometimes have trouble seeing You, much less trusting You when the storms of life are raging all around me. Thank You that the message of Your angel was not just for Paul—it is also for me. Thank You for the purposes You have for my life. Give me courage to speak for You even if I find myself in chains for bearing Your name. It's in Jesus' name that I pray, amen.

# DAY 21

## GOD'S PLACE

*Like a bird that strays from its nest is a man who strays from his home.*

### PROVERBS 27:8

This gem of wisdom—"Don't be like a restless bird flitting to and fro"—is an invitation to a settled life. Being "settled" seems to be a negative for some people, but fulfillment as a Christ-follower is connected to a sense of place. God said to Abraham, "I want you to leave where you are because I have a place for you." I believe God has a place for each of us, a place of service, a place in the body of Christ, even a geographic place. God has a place for you!

## PRAYER

Heavenly Father, thank You that I am not just another one of Your children. Thank You that You know everything about me and have a plan just for me. Thank You that You have a place for each of us. Help us as we seek Your will and wisdom about where that place is. Give us courage as we move out of our comfort zones to go to wherever or whatever You have called us. In Jesus' name, amen.

# DAY 22

## THE GIFT OF CHILDREN

*"Whoever welcomes a little child like this in my name welcomes me."*

MATTHEW 18:5

Jesus introduced a radical idea in Matthew 18. By this time Jesus had a reputation. Crowds gathered wherever He was. When He was traveling through Jericho the most powerful man in town wanted to have lunch with Him. But on this day He attached enormous significance to the life of a child, in a society where children were seen as disposable. Jesus taught that children are valuable and deserve to be treated with dignity, a principle that has shaped Christianity from that day until now.

## PRAYER

Heavenly Father, thank You for the gift of children. Thank You for the joy they bring to our lives. Help us to be the parents and role models You would have us to be. Give me wisdom and strength to be one worthy of their respect and imitation. In Jesus' name, amen.

# DAY 23

## SOLID AND SURE

*Therefore, since we are receiving a kingdom that cannot be shaken, let us be thankful, and so worship God acceptably with reverence and awe, for our "God is a consuming fire."*

### HEBREWS 12:28-29

Scripture says that the Kingdom of God cannot be shaken—not will not be shaken, but cannot be shaken. And we're invited to a perspective that the Kingdom of God is the only stable thing we can invest ourselves in. So here's the challenge for Christ-followers: Imagine yourself beneath the umbrella of the Church of Jesus Christ. You are not just religious, but you have chosen to yield your life to the authority of Jesus Christ. If your life choices, your dreams, your passions, your hopes—if they are indistinguishable from people outside the Kingdom of God, then you will have invested yourself in things that are going to be shaken. To the degree that you invest yourself in the Kingdom of God, you are participating in something that cannot be shaken.

## PRAYER

Heavenly Father, thank You that You are my Strong Tower, my first and last source of trust and security. Show me Your Kingdom purposes, Lord, and give me wisdom to align my hopes and dreams and plans with Your purposes for my life. Help me to speak Your truth faithfully so that I will help others pursue their own callings in Christ. In Jesus' name, amen.

# DAY 24

## WATCH AND WAIT

*But as for me, I watch in hope for the LORD, I wait for God my Savior;*
*my God will hear me.*

MICAH 7:7

Micah has stuck his stick in the ground and said, "Although at the moment my circumstances may not be what I would like, I have chosen to take my stand with God. I'm not giving up. I'm counting on Him to listen to me. And I will wait until I see God bring His deliverance to my life." That is the call of faith. Faith isn't about getting what you want when you want it in the way you want it. Faith is saying, "I have cast my lot with God, and I am going to ride that out because I'm counting on God to hear me."

## PRAYER

Heavenly Father, give me the same faith and persistence that Micah had. When I am in the middle of circumstances that are not what I would like, help me to seek Your will and wait on You. Thank You that You hear me when I cry out to You and always want the best for me, even when I can't see what that is. I rejoice in Your care for me. In Jusus' name, amen.

# DAY 25

## NEW GROWTH, NEW FRUIT

*Like newborn babies, crave pure spiritual milk, so that by it you may grow up in your salvation.*

### 1 PETER 2:2

To gain access to the Kingdom of God through a profession of faith in Jesus Christ is not the end. Peter reminds us that we are expected to grow up in our salvation. When I think of maturing, the word "responsibility" comes to mind—first for yourself, then for others in your sphere of influence, and ultimately as a part of humanity. I don't remember a time when I was particularly glad to get a new responsibility, but every one of those times has enabled me to grow and bring good fruit to my life. Just as we mature physically, we should grow up spiritually, focusing on spiritual things and learning to accept spiritual responsibilities.

## PRAYER

Heavenly Father, thank You that I am a valued part of Your Kingdom purposes and that You entrust me with spiritual tasks. Help me to see my spiritual responsibilities clearly. Give me a joyful heart as I serve You and others. With a grateful heart I ask these things. In Jesus' name, amen.

# DAY 26

## A CALL AND A PURPOSE

*He (God) has saved us and called us to a holy life—not because of anything we have done but because of his own purpose and grace.*

2 TIMOTHY 1:9

To be saved, to be birthed into the Kingdom of God, is to be called of God. Some people think that only "professional Christians" are called. People will say to me, "Pastor, we are so glad God called you." But just as certainly as you believe God would call someone to be a pastor, God has a call on your life. And someday God will ask each of us to give an account for the call on our lives. I want to be ready, don't you?

## PRAYER

Heavenly Father, thank You that You have called me for a purpose in Your Kingdom. You know me better than I know myself, so help me be sensitive to Your plans for me. Give me wisdom and discernment as I work out Your call on my life day by day. In Jesus' name, amen.

# DAY 27

## GOD IS IN FAMILY

*Male and female he created them. God blessed them and said to them, "Be fruitful and increase in number."*

### GENESIS 1:27-28

Our families matter to God. He introduced and defined the principle of the family in Genesis 1, and it carries through the entire story of God's work in the earth. The first family certainly wasn't perfect, and no family since has been. In fact, the greatest pain in our lives can come from the people who are closest to us. However, your family is important to God, and in the midst of the struggles and challenges your family faces, He will meet you there and give you healing and strength.

## PRAYER

Father, I pray that by the Spirit of the Living God You will bring deliverance and healing, restoration and blessing to our families. Thank You that You love me and my family and that You have plans for our good and not our harm. Give us the strength to complete the course You have laid before us. Our hope is in You, Lord. In Jesus' name, amen.

# DAY 28

## A YIELDED SACRIFICE

*Therefore, I urge you, brothers, in view of God's mercy, to offer your bodies as living sacrifices, holy and pleasing to God—this is your spiritual act of worship.*

ROMANS 12:1

The Jewish sacrificial system of this time was at the center of serving God. In the Jerusalem Temple there was an enormous altar where the priest would lay the daily sacrifices, creating a constant aroma of burning flesh. It would have dominated the atmosphere. Before those animals were placed on the altar, they were slaughtered. Paul is using that imagery, but he says, "I want you to offer yourself as a living sacrifice. Present yourself to God and say, 'God, I'm here to serve.'" The grandest way to live is to be yielded to the authority of God, but it's a paradox—how can I gain freedom and liberty by willingly yielding mine to the authority of an Almighty God? Present yourself to God as a living sacrifice. That takes faith. That is your spiritual act of worship.

## PRAYER

Heavenly Father, I present myself to You again today as a living sacrifice. Thank You that because of Jesus' shed blood on the cross, my sacrifice is worthy. Show me each day how I should offer myself to You, because Your ways are not my ways and my vision is limited by my humanity. Thank You for Your mercy. In Jesus' name, amen.

# DAY 29

## THE BEST AGENDA

*Trust in the LORD with all your heart and lean not on your own understanding; in all your ways acknowledge him, and he will make your paths straight.*

### PROVERBS 3:5-6

When I began my Christian journey what I really wanted was the power of God to get my will done on the earth. I had my own plans and my own agenda. I thought Christianity was a pretty good deal: I got the help of an Almighty God to help me get my way. But along the way I've come to understand that's not the goal, because there often is a difference in my agenda and God's agenda. His purposes for us are always the best—guaranteed—and we should trust Him and pursue them with everything we have.

## PRAYER

Heavenly Father, I come before You acknowledging that my understanding is not the same as Yours. I am grateful that You have not left us to wander through life alone but have given us Your Word and the Holy Spirit for guidance. I trust You to make my paths straight so that I may fulfill the purposes You have for me. In Jesus' name, amen.

# DAY 30

## HIS PERFECT PURPOSE

*God sent the angel Gabriel to Nazareth, a town in Galilee, to a virgin pledged to be married to a man named Joseph, a descendant of David. The virgin's name was Mary.*

LUKE 1:26-27

Sometimes God's purposes are very personal events in our lives, and Mary typifies that beautifully. When the angel showed up and said to Mary, "I've got something to tell you," he wasn't there to have a theological discussion. He came with a very personal assignment, and Mary would never be the same again. I'm sure it changed every expectation she had for her life. There will be times when God will put that kind of invitation in front of you, and you'll think, "If I say yes to this, everything's going to be different. It's not what I had planned!" God's purposes for our lives are always best for us, even though we may not be able to see the benefits right away.

## PRAYER

Father, forgive me for the times when You have invited me to have a part in Your purposes and I've seen it as second best. Give me a heart that is open to everything You have for me. Thank You for allowing me to be a part of Your plan. May my days on the earth be fruitful for You. In Jesus' name, amen.

# DAY 31

## NO MORE LEFTOVERS

*Whatever you do, whether in word or deed, do it all in the name of the Lord
Jesus, giving thanks to God the Father through him.*

### COLOSSIANS 3:17

For a long time I thought Christianity was about leftovers—leftover interest, leftover time, leftover clothes, leftover appliances—until I started to serve the Lord, and then I discovered that God doesn't want or need my leftovers. Why do we think Almighty God would involve Himself with us if we're just marginally interested? Too often we give more, and more joyfully, of ourselves to a hobby or sports team than we give to God. God wants our best, and I mean more than money and time. He wants a complete commitment from the inside out, a commitment that comes from your heart with thanksgiving, because "whatever you do" you are doing in His name and for His glory.

## PRAYER

Heavenly Father, forgive me for all the times I have given You less than my best or given with a grudging spirit. It all belongs to You, Lord, and all I am and have is a gift from You, so help me to always give back to You with joy and thanksgiving. In the name of Jesus, amen.

## POWER AND PERSON

*In the beginning God created the heavens and the earth. Now the earth was formless and empty, darkness was over the surface of the deep, and the Spirit of God was hovering over the waters.*

GENESIS 1:1-2

We have a tendency in organized religion to diminish the work of the Holy Spirit. It's clear from the beginning to the end of the Bible that the power of God and the Person of the Holy Spirit are almost synonymous. The Holy Spirit was present for the creative power of God to give shape and order to the world. The Holy Spirit delivered the Israelites from their enemies—sometimes whole armies of enemies. The Holy Spirit enabled Elijah to outrun the chariots of Ahab. The Holy Spirit came upon the prophets and they foretold what God would do. When Mary asked the angel how she would give birth to the Son of God, the angel replied, "The Holy Spirit will come on you, and the power of the Most High will overshadow you" (Luke 1:35). Throughout Scripture the Holy Spirit is the Person through whom the power of God is made evident in people's lives. We will not flourish as Christ-followers apart from the Holy Spirit, so we should be intentional about welcoming Him into our lives.

## PRAYER

Heavenly Father, I offer myself as a living sacrifice, yielded to you. I want to know Your power in my life. I choose to cooperate with the Person and work of the Holy Spirit so that I can fulfill the purposes You have for me in the earth. In Jesus' name I pray, amen.

# DAY 33

## THE DIFFERENCE MAKER

*Do not be anxious about anything, but in everything, by prayer and petition, with thanksgiving, present your requests to God. And the peace of God, which transcends all understanding, will guard your hearts and your minds in Christ Jesus.*

### PHILIPPIANS 4:6-7

I like the candor of Scripture. If the Bible says, "Don't be anxious about anything," we can be sure it's because there are things that will cause us anxiety. This world is filled with evil, and it will touch our lives. Yet Scripture says, "Don't be anxious." Yes, there are things that cause anxiety, but anxiety doesn't have to dominate us. How can that be? Because we are to give our anxieties to God with prayer and petition and thanksgiving, and then the peace of God will guard our hearts and our minds. God is the difference maker. Can you live your life apart from God? Certainly. But our thoughts and emotions are a battlefield, and when you invite God into your life He will fight that battle for you.

## PRAYER

Father, I come before You asking for Your peace that surpasses all understanding. Holy Spirit, I ask for Your intervention into my thoughts when I am feeling anxious. Remind me that the You have promised to guard my heart and mind in Christ Jesus. It's in His name that I ask these things, amen.

# DAY 34

## REMEMBERED AS A SERVANT

*They held harps given them by God and sang the song of Moses the servant of God and the song of the Lamb.*

### REVELATION 15:2-3

One of the things that intrigues me about this verse is that Moses is remembered all the way over in the book of Revelation. They are singing about him in the throne room of God! Think of all the things they could say about him: "Moses, the guy who parted the sea; Moses, the man who talked to God in a burning bush; Moses, the guy who brought water out of a rock; Moses, the one who led a nation out of slavery." Moses' days under the sun are long gone, but he's still being remembered as a "servant of God." How about you? How do you want to be remembered in the ages to come?

## PRAYER

Father in Heaven, I want to live for You today in ways that will cause me to be known as Your servant in the ages to come. Thank You that when the strength is gone from my body and my days under the sun are done, I can still be a part of Your purposes. Thank You for the glorious eternity You have promised to all who believe in Jesus for salvation. In His name I pray, amen.

## THINK ABOUT IT

*His delight is in the law of the LORD, and on his law he meditates day and night. He is like a tree planted by streams of water, which yields its fruit in season and whose leaf does not wither. Whatever he does prospers.*

PSALM 1:2-3

To meditate on something simply means to think about it often. God has said there is a blessing if we'll think about His perspective regularly. I read that, and I want to find that line and figure how to get in it. If it means I have to change what I think about, then let's begin today. It's an amazing promise of Scripture that you and I can lead lives of significance and find stability in our world not because of who we are or what we've achieved, but because we choose to align ourselves with Almighty God.

## PRAYER

Father, give me a greater desire for the eternal things that matter to You, and show me Your perspective on the temporary things of this world. I want to be like that tree, planted by streams that never run dry and yielding fruit for You. Help me to stand steadfast when all around me seems uncertain. In the name of Jesus, amen.

## FAITH FROM DESPERATE PLACES

*Then a man named Jairus, a ruler of the synagogue, came and fell at Jesus' feet, pleading with him to come to his house because his only daughter, a girl of about twelve, was dying.*

LUKE 8:41-42

Did you know faith can come from desperate places? Jairus, a synagogue ruler and a man of authority, not only approached Jesus, an itinerant rabbi, but fell on his face at His feet. This was an incredible expression of humility and desperation and faith. Many times we imagine that faith in God comes from simply studying, and I'm sure sometimes it does. But the reality is that faith is often born in places of desperation, when we feel like our faces are in the dust. If you're in that kind of place today, I want you to know you're not beyond God. He hasn't abandoned you. He's not angry with you. He may have brought you to a place of desperation so that you can have a new revelation of His character. I wouldn't go in search of a desperate place. But if you find yourself in one, know that God is close to you and waiting for you to cry out to Him.

## PRAYER

Heavenly Father, thank You for meeting me in my weakest moments of doubt and uncertainty. I honor You as my refuge and strength, my ever-present help in trouble. I acknowledge that You are always near and waiting for me to humble myself and cry out to You. Give me increasing faith to trust You in all the circumstances of my life. In Jesus' name, amen.

# DAY 37

## THE FEAR OF THE LORD

*Humility and the fear of the LORD bring wealth and honor and life.*

PROVERBS 22:4

If you're trying to track down wealth, honor, and life without humility and the fear of the Lord, they will elude you. But if you will cultivate humility and the fear of the Lord, those things will come to you. If you've been treating God casually through your indifference, if you've entertained sin—if you're unforgiving, envious, greedy, immoral— those are signs that the fear of the Lord is diminished in your life. He is the Almighty Judge of all the earth, so we should lead lives that demonstrate respect and reverence and awe for Him. I don't know of any other single topic in Scripture that has more blessings attached to it than the fear of the Lord. Let the fear of God, the awe of God, grow within you.

## PRAYER

Heavenly Father, I rejoice today in the joy of my salvation. Your Word brings light and life to me. Holy Spirit, direct my steps, illumine my mind, and reveal God's wisdom to me. My hope is anchored in the victory of my Lord and Savior, Jesus of Nazareth. Through my days on this earth may His name be exalted and His kingdom extended. In Jesus' name, amen.

# DAY 38

## KNOWN FOR CHRIST

*"Whoever acknowledges me before men, I will also acknowledge him before my Father in heaven. But whoever disowns me before men, I will disown him before my Father in heaven."*

MATTHEW 10:32-33

There is a lot of emphasis in our culture on personal, private faith. But our faith shouldn't be only private, because it will be very difficult to argue you're a Christ-follower if the people who know you don't know that. Yes, you will be vulnerable because nonbelievers will tell you how Christians should be, and we all have flaws. Declare your allegiance anyway. God will meet you in ways He'll never meet you any other way. And there are some victories and triumphs that will come to you when you're willing to be an advocate for Jesus publically.

## PRAYER

Heavenly Father, I acknowledge today that You are my Lord and Master. You are the Almighty God and worthy of all my praise. May I always be ready to stand up for You in private conversations and in public settings. Give me wisdom and discernment to speak for You in ways that will invite others into Your Kingdom. Thank You for Jesus, who sits at Your right hand and intercedes for me. In His name, amen.

## DAY 39

## GREATER THINGS

*"I tell you the truth, anyone who has faith in me will do what I have been doing. He will do even greater things than these, because I am going to the Father."*

JOHN 14:12

Jesus is speaking to His disciples, men who have been with Him for three years. They've seen Him walk on water and quiet the wind and waves. They've seen Him call a dead man from the grave and cast out demons. Then Jesus says that if they have faith in Him, they'll be able to do even greater things. Because "Jesus Christ is the same yesterday and today and forever" (Heb. 13:8), this power is available in the twenty-first century as it was in the first century. Our objective is simple: Learn how to cooperate with God so that His power is made evident through our lives. That is our only hope to meet the challenges and opportunities we face today.

## PRAYER

Heavenly Father, thank You for the power of Your Word that indwells in every believer. I come before You in humility, recognizing that I am helpless on my own but powerful when I cooperate with You. Give me discernment to know Your purposes for my life and the strength to fulfill them, for Your glory. In Jesus' name, amen.

## A GOD-ASSIGNMENT

*David said to Saul, "Your servant has been keeping his father's sheep. When a lion or a bear came and carried off a sheep from the flock, I went after it, struck it and rescued the sheep from its mouth. When it turned on me, I seized it by its hair, struck it and killed it. Your servant has killed both the lion and the bear; this uncircumcised Philistine will be like one of them, because he has defied the armies of the Living God."*

### 1 SAMUEL 17:34-36

Goliath the Philistine giant had been taunting the Israelite army for forty days. Young David had brought food for his soldier brothers when Goliath bellowed his challenge once again. David was angry at the insult to his God and said to King Saul, "I can take him." When Saul pointed out his youth, David shared his fighting credentials. David had been willing to accept the assignment of watching sheep, and the challenges that went with that humble task prepared him for a future of serving God in bigger ways. Many people hear God's invitations, but not everyone will accept them. Whatever assignments come your way, do them to honor the Lord and He will bless you.

## PRAYER

Father, give me the boldness of young David to defend Your name and reputation, even when the odds seem stacked against me. Remind me of my need to accept all of Your assignments, not just the ones that might seem important in the world's eyes. Grow my faith, Lord, as I see You perform mighty works among Your people. In Jesus' name, amen.

# DAY 41

## OUR SERVANT EXAMPLE

*"The God of Abraham, Isaac and Jacob, the God of our fathers, has glorified his servant Jesus."*

ACTS 3:13

It seems odd to call Jesus a "servant" of God. Jesus is the incarnate Son of God—God come to earth in the flesh. We can see in the attitude He expressed toward God and toward other people that Jesus understood His life to be defined by the mission of serving God. When He was in a place where He was threatened or tempted, He was serving a higher agenda. When He was facing betrayal and arrest and the horror that was coming, He prayed, "Father, I'd really rather not do this. Nevertheless, it's not what I want, but what You want." That's the attitude of a servant, and Jesus lived it out in a remarkable way.

## PRAYER

Heavenly Father, thank You for sending Your Son, Jesus, as our Savior and Lord, our pattern for faith and practice. Show me anew every day how to define my life and ministry as Your servant. Give me humility to always seek Your will and not my own. In Your Son's name I pray, amen.

# DAY 42

## STRENGTH OF YIELDING

*"For I have come down from heaven not to do my will but to do the will of him who sent me."*

JOHN 6:38

People who think that those who are yielded to God, who serve Him, are people who are too weak-willed or simple-minded to do anything else don't understand what it means to follow the Lord. Jesus admitted that He had left the glories of Heaven not to accomplish His own purposes, but the purposes of His Father. It isn't that He was a pushover; He had chosen to yield His will to the purposes of God. Don't imagine that yielding your will to God will make you a weak person. It will take all the strength and courage you have.

## PRAYER

Heavenly Father, I offer myself as a living sacrifice and yield my will to You again today. Give me humility to seek You and Your purposes rather than go my own way. Give me understanding of Your will for me and how to fulfill it. Not my will but Yours, Lord. In Jesus' name, amen.

# DAY 43

## BLESSINGS OVERFLOW

*"Bring the whole tithe into the storehouse, that there may be food in my house. Test me in this," says the LORD Almighty, "and see if I will not throw open the floodgates of heaven and pour out so much blessing that you will not have room enough for it."*

MALACHI 3:10

My understanding of Scripture is that the first tenth of what comes to us belongs to God. Some people claim that's an Old Testament principle that doesn't apply today. But Jesus didn't set aside the principles of the Old Testament—in almost every case, He extended them. I can tell you from personal experience that God is faithful. There have been times when I have had to make life choices based on resources, and God has been faithful to me as I have honored Him. Honor the Lord with what you have. You can trust Him. It will make a difference in your life.

## PRAYER

Father, You are so patient with me as I continue to learn Your lessons about generosity. Teach me, Lord, and show me Your faithfulness and provision for me, and I will praise You all the days of my life. In the name of Jesus, amen.

# DAY 44

## OUTSIDE OUR WALLS

*Paul then stood up in the meeting of the Areopagus and said: "Men of Athens! I see that in every way you are very religious. For as I walked around and looked carefully at your objects of worship, I even found an altar with this inscription: TO AN UNKNOWN GOD. Now what you worship as something unknown I am going to proclaim to you. The God who made the world and everything in it is the Lord of heaven and earth and does not live in temples built by hands."*

ACTS 17: 22-24

We understand that it's not okay for Christ-followers to huddle behind our walls and point our fingers at those who aren't getting it right. We have to go outside our walls and engage the world in which we live. Paul showed us this in Acts 17. He was in Athens, a Greek city filled with pagan temples. Paul went into a public hall to make a presentation for Jesus. He said, "I see how religious you are. In fact, you've built a temple to a God you don't even know. And I'm going to tell you about that God today." He's engaging a group of people who don't know the Jesus-story in a way they can process. You and I have the same privilege of doing whatever we can to open doors for people who have decided Christianity is irrelevant or unknowable or hypocritical, to tell them the good news about Jesus and invite them toward a relationship with Him.

## PRAYER

Heavenly Father, thank You for the example You give to us in the Apostle Paul. I pray for the same boldness to speak for You wherever and whenever I have the opportunity. Show me how to reach the people You place in my path and to represent You well. In Your Son's name, amen.

## DAY 45

### ONLY JESUS

*The next day John saw Jesus coming toward him and said, "Look, the Lamb of God, who takes away the sin of the world!"*

JOHN 1:29

The good news about Jesus is the only story we have to tell, and Jesus is the only solution we're offering. Diminishing God the Father does not make Him more acceptable, and lowering His standards does not make us more acceptable. We are sinners who are utterly, completely dependent upon God's mercy and the saving power of Jesus Christ through His shed blood on the cross. Let's give thanks to Almighty God for His power to take away your sins and mine!

### PRAYER

Father, I come before You in humility to repent of my sin. I thank You for the blood of Jesus Christ that cleanses me and washes me and sets me free. Thank You, Lord, that You have forgiven me and made me righteous in Your sight and cast my sins into the sea of forgetfulness. In the powerful name of Jesus, amen.

# DAY 46

## CHOOSE GOD'S BOUNDARIES

*Blessed is the man who does not walk in the counsel of the wicked.*

### PSALM 1:1

Psalm 1:1 is a very simple statement with a very simple promise: If you will choose not to walk in the counsel of the ungodly, God will bless you. It's our human inclination to walk that way—we have to make a conscious decision not to. The distinctiveness of being a Christ-follower isn't your wardrobe or your vocabulary or your beverage list. It's choosing God's boundaries for your life—for your relationships, for how you do business, for how you spend your time and resources. Whose advice are you taking for your life?  Are you willing to allow God's counsel to fill your heart?

## PRAYER

Heavenly Father, You see my beginning and end and know my every thought. You love me more than I can imagine, and Your will for my life is the best way for me to live in the world. I choose today to live according to the boundaries You have set for my life. Holy Spirit, help me to walk according to the ways of God, today and every day. In Jesus' name, amen.

# DAY 47

## AN INVISIBLE DEADLINE

*The Lord is not slow in keeping his promise, as some understand slowness. He is patient with you, not wanting anyone to perish, but everyone to come to repentance. But the day of the Lord will come like a thief.*

### 2 PETER 3:9-10

God's desire is that every person would come to repentance, so we should care about that too. If we're faithful servants of the Most High God, it will be important to us that people come to know God and Jesus as Lord. Sometimes if you listen to those of us who are Christians, it's almost like we're happy that people don't know God because we want them to get what they deserve. God cares about people, and we have to care about people too. And we should feel an urgency about that, because the day of the Lord's coming is unknown to us.

## PRAYER

Heavenly Father, how patient You are with me and my generation! Your desire is for every one of us come to faith in You, so awaken in me that desire again and again. Thank You that You want to call each one of us Your beloved child. Help me to be a faithful witness to Your love and compassion in every avenue I walk today. May Your Kingdom increase, Lord! In the name of Jesus, the Savior of the world, amen.

# DAY 48

## GRASP FORGIVENESS

*Bear with each other and forgive whatever grievances you may have against one another. Forgive as the Lord forgave you.*

COLOSSIANS 3:13

Forgiveness is very important to God. When God says forgive, He doesn't mean just to forgive someone when you're in a generous mood or only when someone apologizes and asks for your forgiveness. He said if anybody has offended you in any way, forgive them. That's not excusing what happened—perhaps the person should have done better. But God knows that resentment and bitterness will wear you down. He wants you to let it go and wipe the slate clean, just as He has done for us.

## PRAYER

Father in Heaven, how grateful I am for the forgiveness You have shown to me through Christ, forgiveness I did not deserve but You gave freely. Help me to show that same spirit of love and generosity to those I feel may have offended me in some way. Have mercy on me, oh God, according to Your great compassion! In Jesus' name, amen.

# DAY 49

## WORKS IN PROGRESS

*"I will cleanse you from all your impurities and from all your idols. I will give you a new heart and put a new spirit in you; I will remove from you your heart of stone and give you a heart of flesh."*

### EZEKIEL 36:25-26

God spoke these words to the people of Israel through His prophet Ezekiel, but they apply to us as well. God is reminding us that His Church is not a collection of perfect people and that we are still in process. If we don't acknowledge that, then church becomes a pretty façade, and we are just pretending. The good news of God's Word is that His power is available to help you and me change. Repentance is so significant because it enables us to present ourselves to God so that we can be transformed. We don't have to hide who we are or what we've been. He is simply waiting for us to ask Him for a new heart and a new spirit.

## PRAYER

Heavenly Father, thank You for Your promise of cleansing and a new heart and a new spirit. I acknowledge my many weaknesses and ask that You would cleanse and renew me again today. I thank You for the power of Your Word within me. Help me to live today so that people would see the new heart that comes from You. In Jesus' name, amen.

## KINGS AND AUTHORITY

*I urge, then, first of all, that requests, prayers, intercession and thanksgiving be made for everyone—for kings and all those in authority, that we may live peaceful and quiet lives in all godliness and holiness. This is good, and pleases God our Savior, who wants all men to be saved and to come to a knowledge of the truth.*

### 1 TIMOTHY 2:1-4

It's fashionable in many circles to be angry and complain about the circumstances that surround us. And many of those circumstances are frustrating! In spite of that, God has blessed us. Let's commit to pray "for kings and all those in authority" more than we complain about them. And it's good to remember that while governments rise and fall, a believer's true security comes from Almighty God, who holds the future in His hands.

## PRAYER

Father, I see people in authority who appear indifferent to Your purposes. You want all to be saved, however, so I know that no one is beyond Your reach, beyond Your purposes if they would turn to You. That's my prayer today, Lord: That many of those in positions of power would come to know You as Savior and that we would see a great movement for Almighty God among "kings and all those in authority." In the name of Jesus, amen.

# DAY 51

## STAND UP ANYWAY

*They will tell of the power of your awesome works, and I will proclaim your great deeds.*

### PSALM 145:6

Following God can be intimidating. I don't like to be vulnerable, to be inadequate, to do the very best I can and still fall short because I don't have the ability to deliver the goods. Week after week I say to people, "I believe God can change your life. He can bring strength to your body, heal your marriage, deliver your children." On my best day, I can't do any of those things. So I stand up as a representative for a product I can't deliver. The temptation is to dial it back, water it down, don't ask people to believe or to hope. It's frightening to stand up for the Lord. I understand that. Let's stand up anyway. He will bless us when we do.

## PRAYER

Heavenly Father, You are great and greatly to be praised! You are mighty and powerful, yet full of mercy and lovingkindness toward Your children. How patient You are with me in my weakness. Give me courage to stand up for You and declare Your mighty works, believing Your promises for myself and for all who call out to You for mercy. In Jesus' name, amen.

## SMALL TREASURES

*"See that you do not look down on one of these little ones. For I tell you that their angels in heaven always see the face of my Father in heaven."*

MATTHEW 18:10

Do you believe in angels? Jesus did. Scripture teaches that angels are ministering spirits sent into the world to help us. Jesus said that there are angels assigned to children and that those angels have unique access to Almighty God. I always consider it a privilege to interact and pray with children because they hold a unique place in God's economy. Let's be careful to treasure the time we have with the children in our families and under our influence.

## PRAYER

Heavenly Father, thank You for sending angels to minister among us. Thank You for Your love and watchful care. Lord, I'm especially grateful for Your great love for children. Help us to be the kind of Christ-followers who live for You in a way that children would see You in us. In Jesus' name, amen.

# DAY 53

## HOLY SPIRIT POWER

*Jesus returned to Galilee in the power of the Spirit, and news about him spread through the whole countryside.*

LUKE 4:14

Jesus was thirty years old and had been living in relative obscurity as Joseph and Mary's son. Then He went to John, who baptized Him in the Jordan River. The Holy Spirit descended upon Jesus in the form of a dove, and God said, "This is My Son—I'm pleased with Him." That's when Jesus "went public" and the miraculous part of His life began. Healing people, casting out spirits, walking on water, calling dead people to life—all of those things followed the descent of the Spirit in Jesus' life. If Jesus needed the help of the Holy Spirit to let the power of God be unleashed in order to accomplish God's purposes for His life, you and I most certainly do as well.

## PRAYER

Father, thank You for Your gift of the Holy Spirit to all of us who belong to You. I come before You asking for a greater humility and awareness of my need for the Spirit and a greater willingness to rely on the Spirit's power to accomplish Your purposes through me. Use me to make a difference for Your Kingdom, Lord. In the name of Jesus I pray, amen.

# DAY 54

## SECURE HOPE

*"For I know the plans I have for you," declares the LORD, "plans to prosper you and not to harm you, plans to give you hope and a future."*

JEREMIAH 29:11

Everyone needs hope. Hope gives a momentum to your spiritual life that's not there otherwise. Hope is not just the determination to get your way or a refusal to quit or the drive to complete your agenda. Our hope is not linked to our circumstances or the people around us or even our own ability. Our hope is secured by the faithfulness of Almighty God, who says, "I have a plan for you." Hope says, "I will live out the promises of God. They will define my future. If God says I'm forgiven, I'm forgiven. If God says I'm cleansed, I'm cleansed. If God has given me this assignment, I can see this assignment through." Let God's promises inspire the hope in your life. Your circumstances may be difficult, but Almighty God cares about who you are. If you'll allow Him, His promises will bring hope to you.

## PRAYER

Heavenly Father, I am so grateful that You love me so much that You have designed a plan that is perfect for my life. Even when I have veered from Your purposes and gone my own way, You have been there to pull me back in and love me in spite of my willfulness. Holy Spirit, help me to discern God's plans for my life because I want to be a part of Your purposes in the earth. In the name of Jesus, amen.

# DAY 55

## A NEW YOU

*Therefore, if anyone is in Christ, he is a new creation; the old has gone, the new has come!*

### 2 CORINTHIANS 5:17

When you surrender your life to Christ some people will wonder about the new you. Some will understand. Some won't. Some will make fun. Some will be jealous. Some will throw rocks. When you follow the Lord you'll have to be willing to stand out a little because what you live for and hope for will make you different. In fact, your life should cause other people to want to get to know the Lord. Some people will ask you for more information, and some of those will follow Jesus with you!

## PRAYER

Heavenly Father, thank You for making such a change in me that people look and wonder about the difference. Give me strength to be a faithful witness for You when others do not understand or mock or even throw rocks. May people always be able to tell that I am a follower of Jesus. In His name I ask these things, amen.

# DAY 56

## CELEBRATE GOD'S GOODNESS

*I will tell of the kindnesses of the LORD, the deeds for which he is to be praised, according to all the LORD has done for us.*

ISAIAH 63:7

Sometimes God's invitations to us are simply to observe how He's working in other people's lives and then celebrate and report. If we're not careful we can miss these opportunities because they may not feel like they have much to do with us. You may be just going about your daily tasks, minding your own business, when God says, "Hey, I'm doing something for your friend over there—why don't you go celebrate with him?" Your own life may not be completely transformed by what you see, but you should take the opportunity to see God at work and then praise Him for "all the Lord has done for us."

## PRAYER

Heavenly Father, thank You for all the ways You bless me and the people around me—the big things we can all see and the small things You invite me to witness. Help me to remember that every good thing comes from You. Give me a heart of love and generosity toward others so that I would be as eager to celebrate when You bless them as I am when You bless me. In the name of Jesus, amen.

## PURSUE THE POWER OF GOD

*As Jesus was on his way, the crowds almost crushed him. And a woman was there who had been subject to bleeding for twelve years, but no one could heal her. She came up behind him and touched the edge of his cloak, and immediately her bleeding stopped. "Who touched me?" Jesus asked...*
*"Someone touched me; I know that power has gone out from me."*

LUKE 8:43-46

This is an incredible scene. A desperate woman had come to Jesus, believing that she would be healed if she could just touch Him. And when she pushed through the crowd and touched His garment, He felt the power of God flowing out of Him. It wasn't something mythical or theoretical but a physical force. Sometimes we'd rather get together and talk about His power than invite His power into our lives. That's unfortunate, because we need the power of God to bring change and transformation to us and to our world. We're desperate for it, so let's begin by pursuing it with the same determination this woman showed.

## PRAYER

Heavenly Father, You are the all-powerful God of creation. The world was made and is held together by the power of Your command. Lord, remind me every day that You love me as a child, and Your desire is to show Yourself strong on my behalf. And when You do, Father, I'll give You all the praise and honor. In Jesus' name, amen.

## THE POWER OF JUST ONE

*"I have seen these people," the LORD said to Moses, "and they are a stiff-necked people. Now leave me alone so that my anger may burn against them and that I may destroy them. Then I will make you into a great nation." But Moses sought the favor of the LORD his God . . . then the LORD relented and did not bring on his people the disaster he had threatened.*

EXODUS 32:9-14

The Israelites were in the wilderness, and Moses was on Mount Sinai with God. He'd been gone so long that the people thought something had happened to him and he wasn't coming back. It didn't take long for them to begin to engage in all sorts of immorality and ungodly things. They even made a golden calf and worshipped it. God was very angry and said, "I'm going to destroy them all, Moses. I'll just start over with you." Moses replied, "Don't do it, Lord, because the Egyptians will hear and they'll say You couldn't finish what You started." And God relented. When we find ourselves in the midst of a generation that's made ungodly choices, choosing to follow God can make all the difference. You say, "I don't see how. I'm just one person, and I don't have much influence." Don't discount the power of God in you. He is searching for people who will follow Him.

## PRAYER

Father God, I want to be known as someone who will follow You no matter where You lead—to the mountaintop or through the wilderness. Help me to be faithful to You in all of life's circumstances, even when I don't understand Your plan. Give me the faith of Moses, Lord, so I will have the persistence to plead with You and not give up on myself or others. In the name of Jesus, amen.

# DAY 59

## SET APART

*Joshua told the people, "Consecrate yourselves, for tomorrow the LORD will do amazing things among you."*

JOSHUA 3:5

"Consecration" is a big word that simply means "to set yourself apart to God." When Joshua got ready to lead the children of Israel into the Promised Land, God said, "That's your inheritance. I've given it to you and your children forever." But before they could live in the Promised Land they had to cross the flooded Jordan River and then actually go to war to occupy their inheritance. Before they started that process, Joshua said, "Take three days, and consecrate yourself. Get yourself ready. Prepare your hearts." He knew they would need God's blessing in order to fulfill His plan for them. We too should cultivate the mindset of setting ourselves apart for Him because we are not just business people or family people, we are people of God who need His direction and blessing in order to fulfill His purposes for our lives.

## PRAYER

Heavenly Father, I yield my life to You. Having a part in Your plan for the earth will be my highest honor and greatest reward. Lord, show me where You are at work in my world and how I can be a part of that. I ask this in the name of Jesus, amen.

## DAY 60

### A DIFFERENT SYSTEM

*Jesus sat down opposite the place where the offerings were put and watched the crowd putting their money into the temple treasury. Many rich people threw in large amounts. But a poor widow came and put in two very small copper coins, worth only a fraction of a penny. Calling his disciples to him, Jesus said, "I tell you the truth, this poor widow has put more into the treasury than all the others. They all gave out of their wealth; but she, out of her poverty, put in everything—all she had to live on."*

MARK 12:41-44

Jesus was on the Temple Mount watching the people give their gifts. It was a public offering, and some very large gifts were being given that day. A woman came—a widow—and put two coins in, worth less than a penny. When Jesus told the disciples that the woman had given more than all the others, the disciples were confused and Jesus had to explain to them that God's accounting system is not like ours. Don't allow the enemy to rob you of the opportunity to participate in what God is doing. Your sacrifice has great value in God's sight.

## PRAYER

Heavenly Father, thank You for allowing me to have a part in Your purposes in the earth. Thank You that You do not look at outward appearances but my heart. Lord, I am so grateful that Your accounting system is not the same as mine. Thank You for Your patience with me as I strive to see the world through Your eyes and look beyond outward appearances to the hearts of people. In Jesus' name, amen.

G. ALLEN JACKSON

# DAY 61

## GOD'S TRUTH

*"You are a king, then!" said Pilate. Jesus answered, "You are right in saying I am a king. In fact, for this reason I was born, and for this I came into the world, to testify to the truth. Everyone on the side of truth listens to me." "What is truth?" Pilate asked.*

JOHN 18:37-38

I love the courage of Jesus. I imagine He looked Pilate directly in the eye during this conversation. Jesus had already told Pilate that His Kingdom wasn't of this world, and Pilate was in a difficult position. He needed the political support of a group of people who wanted Jesus executed, and yet he thought Jesus was innocent. Pilate thought he had Jesus backed into a corner, but Jesus pushed right back at him. And then Pilate uttered perhaps his most-quoted phrase: "What is truth?" Jesus forced him to decide what he would do, and Pilate will be forever known as the man who sent Jesus to His death. We're faced with the same dilemma Pilate was—the direction, the trajectory, the momentum of our lives will be determined by what we do with the truth about Jesus.

## PRAYER

Heavenly Father, thank You that You sent Your only, beloved Son to live among us. Thank You that Your Son willingly died for my sins and was raised from the dead so that I might have eternal life with You. Thank You that He lives forever at Your right hand, interceding for me. This is the truth that I know from Your Word, and I stand on it today. May it direct my every step. In the glorious name of Jesus I pray, amen.

# DAY 62

## GOD'S TIMELESS WORD

*"I will display my glory among the nations, and all the nations will see the punishment I inflict and the hand I lay on them."*

EZEKIEL 39:21

We hear a lot of talk about globalization and how we no longer live in isolation. We drink our morning coffee while we watch events unfold in Europe and the Middle East and hear how trading in the Asian markets will affect us. We act as if this is something new, but Ezekiel—a near Eastern, Hebrew prophet who lived about five centuries before the birth of Jesus—is relaying a message from God about all the nations of the world having a common experience. And he's describing the season in which you and I live. Don't ever be embarrassed because you believe the Word of God. It teaches us that God had a plan for the world long before the recent discussions of globalization, and He is working it out moment by moment.

## PRAYER

Heavenly Father, I thank You for Your Word. I do not consider it antiquated but relevant to my life today. Give me a hunger and thirst for Your Word and the truth it brings to our lives. May it help me in every season. In Jesus' name, amen.

## BEARING GOOD FRUIT

*"I chose you and appointed you to go and bear fruit."*

JOHN 15:16

Before the earth ever saw its first sunrise or sunset, God chose you and planned that you would have a part in growing His Kingdom. And He has gifted you with a unique toolkit of spiritual gifts, personality, temperament, skills, and abilities that will help you. I will never play tight end in the NFL, but I have other gifts and abilities that are uniquely part of who God made me to be. When we're birthed into the Kingdom of God, a significant step in our journey of discipleship—of practicing faith—is to say to the Lord, "I want to understand who You've made me to be, not just who I want to be." Let's rejoice in the liberty of that, and go and bear fruit!

## PRAYER

Heavenly Father, thank You that You chose me to go and bear fruit. I submit my life to be used for Your purposes. I thank You that I have been uniquely created with gifts to be used for growing Your Kingdom. I want to understand who You've made me to be, not just who I want to be. In Jesus' name, amen.

## AN EXPECTATION OF HOLINESS

*But just as he who called you is holy, so be holy in all you do; for it is written: "Be holy, because I am holy."*

### 1 PETER 1:15-16

People don't talk much about holiness anymore. Holiness is probably not a common conversation in the break room. You probably won't hear your favorite television characters discussing it or see it lifted up as the ideal in advertisements. However, God has unchanging expectations for how His people should live, and holiness is one of them. While you can never earn your way into the Kingdom of God, your behavior is a reflection of the value you attach to God's wonderful gift of redemption. If you are casual with the things of God, it very clearly says you don't value what Jesus did for you. But if you are endeavoring to let holiness emerge in your life, it suggests you attach great value to it. Scripture says it in the plainest of language: "Be holy in all you do." So let's take the boundaries God gives us and treat them personally, no matter what our culture says.

## PRAYER

Heavenly Father, Your holiness and perfection are beyond anything I can imagine, yet You call me to be holy as You are holy. I am thankful that You have not left me to strive on my own but have given me the gift of Your Word as a light for my path and the Holy Spirit as a guide for my thoughts and actions. Lord, may I live in such a way that people who see me know that I am Your follower. In Jesus' name, amen.

# DAY 65

## STANDING UP, STANDING OUT

*"Let your light shine before men, that they may see your good deeds and praise your Father in heaven."*

MATTHEW 5:15

It seems easier to travel around the world to talk about Jesus than to go to work and own your faith with people you see every day. You think, "I can't tell them my Jesus-story because they know what I'm really like." But that's precisely the reason why you can. I think of this assignment in three simple words: **Serving** is what you do. **Support** is standing with someone when they're going through a tough season. And **sharing** is what you say. Before you even talk about your Jesus-story, show it with your behavior. The sermons you live are just as significant as the ones you speak.

## PRAYER

Heavenly Father, thank You for giving me a Jesus-story. Give me discernment into the lives of the people around me and boldness to speak for You. Holy Spirit, guide my words and actions as I seek to live and speak my Jesus-story today. In His name I ask these things, amen.

# DAY 66

## YOUR ASSIGNED ARENA

*But the plans of the LORD stand firm forever, the purposes of his heart through all generations.*

PSALM 33:11

How many times have you read your Bible and thought to yourself how remarkable it would have been to be a part of God's story in the earth? That's precisely the invitation before us! Like David or Esther or Mary or Paul, we are here for the purposes of the Kingdom of God. The greatest opportunity for a human being in this generation is to participate with God in His purposes in the earth and facilitate the return of the Lord. Whatever arena of influence God has given you, use that arena to be an advocate for Jesus. You'll be preparing the way for the coming King.

## PRAYER

Heavenly Father, how generous You are to allow us to have a part in Your plans and purposes in the earth. Give me wisdom to know Your plans for me and perseverance as I serve You. I joyfully await the coming of King Jesus, in whose name I pray, amen.

# DAY 67

## TRUTH BUCKLED TIGHTLY

*Put on the full armor of God so that you can take your stand against the devil's schemes... Stand firm then, with the belt of truth buckled around your waist...*

### EPHESIANS 6:11, 14

Ephesians 6 includes this famous passage describing the reality of spiritual conflict—it is a battle "against the spiritual forces of evil in the heavenly realms." We are told that to thrive during evil days we must wear the armor of God. It's worth noting that the first piece of armor mentioned is the belt of truth. Evil will touch all of our lives, and your spiritual effectiveness will be limited if you don't have the belt of God's truth firmly in place. And it's a personal thing. Each one of us will have to decide whether we will believe God's truth and wear it as armor as we stand our ground for God in the world.

## PRAYER

Heavenly Father, open my eyes. Let me see Your truth. May it be the first thing I reach for when I am faced with scoffing and confusion and hostility and even my own uncertainties. Help me to stand firm, Lord, for I want to represent You well and bring honor to You. In Jesus' name, amen.

## JESUS AS AUTHOR

*Let us fix our eyes on Jesus, the author and perfecter of our faith, who for the joy set before him endured the cross, scorning its shame, and sat down at the right hand of the throne of God.*

### HEBREWS 12:2

Jesus is the author of your story. He created you for this time and this place to do something significant in His Kingdom. He's written not an average story for you, but an extraordinary story. He's also the perfecter of your faith who has the power to make the ending work. Storms, demons, sickness, death—none of those intimidated Jesus while He was on earth, and they are not intimidating Him today as He sits at the right hand of God. There will be some challenges between where you are now and God's best for you. Jesus endured death on the cross before His joy was complete. He's held up to us as an example, so let's fix our eyes on Him and trust Him to write our stories.

## PRAYER

Heavenly Father, it is so easy for me to focus my attention on things other than You—my circumstances, my feelings—a lot of "me" it seems. Give me a renewed focus on You and Your purposes, no matter where that leads me, for You are my victory in this life and the next. In the name of Jesus, the author and perfecter of my faith, amen.

## WASHED, SANCTIFIED, JUSTIFIED

*Do you not know that the wicked will not inherit the kingdom of God? Do not be deceived: Neither the sexually immoral nor idolaters nor adulterers nor male prostitutes nor homosexual offenders nor thieves nor the greedy nor drunkards nor slanderers nor swindlers will inherit the kingdom of God. And that is what some of you were. But you were washed, you were sanctified, you were justified in the name of the Lord Jesus Christ and by the Spirit of our God.*

### 1 CORINTHIANS 6:9-11

This is written to the church in Corinth, but it's as fresh as today's news. Paul reminds us even though life seems to be going well for the wicked, they're not going to have a happy ending. To keep pride from creeping in, his list of wicked behaviors puts being greedy along with adultery. But he gives the good news: "That's what you were, but you've been washed, sanctified, and justified." He reminds us we have the power of Almighty God, the Creator of the universe, to help us change. Remember that you too have been washed, and sanctified, and justified. Even when living inside His boundaries seems hard, ask Him to help you, and He will.

## PRAYER

Heavenly Father, thank You that because of Jesus' death on the cross for me I have been washed, sanctified, and justified. Help me as I struggle against my weaknesses to live for You within Your boundaries for a righteous life. Help me to be the person on the inside that I want the world to see on the outside. I'm so grateful that You have promised the Holy Spirit to guide me during all my days on the earth. In the name of Jesus I pray, amen.

## LIFE FULLY LIVED

*I have set before you life and death, the blessing and the curse. So choose life in order that you may live, you and your descendants, by loving the LORD your God, by obeying His voice, and by holding fast to Him.*

DEUTERONOMY 30:19-20 • NASB®

The children of Israel have been out of Egypt for a long time. They've eaten manna God provided and followed His pillar of cloud and pillar of fire. God sustained them in the desert for many years, and they know they are His people. Moses, in one of his last addresses to the Israelites, says, "You've got to choose: life or death, blessing or curse. Choose life." We also need to be reminded that a healthy spiritual life does not consist of a single decision in the past. We say a prayer somewhere along the way and think, "Well, I made my God-choice. Now I can go live my life." That's not the message of Scripture. It invites us to lead a life of choosing Him, day by day and moment by moment. Wherever you are in your spiritual journey, there's an opportunity to choose God more fully than you've known Him before.

## PRAYER

Heavenly Father, today I choose life and blessing. Thank You for all the ways You provide for me and lead me. I commit today to love You more deeply, obey You more fully, and hold fast to You when my strength fails. Thank You for Your promise of life. Thank You for the invitations You place before me and the opportunities You give me to cooperate with You. In Jesus' name, amen.

# DAY 71

## A SINGLE-MINDED FOCUS

*You were running a good race. Who cut in on you and kept you from obeying the truth?*

GALATIANS 5:7

One of the difficulties we all face as we are growing up in the Lord is keeping a single-minded focus. I've read that the more options we have, the less likely we are to do something significant, because when things get tough we just move on to the next option. We have so many church options that we have the luxury of arguing among ourselves about music and which translation of the Bible to read, and moving on when something doesn't suit us. This verse reminds us that our faith-life needs the purposeful determination of a runner in a race in order to maintain a forward momentum and accomplish the purposes that God has for us. Let's minimize the distractions and keep our eyes on the goal!

## PRAYER

Heavenly Father, I want to keep my eyes on You. Help me to run a good race toward eternity and ignore all the things that would distract me from that goal—people, circumstances, emotions, false promises of the world, the busyness of daily life. In all things I give You the glory and honor. In Jesus' name, amen.

# DAY 72

## REAL FREEDOM

*To the Jews who had believed him, Jesus said, "If you hold to my teaching, you are really my disciples. Then you will know the truth, and the truth will set you free." They answered him, "We are Abraham's descendants and have never been slaves of anyone. How can you say that we shall be set free?"*

JOHN 8:31-33

Jesus is talking to a group of people who believe in Him, and they are offended. They've already accepted His message, and He says, "If you follow my teachings and really are my disciples, my truth will bring greater freedom to your life." They reply, "Wait a minute! We come from the right group. We've got the right DNA. We've never been enslaved by anyone. How dare you say we need to be set free!" If you're a Christ-follower, you know the freedom that comes from acknowledging your sin and being forgiven and welcomed into the Kingdom of God. But God has more freedom for you! Beyond accepting the truth of Jesus as Savior, He wants you to apply His truth to every aspect of your life and experience the joy that only comes from living in the freedom of a life fully devoted to His purposes.

## PRAYER

Heavenly Father, thank You for the freedom You generously bestow on all who believe in the power of Jesus to save. Forgive me for the times I have been complacent and content with so little of Your freedom. Expand my awareness of You, Lord, so I can experience all of the joy life in You brings. In Jesus' name, amen.

# DAY 73

## GOD'S TRIUMPH

*"Although you have been forsaken and hated . . . I will make you the everlasting pride and the joy of all generations."*

ISAIAH 60:15

"You're going to be hated by everybody." God is speaking very plainly to the Jewish people about how they can expect to be treated. Historically, that unreasoning hatred has worn many labels: the Spanish Inquisition, the Russian pogroms, Hitler's Final Solution. And anti-Semitism is still alive and well today. But then He says, "In spite of that hatred, I'm going to use you to bring joy to every generation." That's a wonderful promise because if God can do it in the lives of the Jewish people, He can do it in your life and mine. When you are in one of those places that feels painful, that feels unfair and unjust, remember that God can turn that into triumph for you.

## PRAYER

Heavenly Father, thank You for the Jewish people. You are faithful and just in all Your ways to every generation. Give me a renewed boldness to proclaim You as the source of everything good in my life. Help me to live so that I may be called Your pride and joy. I pray for the peace of Jerusalem, that You may rule and reign in the hearts of all Your chosen ones. In Jesus' name, amen.

## STANDING TOGETHER

*You are . . . members of God's household, built on the foundation of the apostles and prophets, with Christ Jesus himself as the chief cornerstone. In him the whole building is joined together and rises to become a holy temple in the Lord. And in him you too are being built together to become a dwelling in which God lives by his Spirit.*

### EPHESIANS 2:19-22

An effective, vibrant, and growing church that results in transformed lives is no more an accident than a productive garden or a well-disciplined child. It's because a group of people intentionally stand together, with Jesus as their Cornerstone and the Holy Spirit as their Guide, and trust God and work together for that outcome. It's almost impossible to watch the news without seeing acts of almost unimaginable hatred. A local task force, an international coalition, a political or military response—none of those things will bring victory beyond the values that are foundational to the Church of Jesus Christ. I have never known a greater need for the churches of Jesus Christ to have a voice than in this season, so let's stand together in unity and work for His purposes.

## PRAYER

Heavenly Father, although You are shaking all things which can be shaken, You have a Kingdom that cannot be shaken. I choose to trust in and rely on You. May Your Church rise up and be the Body of Christ in our communities and around the world. May Your purposes be fulfilled in the earth. Come, Lord Jesus. In His name I pray, amen.

# DAY 75

## FOLDERS

*For the grace of God that brings salvation has appeared to all men. It teaches us to say "No" to ungodliness and worldly passions, and to live self-controlled, upright and godly lives in this present age, while we wait for the blessed hope—the glorious appearing of our great God and Savior, Jesus Christ.*

TITUS 2:11-13

It's easy as an American Christian to think that we can know God and love God but keep Him tucked away in a God-folder where we file "attended church" and "gave an offering" or "volunteered for an event." But we also have a separate family-folder, a friends-folder, a fun-folder, and a business-folder, and they're all neatly organized. Being a Christ-follower means that you don't have a God-folder, but that you put God in all your folders—family, friends, work, fun, finances, etc. None of us begins our faith-journey with a life wide open to God, but as we learn more about His love and His faithfulness we will welcome Him gladly into every "folder" of our lives.

## PRAYER

Heavenly Father, I ask You to forgive me for keeping You separate from the more broad areas of my life. I want to live a life that is open to Your perspective. Show me the places or "folders" where I need more of You, and give me the wisdom to know how to begin the process of inviting You into my whole life. I thank You that You are patient to help me one step at a time. In Jesus' name, amen.

## EYE ON THE PRIZE

*Do you not know that in a race all the runners run, but only one gets the prize? Run in such a way as to get the prize.*

1 CORINTHIANS 9:24

If we're going to do something extraordinary for the Lord and finish well, we're going to need perseverance. I admit that can be a struggle for me because I like to see results quickly. But I understand the benefit of it, so I work on incorporating it into my toolkit. If you and I are going to complete what God called us to do, we've got to find a way to persevere. Most of us have a good story about how we began our God-journey, but too many of us don't have much to say about what happened after that. If you're in that category, I encourage you to shift your focus to how you want to end the race and then run with that in mind. Because the prize doesn't go to the people who start—the prize goes to the people who finish.

## PRAYER

Heavenly Father, teach me perseverance when I am tempted to give up. Sharpen my vision when I cannot see Your path clearly and am tempted to go my own way. Give me strength to run my race with the end clearly in focus. And with every step I take, may I bring glory to You. In the name of Jesus, amen.

# DAY 77

## PERFECT TIMING

*Praise be to God, who has not rejected my prayer or withheld his love from me!*

PSALM 66:20

In my years as a Christ-follower, I have come to trust the faithfulness of God. In every event and every circumstance, I have come to understand that God is faithful. But I've also come to understand that His timing and my timing are often different. If you're in one of those timing gaps where you think God might not be paying attention to your circumstances or your calendar, I would encourage you not to give up. Don't throw away your confidence in God, the scripture says, because in all things He's working for your good. I can always look back and see God's involvement in my circumstances, but in the moment, I've sometimes felt He was overlooking me. Be assured that God loves you and is watching over your life.

## PRAYER

Heavenly Father, how grateful I am that You are watching over me, loving me. Thank You for the assurance that You are working all things for my good. Help me to not lean on my own understanding but trust in You during the times when I cannot see You at work. I rejoice in Your faithfulness! In Jesus' name, amen.

# DAY 78

## STAND TOGETHER

*Encourage one another and build each other up.*

### 1 THESSALONIANS 5:11

Unfortunately, many of us are trained to judge one another rather than encourage one another. I'm not advocating sloppy Christianity, but the reality is that none of us are perfect. I ran a 5K with a friend a few years ago, and I discovered that the encouragement of spectators along the way helped me cross the finish line. I tried to hold it together during the last fifty yards because I didn't want to disappoint the complete strangers who were cheering me on! I discovered something that day: I like encouragement. Wouldn't it be wonderful if we as Christ-followers decided to be that kind of people, encouraging each other to persevere in the faith and cheering each other on toward the finish line? If you're reading this today and you're at the end of the rope, I want to say something to you—don't stop. Finish the race!

## PRAYER

Heavenly Father, You are faithful and constant, an ever-present encourager to me. I thank You that You are concerned for me and watching over my life. Help me to stay the course You have set for me and encourage others in their faith. And we will stand together and shout Your praises. In the name of Jesus, amen.

# DAY 79

## ETERNAL FRUIT

*Do not conform any longer to the pattern of this world, but be transformed by the renewing of your mind. Then you will be able to test and approve what God's will is—his good, pleasing and perfect will.*

ROMANS 12:2

What is God's purpose for your life? He isn't working in you just to get you to Heaven—He's working in you so that your eternity will be fruitful for Him. And the goal is your transformation. We're pretty self-absorbed little people when we're born into this world, and we need help to grow and change. If you will choose to follow the Lord, He will initiate spiritual transformation in your life. It's about more than saying the Sinner's Prayer or joining a church. It's about maturing in your faith to the point where you can discern God's will for you and then have the determination to do it. God will be faithful to His part of that bargain because His desire is for you to be a spiritually mature Jesus-follower.

## PRAYER

Heavenly Father, I need Your transforming work in my life. Renew a steadfast spirit in me and give me a clean heart to follow You. Forgive me for my indifferent attitude and stubbornness. I choose to yield to You in all areas of my life. Thank You for Your faithfulness and guidance. In Jesus' name, amen.

# DAY 80

## PRAYER MAKES A DIFFERENCE

*"Now, Lord, consider their threats and enable your servants to speak your word with great boldness. Stretch out your hand to heal and perform miraculous signs and wonders through the name of your holy servant Jesus." After they prayed, the place where they were meeting was shaken. And they were all filled with the Holy Spirit and spoke the word of God boldly.*

ACTS 4:29-31

The book of Acts is the story of the Church as it emerged after Jesus' ascension. They were under a great deal of scrutiny, and Peter and John had been brought before the ruling council and ordered to stop talking about Jesus. After they were released they went to their people to give a report, and then they prayed. This passage includes the end of their prayer. And then we see what happened: Their meeting place began to shake, they were all filled with the Holy Spirit, and they spoke the Word of God boldly. The sequence is very clear: prayer, shaking, anointing, boldness. Prayer makes a difference! Cultivate the habit of considering your life and the lives of those around you, then acknowledge the times when prayer has made a difference. The world is hungry for news of God's goodness, and answered prayers are a great starting point for a conversation about what He has done for you.

## PRAYER

Heavenly Father, thank You that You hear my prayers. I choose to cultivate a consistent prayer life, and I invite Your Holy Spirit to guide me. I thank You for the times You have answered my prayers and made a difference in the lives of others. Give me boldness to pray with those in my sphere of influence. In Jesus' name, amen.

## STAND ON TRUTH

*There are six things the LORD hates, seven that are detestable to him:*
*haughty eyes, a lying tongue, hands that shed innocent blood, a heart that*
*devises wicked schemes, feet that are quick to rush into evil, a false witness*
*who pours out lies and a man who stirs up dissension among brothers.*

### PROVERBS 6:16-19

If there is something that God hates, I don't want to stand before Him with three or four of those things in my pocket. In this list of things "the Lord hates," one of them is specifically a lying tongue, but the majority of them have to do with deception, falsehood, and manipulation. Even when those around you don't hold the truth in high regard, I want to encourage you as a Christ-follower to be a person who values the truth—in the words you speak, in the way you do business, in the way you conduct yourself in your home, and as you go about your day. If you will make that conscious, daily decision, God will make His truth available to you—and meditating on that will help you avoid doing the other things on the list!

## PRAYER

Heavenly Father, You are Truth and all truth comes from You. As the Psalmist said, all Your words are true, and all Your righteous laws are eternal. Help me to remember Your truth and walk in it today, Lord, that I might live in Your freedom and fulfill Your purposes for me in the earth. It's in Jesus' name that I pray, amen.

## TAKE THE JOURNEY

*God has chosen to make known among the Gentiles the glorious riches of this mystery, which is Christ in you, the hope of glory.*

COLOSSIANS 1:27

Scripture says the people in whom God dwells are the hope of the world. Hope for the planet is not in the buildings where we gather for a few minutes on the weekend, but in Jesus-followers scattered throughout the world. In spite of our humanity, Christ in us is the difference, and we must never lose sight of that. You are of tremendous significance for God's purposes at this unique point in human history, and if you'll choose to take the journey with Him with enthusiasm and hope, God will meet you and walk alongside you. His power will be unleashed, and you'll see remarkable things happen through you.

## PRAYER

Heavenly Father, may all those I interact with today know without a doubt that Jesus is Lord of my life. May my words and actions bring glory to Your name and extend Your Kingdom. Lord, thank You for allowing me to have a part in Your purposes in the earth in this generation. In the name of Jesus I ask these things, amen.

# DAY 83

## AT THE TOP OF THE LIST

*He must become greater; I must become less.*

JOHN 3:30

Many of us have wrongly believed that being a Christ-follower means reciting a prayer and perhaps being dunked in a pool of water then returning to live our lives on our own terms with little interest in the things of God. And being a Christ-follower is not even about where you sit for a few minutes on the weekend. That is a deception. To be a Christ-follower means you not only believe that Jesus of Nazareth is the Christ, the Messiah, but you choose Him as Lord. He becomes your new priority. He gets first place. His agenda becomes your agenda. His moral perspectives become your moral perspectives. His passions become your passions. Thankfully, He has not left us to navigate these things on our own but has given us His Word as an instruction manual and His Holy Spirit as our Helper and Guide.

## PRAYER

Heavenly Father, thank You for Your great mercy and love. My desire is to know and love Your Word and apply the truths in it to my life. Thank You also for sending Your Holy Spirit as my Guide. In Jesus' name, amen.

# DAY 84

## THE RIGHT SIDE OF AUTHORITY

*Then Jesus came to them and said, "All authority in heaven and on earth has been given to me."*

MATTHEW 28:18

This is one of my favorite statements in the Bible. It's after the resurrection, and Jesus is telling His disciples, "The game has changed now, guys. All of the authority of heaven and earth has been given to Me." We understand authority and power. The UN, the World Bank, and the Pentagon are expressions of authority and power. Not to diminish those things—their authority and power is very real—but Jesus is a greater authority with greater power. And there is a day coming, Scripture assures us, when every knee will bow and every tongue will confess that Jesus Christ is Lord. Let's act now to get on the right side of His power, for eternity with or without Him awaits us all.

## PRAYER

Heavenly Father, I acknowledge Your power that is greater than any other the world has ever known. How I want to live a life that honors You! Thank You for the grace and mercy You show to me in my weakness. Thank You for the freedom I have in Christ to live an abundant life of blessing and purpose. In His name I pray, amen.

# DAY 85

## ALL CIRCUMSTANCES

*David stayed in the desert strongholds and in the hills of the Desert of Ziph. Day after day Saul searched for him, but God did not give David into his hands.*

### 1 SAMUEL 23:14

The prophet Samuel had anointed young David to be king, but there was a problem: Israel already had a king, Saul, and he was not interested in vacating the throne. So for more than twenty years David lived as the anointed king of Israel while a man who was hostile to him occupied the throne. He had some seasons of success during those years. He took down Goliath. Some of the finest warriors in Israel migrated toward David and followed his leadership. But he was living as a fugitive in the desert. You might think that after God's prophet had anointed him king, everything would go his way. But God let him spend twenty years as a fugitive instead. Sometimes embracing God's truth for your life means that things may not be easy, but you're willing to give the very best you have to see the purposes of God emerge.

## PRAYER

Heavenly Father, thank You for the example of David, who stood firm in Your plan for him even when he could not see it being fulfilled. Help me to do that too, Lord, when Your path for me seems difficult or leads me through desert places. I choose to serve You in all circumstances. In the name of Jesus, amen.

# DAY 86

## A POWERFUL FORCE

*"Then you will know the truth, and the truth will set you free."*

JOHN 8:32

The truth is a powerful force in our lives. We have to make a conscious decision to become people of truth as we interact with one another. There will be times it will seem to put us at a disadvantage, but it's worth it. Because if we own the truth, we gain a freedom that comes from Almighty God. And when you and I begin to esteem the truth—to give it value and make it a significant objective in our lives—God will make His truth known to us, and that opens an entirely new set of possibilities for our lives. Some of us need to repent and say to the Lord, "I'm sorry. I've been a deceiver and a manipulator. Forgive me." If you will repent and begin to practice truthfulness, God's truth will bring freedom to you.

## PRAYER

Heavenly Father, You are Truth. Your Word is truth, and You desire that Your children walk in the truth. Give me boldness to speak Your truth so that people will hear of Your salvation. Season my words with Your grace so that I might draw people to You. Open doors of hope and renewal and restoration so that people will experience wholeness as never before. I ask these things in the name of Jesus, amen.

## FAITH REQUIRES PRACTICE

*Whatever you have learned or received or heard from me, or seen in me—
put it into practice.*

PHILIPPIANS 4:9

We as disciples are called to be practitioners of our faith. "Church" language works against us, though, because we've been taught that church is something we "attend." Our faith is not something we "attend"—we don't go to watch Christianity like we watch a ballgame. But we've brought that mentality to our faith-life, and we've imagined that the objective is to sit on the sidelines and evaluate. That is not biblical. Church isn't about a building. Church isn't what happens behind a podium. We are the Church—you and I—and we are to take everything we experience inside the church building and put it into practice outside the church building.

## PRAYER

Heavenly Father, thank You for Your Church throughout the earth. Strengthen Your Church to preach the Gospel and to hold fast to Your promises. Provide wide and effectual doors for Your believers to tell about You in all circumstances. In Jesus' name, amen.

## THE SOURCE OF ALL

*"Who am I, and who are my people, that we should be able to give as generously as this? Everything comes from you, and we have given you only what comes from your hand."*

### 1 CHRONICLES 29:14

If you have been blessed financially, I know you can receive many requests for financial support for legitimate, worthy things. If you find yourself in that position, I would encourage you to prayerfully go to the Lord and ask, "What does sacrifice look like for me?" Candidly, He doesn't need your resources, for everything we have comes from Him. What He needs is your heart, and if your heart is open to Him, your resources will flow out. God wants all of us to participate in His Kingdom purposes in a way that recognizes Him as the source of all that is good in our lives and expresses our gratitude to Him. When you give back to God in a tangible expression of your faith, you will give Him the opportunity to bless you beyond your imagining.

## PRAYER

Heavenly Father, Your Word says that every good thing is from You. I come before You in gratitude and humility, acknowledging You as the source of every good thing in my life. I trust You to show me what a sacrifice looks like in my life, and I make a commitment to be obedient to what You show me. In Jesus' name, amen.

# DAY 89

## JUST WHATEVER

*When the wine was gone, Jesus' mother said to him, "They have no more wine." "Dear woman, why do you involve me?" Jesus replied. "My time has not yet come." His mother said to the servants, "Do whatever he tells you."*

JOHN 2:3-5

This story is set at the beginning of Jesus' public ministry. He and His mother and His disciples were at a wedding in Cana, and the hosts ran out of wine. I don't know all that Mary knew about Jesus, but she knew that it wasn't just business as usual with Him. Mary informed Jesus of the situation then turned to the servants and said, "Do whatever he tells you." I can just see the gleam in her eye as she sat back to watch what would happen. Jesus told the servants to fill six large jars with water, and soon the host was impressing his guests with "choice wine." Mary's "whatever" shows a faith that is transformational, a faith that takes the boundaries of our lives and makes them doorways of possibility. My advice on cooperating with Jesus is to just do whatever He tells you. Because when you say yes to Jesus, it changes things.

## PRAYER

Heavenly Father, thank You for this day. Thank You for Your great love that knows no end. Thank You for being my Provider who wants to bless me in ways I cannot imagine. Lord, give me a "whatever faith" that turns boundaries into doorways of possibility. Show me Your plan for my days in the earth, that I might walk in Your ways. In Jesus' name, amen.

## COMPLETE PROVISION

*For this reason he had to be made like his brothers in every way, in order that he might become a merciful and faithful high priest in service to God, and that he might make atonement for the sins of the people.*

HEBREWS 2:17

Jesus' death for you and me on the cross is the expression of God's provision for our lives—completely, for time and eternity. God's provision for us is wrapped up in one word: "atonement." We can understand this "church word" by breaking it into syllables: at-one-ment. It simply means we are brought into a relationship in which we are reconciled, or "at one," with God. To grasp the full magnitude of this, we have to think about the character of God. He is the Almighty Creator, the God who hung the stars in space and knows them by name, the God who is not bound by time or the physical laws that restrict us. The God of the universe has made it possible for you and me to be "at one" with Him. The extravagance of God's provision for us is impossible to exaggerate or overestimate. And He offers it freely to you and to me.

## PRAYER

Heavenly Father, thank You for the extravagant provision You made for me through the death of Your Son, Jesus. Give me a new awareness of the privilege of being "at one" with the God of the universe. Help me to lean on You and Your provision, for You truly are all I need. In Jesus' name, amen.

# DAY 91

## GROWTH STAGES

*Encourage the timid, help the weak, be patient with everyone.*

1 THESSALONIANS 5:14

In order to participate in the Kingdom of God, you have to be born into it. There is no other way. And after that spiritual birth comes spiritual infancy. This is true for all of us, no matter the age we become a Jesus-follower. We have all the equipment necessary to participate, but it's not fully formed, and we have to learn to trust God. It's something we grow into, and we all mature at different rates. Don't be critical of those who are struggling with their faith. They may not believe in the same way you believe, or as fully as you believe. Encourage them, just as you encourage a child who is learning something new. And in a similar way, if you meet someone whose trust has developed beyond yours, who trusts God in ways that you don't yet, don't be angry with them or mock them. Learn what you can from them and aspire to grow in your own faith.

## PRAYER

Heavenly Father, I praise You that You accept us into Your family as children. Thank You for Your patience as we mature in our faith and grow to trust You in greater ways. Give me that same patience as I encourage others to love and trust You more fully. Guide me into a greater understanding of Your nature and Your plans and purposes for my life, so that I might bring honor to Your name. In the name of Jesus I pray, amen.

## SUPREMELY CREATIVE

*How many are your works, O LORD! In wisdom you made them all.*

PSALM 104:24

The creativity of God astounds me! When I think about God's interaction with human beings, one of the first words that comes to mind is "extravagant." When God created flowers, He didn't create one or two kinds. He created hundreds of thousands of different flowers with different shapes and colors and sizes and scents. They bloom in different seasons and in different places. The same is true of trees: God created hundreds of thousands of different kinds in every size and shape. And think of fruits and vegetables. They come in so many colors, textures, shapes, and flavors. It seems that God's creativity just in the realm of plants is virtually endless, and it certainly surpasses anything humans could do. Genesis says that God created all of this for us—for our nourishment, our shelter, and our enjoyment. What a wonderful God!

## PRAYER

Heavenly Father, I marvel at the extent of Your extravagant provision. Open my heart daily to the wonder of Your world. Give me a new appreciation for all You have done—from the magnitude of the distant galaxies to the flavors of the fruits and vegetables I enjoy. Thank You for the creativity and imagination You have placed within humanity because we are made in Your image. May my creativity always bring glory to You. In Jesus' name, amen.

# DAY 93

## AWKWARD TRUTH

*"Therefore let all Israel be assured of this: God has made this Jesus, whom you crucified, both Lord and Christ." When the people heard this, they were cut to the heart and said to Peter and the other apostles, "Brothers, what shall we do?"*

ACTS 2:36-37

The events of Acts 2 occurred during Pentecost, a Jewish holiday celebrated fifty days after Passover. Verse 2 says "God-fearing Jews from every nation under heaven" were in Jerusalem for the occasion. The Holy Spirit had been poured out on the believers in the city, and a crowd had gathered. In the midst of this, Peter stood and said, "You crucified the Messiah." That's a tough message for people who had been keeping God's rules and looking forward to the coming of a messiah for hundreds of years. Even today, the Jesus-story is awkward and uncomfortable until you decide to receive it—that you're a sinner who needs a Savior. Jesus died on a cross not simply because the Romans put Him there; He died on a cross because of my ungodliness. That message hasn't been diminished by two thousand years, and it still takes courage to stand for Jesus.

## PRAYER

Heavenly Father, I thank You for the Jesus-story. I choose to receive it and to receive Jesus as Lord. I believe that Jesus died on a cross for my sins. I recognize that I cannot earn His salvation. I need a Savior. I ask You to be Lord of my life. I want to serve You in every area of my life. In Jesus' name, amen.

# DAY 94

## FULLY YIELDED

*I want to know Christ and the power of his resurrection and the fellowship of sharing in his sufferings, becoming like him in his death.*

PHILIPPIANS 3:10

Paul is making an interesting statement. The first part of it, "I want to know Christ," most of us would agree with. Then, "I want to know the power of his resurrection." Most of us are advocates for the power of God, for healing and deliverance and the things that God's power can accomplish on our behalf. Then comes the tough part: "I want to share in the fellowship of His sufferings." And then he says something that seems really uncomfortable: "Becoming like him in his death." At the point of Jesus' suffering and death, He was completely yielded to Almighty God and His Father's agenda. Jesus said, "God, I'd rather go any other way but this way, but if You need Me to go this way, let's go." And Paul said, "I want to do that." Being yielded to Christ is not about pulpits or rooms filled with people. It's about a God-purpose for your life, a Jesus-story to be told.

## PRAYER

Heavenly Father, give me the faith and perseverance of Paul, that I might know You fully and desire Your will in my life above all else. Thank You for the people You place in my path so that I might share my Jesus-story with them. Give me courage to tell them about You. In His name I pray, amen.

# DAY 95

## TRUST IN RIGHTEOUSNESS

*For whoever keeps the whole law and yet stumbles at just one point is guilty of breaking all of it.*

JAMES 2:10

We have all seen Christians work hard to follow a set of self-imposed rules in order to achieve their standard for righteousness. One thing I've learned about religious rules is that my rules make sense and yours don't! We all have a rationale for our rules, but we look at someone else's and think, "Why would anyone think that?" But no matter our particular list, our rules only serve to make us aware that we can't keep them, no matter how hard we try. Believers are made righteous only through the death of Christ for our sins. This righteousness is God's gift to us, and we must learn to trust Him in that. Trust is a learned response that is developed over time, and the same is true for trust in God. It's a seed that is planted, nurtured, and grows stronger as we witness His faithfulness in our lives.

## PRAYER

Heavenly Father, thank You for the cross. I choose today to trust in You. As I make that commitment I ask You to nurture and grow the trust that I have today into something stronger. Use my life to further Your purposes in the earth. May Your Kingdom come and Your will be done. In Jesus' name, amen.

# DAY 96

## PACK YOUR BAGS

*"Commemorate this day, the day you came out of Egypt, out of the land of slavery, because the Lord brought you out of it with a mighty hand."*

EXODUS 13:3

God required the Jewish people to celebrate a series of annual events that would foster their trust in His provision for them. Passover commemorates when the Spirit of God passed through Egypt and brought death to the firstborn in the land. The Hebrew children were spared when families followed God's command to sacrifice a lamb and mark their doors with its blood. This event resulted in Pharaoh releasing them from slavery and was a prototype of the deliverance that Jesus would later bring on our behalf. But their deliverance was from more than just slavery; God delivered them from being powerless over their condition. There were strong men and intelligent, capable women among them, but they were powerless to change their circumstances. And then Moses walked in and said, "Pack your bags." It's a picture of what Jesus does in our lives. Apart from Jesus we can be physically strong, intelligent, and capable, but bound by something that we are powerless to shake off. Only He has the power to deliver us.

## PRAYER

Heavenly Father, thank You for the power of the cross and the deliverance that is available to me today. I choose to "pack my bags" and follow You. Give me a hunger to read Your Word and the will to be obedient to it so that You can show me the way to a better life. In Jesus' name, amen.

## DAY 97

### A PERFECT LAMB

*The next day John saw Jesus coming toward him and said, "Look, the Lamb of God, who takes away the sin of the world!"*

JOHN 1:29

Jesus as "the Lamb of God" is imagery that is a little blind to us. We think of lambs as cute and cuddly, but during first-century Hebrew worship lambs were an annual sacrifice offered to God in exchange for His forgiveness of sin. During Passover, every family was commanded to kill and roast a lamb as a sacrifice and a ritual meal. Can you imagine as many as 100,000 lambs roasting in the city of Jerusalem? The air would be filled with the aroma. So when John the Baptist declared that Jesus was "the Lamb of God, who takes away the sin of the world!" the people had a very vivid picture of what that sacrifice would mean.

### PRAYER

Heavenly Father, thank You for Your Son and the sacrifice He made on my behalf. I thank You that Jesus made a sacrifice that would stand for eternity. I thank You that everything provided on the cross is complete and finished—nothing left to add—and I have access to every provision made. Help me to understand and receive all that You've done for me. In Jesus' name, amen.

## BEYOND EXPECTATIONS

*We preach Christ crucified: a stumbling block to Jews and foolishness to Gentiles.*

### 1 CORINTHIANS 1:23

Paul's first-century Jewish audience lived in a nation that was occupied by Romans. They were looking for a messiah who would come as a conquering king—overthrowing the Romans and restoring their independence—politically, economically, and spiritually. It was unthinkable for a Jewish person to believe that their messiah had come to earth only to be killed by Romans. And for the Greeks and Romans, who believed in a pantheon of gods who toyed with human beings, it was utter foolishness to imagine that God would send His Son to the world to be executed by humans. Here we are two millennia later, and those two responses are still fully in play. If we don't guard our hearts, we too will be tempted to reject Jesus if He doesn't line up with our expectations. We want Him to be what we want, do what we want, and give us what we want; and if that doesn't happen, we turn away. We have to choose to believe in Him and believe everything about Him. What we believe about Jesus really does make a difference.

## PRAYER

Heavenly Father, thank You for the life, death, and resurrection of Jesus Christ, Your Son. Give me wisdom to guard my heart so I will not reject Jesus or put my own desires and expectations of life ahead of Your plan. I yield my life to You and Your will. In Jesus' name, amen.

# DAY 99

## OUR WAY OUT

*The heart is deceitful above all things and beyond cure.*
*Who can understand it?*

JEREMIAH 17:9

Why do most of us who come to church and carry Bibles and pray still have so many problems? The Bible's diagnosis is very straightforward, and it's captured in one word: sin. Sin still flourishes on planet Earth. We struggle not only with our actions, but with our thoughts and emotions and attitudes. The Bible says that even Jesus was tempted. Since Jesus was perfect, obedient, and sinless but still suffered with temptation, we should not be surprised when we are tempted. Jesus' death on the cross made provision so that the consequences of sin no longer have a hold over our lives. Praise God that He has given us a remedy for the sin problem!

## PRAYER

Heavenly Father, I come before You in humility, asking for Your forgiveness for the times my life has not brought glory to You. I pray that my life would reflect You so that others will see and wonder about Your power in my life. Thank You for the Holy Spirit who directs and convicts me. I praise You for the blood of Jesus. It is in His name that I pray, amen.

# DAY 100

## OPINIONS DO NOT MATTER

*But these are written that you may believe that Jesus is the Christ, the Son of God, and that by believing you may have life in his name.*

JOHN 20:31

What you believe makes a difference across the breadth of your life. The scientific community has established that smoking will harm your health, yet people still choose to smoke. Why? They don't believe the warnings apply to them. What you believe makes a difference. That's true in all kinds of places, and it's true spiritually. We live in an age of skepticism. It's far more fashionable to be a critic and a skeptic than to be a believer. But the best things of God come to those who choose to believe in Him. It's not about my opinion or your opinion. Our opportunity is to take God's Word and let it begin to define the boundaries of who we are. It's the greatest way I know to live. Choose to believe. Choose to put your faith in the Living God.

## PRAYER

Our Heavenly Father, I pray that by Your Spirit You will ignite something within me today, something that will give me the courage to believe, to lay aside skepticism and the reasons for withholding myself from Your purposes. I need Your help. I've been disappointed, discouraged, and betrayed. Holy Spirit, help me to overcome unbelief, to put my hope, trust, and faith in a Living God as never before. Thank You for what You'll do on my behalf. I trust You. In Jesus' name, amen.

# DAY 101

## A REMARKABLE EXCHANGE

*God made him who had no sin to be sin for us, so that in him we might become the righteousness of God.*

### 2 CORINTHIANS 5:21

God orchestrated a divine exchange, where the perfect, sinless, obedient Son of God received what we deserved in order that we might receive what He deserved. And the exchange included far more than just the forgiveness of sins. Jesus was punished that we might be forgiven. He suffered physically that we might know healing and health. He was made sin with our sinfulness that we might be righteous with His righteousness. He was made a curse that we might have His blessings. He endured our poverty that we might know His abundance. He bore our shame that we might share in His glory. He endured our rejection that we might have His acceptance. It was a remarkable exchange, the likes of which the world had never experienced before nor will again.

## PRAYER

Heavenly Father, thank You for the exchanges made possible because of Jesus' obedience on the cross. Only that exchange could take the limits of my life and turn them into doorways of possibility. I choose to put my faith in Him, and open my heart to believe. In Jesus' name, amen.

# DAY 102

## FREE INDEED

*You know of Jesus of Nazareth, how God anointed Him with the Holy Spirit and with power, and how He went about doing good and healing all who were oppressed by the devil, for God was with Him.*

ACTS 10:38 • NASB®

This is an interesting description of Jesus. During Jesus' days on the earth, God was with Him and empowered Him to go about doing good and healing all who were oppressed by the Devil. The Bible also tells us that Jesus Christ is the same yesterday, today, and forever. He hasn't changed and never will change. And what He did in the first century, He is doing in the twenty-first century. So Jesus is in the earth today— in our families, our churches, our communities—to do good and to deliver all who are oppressed. We sometimes think that Christianity will impose restrictions on our lives that will make us less fulfilled, less joyful, less content. That's obviously not true when Jesus Christ is living and working among us, doing good and bringing about God's purposes in our lives.

## PRAYER

Heavenly Father, open my heart to believe in Jesus, to know that He is alive and well—my High Priest, my Intercessor—the One who gave His life that my life might be transformed. Thank You that neither sickness nor demonic oppression nor any dark force can stand before the mighty name of Jesus Christ, our Lord and Savior. Let Your victory fill my life. In Jesus' name, amen.

# DAY 103

## A LIFE WELL-LIVED

*David son of Jesse was king over all Israel. He ruled over Israel forty years—seven in Hebron and thirty-three in Jerusalem. He died at a good old age, having enjoyed long life, wealth and honor. His son Solomon succeeded him as king.*

1 CHRONICLES 29:26-28

King David lived in Jerusalem about a thousand years before Christ. One of the archeological debates today is that the enemies of King David, people who don't want to acknowledge that he lived, worked very hard to destroy any archeological evidence of his kingdom. I often smile about that. His enemies are still afraid of him, and he's been dead three thousand years. What a testimony about the impact of his days in the earth! If you will cooperate with the purposes of God, you'll make an impact far beyond your days—not because you live in the center of civilization, or because your skill set is so phenomenal, but because of your affiliation with Almighty God.

## PRAYER

Heavenly Father, I long to make an impact for You beyond my days in the earth. I pray for a willing spirit that I may daily yield my plans to Yours. Make my path plain, Lord, and Your purposes clear to me that I might honor You with my days. In the wonderful name of Jesus, amen.

## NEW PLACES, NEW ADVENTURES

*He got up, rebuked the wind and said to the waves, "Quiet! Be still!" Then the wind died down and it was completely calm. He said to his disciples, "Why are you so afraid? Do you still have no faith?" They were terrified and asked each other, "Who is this? Even the wind and the waves obey him!"*

MARK 4:39-41

In the first century, it was very common for the pagans to worship the wind and water and the sun and stars. Jesus and His disciples were on a lake when a violent storm blew up. The disciples were afraid they were going to drown. So they woke Jesus up. He calmed the wind and waves, then questioned their faith. We assume that Jesus' work in our lives will be calm and familiar, perhaps in the context of a small group or worship service. In this case, Jesus stretched the disciples' imaginations to the point that they were terrified, even as they were experiencing a miracle. Following God and learning about His power and authority may take you to some places that are not familiar and perhaps some places that are uncomfortable or even terrifying. No matter the circumstance, we can rest in His great love for us and His plan for our lives.

## PRAYER

Heavenly Father, thank You that the world is Yours and under Your authority. How great is Your command that even the wind and the waves obey You! I confess that even as I shake my head at the disciples' unbelief, I imagine that I would have been as terrified as any of them. Help me to trust in You when I am doubting and afraid. In Jesus' name, amen.

# DAY 105

## BELIEVE ME

*"Believe me when I say that I am in the Father and the Father is in me; or at least believe on the evidence of the miracles themselves. I tell you the truth, anyone who has faith in me will do what I have been doing. He will do even greater things than these, because I am going to the Father."*

JOHN 14:11-12

If Jesus begins by saying "Believe me," you know what follows is going to stretch us a bit. And His assertion in this passage is mind-blowing: Those who believe in Him can do the things He had been doing. And what He didn't say is as important as what He did say. He didn't say, "Those who believe in me will gather on Sunday mornings in a building and sing songs and listen to a sermon." He didn't say, "Those who believe in me will keep the rules better." He said, "Those who believe in me will do the kind of things I have been doing—even greater things." Jesus' legacy wasn't only about showing us what He could do; it was also about unleashing His power within us to be His hands and feet and voice in the earth.

## PRAYER

Heavenly Father, I thank You that you help me to believe. I open my heart to cooperate with You. Impart Your power in me so I can be used as a voice in the earth for Your purposes. Use me today to encourage someone to look toward You. In Jesus' name, amen.

# DAY 106

## WE HAVE A PROBLEM

*He himself bore our sins in his body on the tree, so that we might die to sins and live for righteousness.*

### 1 PETER 2:24

One of the roles and responsibilities of the Church of Jesus Christ is to say to the world, "We have a sin problem, and we need a Savior." This is a challenge because we live in an age where tolerance is the ultimate virtue. Tolerance used to mean that we could hold different opinions and still deal with one another with respect. It has come to mean that there is no right and wrong—that you should have my permission, even my blessing, to do whatever you want to do. But that is not the message of Scripture. There is no point in the crucifixion and resurrection if sin is not a problem. We have a responsibility before Almighty God to say there is right and wrong—not in condemnation or judgment but in love and concern. We must have the courage to say, "We have a sin problem, and we need a Savior. Do you know Him?"

## PRAYER

Heavenly Father, thank You that You sent a Savior who gave His life that mine might be transformed. I repent of all my sins. Thank You that sin's mastery over my life was broken through the redemptive work of Jesus on the cross. Open my heart and mind to what Jesus has done for me. Holy Spirit, grant me a fresh revelation of my Lord and Redeemer. In Jesus' name, amen.

# DAY 107

## CHALLENGED TO FOLLOW GOD

*His brothers then came and threw themselves down before him. "We are your slaves," they said. But Joseph said to them, "Don't be afraid. Am I in the place of God? You intended to harm me, but God intended it for good to accomplish what is now being done, the saving of many lives. So then, don't be afraid. I will provide for you and your children." And he reassured them and spoke kindly to them.*

### GENESIS 50:18-21

The purposes of God can bring significance to the challenges you face in life. Joseph's father, Jacob, was one of the Patriarchs—a heavy-hitter in God's story. But there was some major dysfunction in his family. Jacob played favorites with his children, and Joseph's jealous brothers sold him into slavery. Through God's providence, Joseph became the pharaoh's right-hand man and eventually saved his brothers and their families from starvation during a famine. Joseph faced a lot of challenges, but he was always determined to honor his God. If we're going about our daily tasks and facing our challenges with an attitude of, "God, I choose You. I want to honor You. I want to cooperate with You," the purposes of God will come forth.

## PRAYER

Heavenly Father, I choose You. I choose to honor and cooperate with You. I pray that Your Kingdom purposes would be accomplished in my days in the earth. Give me perseverance to keep my eyes on You when I face the challenges of life. In the midst of my circumstances, give me a revelation of Jesus that will bring meaning, hope, and a pathway toward freedom. May I always bring honor to You. In Jesus' name, amen.

# DAY 108

## A NEW DESTINATION

*And after He had said these things, He was lifted up while they were looking on, and a cloud received Him out of their sight. And as they were gazing intently into the sky while He was going, behold, two men in white clothing stood beside them. They also said, "Men of Galilee, why do you stand looking into the sky? This Jesus, who has been taken up from you into heaven, will come in just the same way as you have watched Him go into heaven."*

ACTS 1:9-11 • NASB®

The disciples have been with Jesus through His crucifixion and resurrection. Now He was standing with them on the Mount of Olives. He gave them some final instructions, then stopped talking and began to rise through the air until they couldn't see Him for the clouds. Can you imagine? Jesus had constantly stretched the disciples' thinking. They had known Him on the earth, and when He lifted off, He was showing them there was a new destination. Because of Jesus, our lives are not bound just in time. Because of Jesus, our lives become momentary offerings while we are awaiting a greater reality. The cross truly changes everything.

## PRAYER

Heavenly Father, how I long for Jesus' return in glory! Help me to see beyond the circumstances of my days and live in expectation of eternity with You. Come, Lord Jesus! In His name I pray, amen.

# DAY 109

## JOB QUALIFICATIONS

*If someone else thinks he has reasons to put confidence in the flesh, I have more: circumcised on the eighth day, of the people of Israel, of the tribe of Benjamin, a Hebrew of Hebrews; in regard to the law, a Pharisee; as for zeal, persecuting the church; as for legalistic righteousness, faultless. But whatever was to my profit I now consider loss for the sake of Christ.*

PHILIPPIANS 3:4-7

Paul began his Jesus-story as a Pharisee named Saul of Tarsus. Saul was one of the meanest men we meet in Scripture, and then he met Jesus and became one of the most tenacious advocates for the faith we've ever known. In this passage he's sharing his impressive resume. God turned Saul's life in a different direction and used his background and training for His purposes. All of the things that made Saul a great Pharisee made him a great Jesus-follower. He advocated for Jesus with the same tenacity he had persecuted the Church. If you've accumulated knowledge and developed skills with no intention of using them for the Lord, I promise you Jesus can repurpose all that. He knows how to redeem time spent in other pursuits, and He knows how to repurpose your life experiences.

## PRAYER

Heavenly Father, thank You that You are in the business of repurposing our lives. Show me how I can serve Your purposes in the earth. Give me a willingness to use everything I have to extend Your Kingdom, even the parts of my life that don't seem very useful. May Your Kingdom come. In Jesus' mighty name, amen.

# DAY 110

## MAXIMUM PROVISION

*He who did not spare his own Son, but gave him up for us all—how will he not also, along with him, graciously give us all things?*

ROMANS 8:32

God has been incredibly extravagant toward us, and it's unfortunate that we often don't imagine Him in those terms. We act like extravagance is a bad thing. Sometimes when I talk to people about God's provision, they say, "But God might not want me to have that." If He didn't withhold His Son from you, what would He withhold? We worship an extravagant God, and what He's done toward us is not minimalistic in its nature, presentation, or scope. 2 Peter 1:3 says, "His divine power has given us everything we need for life and godliness." What a generous God we serve!

## PRAYER

Heavenly Father, thank You for Your great love for me. Thank You for providing Your own Son as a sacrifice that I might live in freedom and with joy in the earth and for eternity. Thank You for providing for my needs. I praise You that You are not distant or aloof, but attentive, watching over the details and circumstances of my life. Open my eyes to see and my heart to understand all that You have for me. I will praise You all of my days. In Jesus' name, amen.

# DAY 111

## AN INHERENT PURPOSE

*Here is the conclusion of the matter: Fear God and keep his commandments, for this is the whole duty of man.*

### ECCLESIASTES 12:13

Are you looking for a life purpose? Here's advice from King Solomon, known for his great wisdom: Respect God. Live with reverence for God. Do what's right in the eyes of God. In all the assignments of your life—employer, employee, father, mother, son, daughter, brother, sister, church member, team member, committee member, friend, I could go on—do what's right. Fulfill your responsibilities in a way that shows respect for Almighty God. The principle isn't hard, but it will take everything you have. You don't have to wander the world looking for His purpose for you. He has already given you one.

## PRAYER

Heavenly Father, my desire today is to show respect and reverence for You in all that I do. In all the assignments You have given me, show me how to fulfill them in a way that reflects Your love for people. May others be drawn to You through my actions and attitudes, that Your Kingdom would be extended. In the name of Jesus, amen.

# DAY 112

## OUR MIGHTY BRIDGE

*"Do not think that I have come to abolish the Law or the Prophets; I have not come to abolish them but to fulfill them."*

MATTHEW 5:17

Have you noticed that there are a lot of rules and regulations in the first books of the Old Testament? It took considerable effort to be God's people back in the day. "Wear this. Don't eat that. Go outside the camp for this. Find a priest for that." Whew! But there was a purpose for all of those rules: Without the Mosaic Law and the sacrificial system, without God's detailed explanation of His holiness and what we have to do to bridge the gap between Him and us, we wouldn't have understood the necessity or significance of Jesus' death. The Law makes us aware that even the holiest of us could not keep it perfectly. And when we put Jesus in the context of the story, we recognize that His death did something for us that we could not do for ourselves: bridge the gap between us and God.

## PRAYER

Heavenly Father, I am so grateful that You are a merciful God who has not left us to strive toward holiness on our own. I praise You that through Your intervention we've been made righteous, justified in Your sight. Thank You for the saving work of Jesus that makes me not only accepted in Your family, but loved as Your dearest child. I come to You in the powerful name of Jesus, amen.

# DAY 113

## GOD USES IMPERFECT PEOPLE

*Let the peace of Christ rule in your hearts, since as members
of one body you were called to peace. And be thankful.*

### COLOSSIANS 3:15

Sometimes we think that as believers, our lives should all look the same. We don't have Pharisees and Sadducees who define righteousness by a set of rules, but our immersion in Christianity has caused us to create our own standards of righteousness. And when our life experience stands outside of those standards—the perfect family, the perfect education, the spotless history—we imagine that our opportunities are diminished or that we have suffered unjustly. We become angry at God and hold Him at a distance. It's as if there is a deficit in our account with God, and we're not going to serve Him with too much enthusiasm until He overcomes that deficit. This feeling is very common in the hearts of those of us who fill churches. We're all vulnerable to that kind of comparative analysis, but the idea that you have been treated unjustly by Almighty God is a tool of Satan. If you're in that place, I want to invite you to make peace with God and to thankfully seek out the purposes God has for your life.

## PRAYER

Heavenly Father, Thank You for Your plan for my life—a plan to give me a hope and a future. I repent for my attitude; I repent for being angry with Your timing. I ask You to forgive me. I want to cooperate with You in Your timing with Your plans for my life. In Jesus' name, amen.

# DAY 114

## THE AWKWARD REALITY

*"By faith in the name of Jesus, this man whom you see and know was made strong. It is Jesus' name and the faith that comes through him that has given this complete healing to him, as you can all see. Now, brothers, I know that you acted in ignorance, as did your leaders. But this is how God fulfilled what he had foretold through all the prophets, saying that his Christ would suffer. Repent, then, and turn to God, so that your sins may be wiped out, that times of refreshing may come from the Lord."*

ACTS 3:16-19

This miracle naturally drew a crowd, and Peter took the opportunity to call the people to repentance and belief. Peter says, "If you don't repent, if you don't turn to God, you will miss His Kingdom." The Jesus-story is an awkward story. It's good news, because He's made it possible for us to participate in the Kingdom of God. But we have to grapple with the awkward reality that we're not going to do this one on our own. We'll never deserve it, and that message is uncomfortable in every generation. We need Jesus to participate.

## PRAYER

Heavenly Father, I do not want to be a religious person. I want to be a Christ-follower, one following after Your will over my own. I repent of all my sins. Today I choose to specifically repent for _____. I ask for Your forgiveness, and I thank You that You do forgive me. May my life be a reflection of Your great power. In Jesus' name, amen.

# DAY 115

## THE STANDARD FOR OUR LIVES

*Let us examine our ways and test them, and let us return to the LORD.*

LAMENTATIONS 3:40

I once went to the hospital to pray for a man who was going to have serious surgery. I said, "I wouldn't want you to face that surgery and the possibility of eternity without peace with God. Do you know if you were to die on the operating table, are you prepared to meet the Lord?" He looked me in the eye and said, "Preacher, I'm a whole lot better than the man who lives across the street." And I said, "Well, I don't know your neighbor, but unless he's God, he's not the standard." You may be like this man and have the kind of neighbors who make you feel pretty good about yourself. Unfortunately, the only comparison that matters for eternity is our righteousness compared to God's holiness. Jesus came not only to show us the righteousness of God but to bridge the gap between us and Him—a gap that we could never bridge on our own.

## PRAYER

Heavenly Father, thank You that You give me all I need to live for You. Thank You for the standard we have in Jesus—who shows us how to live for You. Thank You for the gift of Your Word, which teaches me Your character and Your purposes in the earth. Thank You for the Holy Spirit, who guides my steps. May my life show my obedience to You. In Jesus' name, amen.

## GLIMPSES OF GLORY

*For all have sinned and fall short of the glory of God.*

ROMANS 3:23

We were created to bring glory to Almighty God, but we all fall short of that. That is universal; no one is exempt. But even in a fallen world, we get glimpses of that glory. When parents see their newborn child, there is a sense of an almost unbridled joy. It's a "Yay, God!" moment. Only God can do that. When God imagined you before the creation of the world, He intended that you would cause people to think, "Yay, God!" Instead we often cause people to think, "Oh, me." We live in a fallen world. The problem is sin, and the only resolution, the only remedy, is Jesus' death on the cross—a complete, total, absolute, finished, irrevocable defeat of sin.

## PRAYER

Heavenly Father, I come before You in humility to repent of my sin. Where I have chosen ungodliness, where I have chosen to set aside Your counsel, I am sorry and ask You to forgive me. I praise You for the great honor of bearing the name of Jesus. Thank You that I am washed clean because of His sacrifice for me. May I be found faithful today. In His name I pray, amen.

## JUST DO IT

*"And when you stand praying, if you hold anything against anyone, forgive him, so that your Father in heaven may forgive you your sins."*

### MARK 11:25

Forgiveness is the act of setting someone free from an obligation they may owe you. You may feel they owe you an apology or restitution, or maybe you would like an explanation. It's typically the result of a wrong done against you. The Bible has a lot to say about forgiveness, and perhaps the best news is that it can be achieved quickly. Sometimes we have to walk through a shadowed valley. Sometimes we need to be still and know that the Lord is God. But with forgiveness the message is "Just do it!" Don't stop to pray about it or collect the evidence. If unforgiveness and bitterness and hatred and resentment have held you in emotional bondage, choose to forgive. And when you forgive others, God will forgive you.

## PRAYER

Heavenly Father, I repent for all my sins and ask You to forgive me. I thank You that You forgive me. In obedience, I choose to forgive all who have wronged me. I cancel the debt they owe me and lay down all bitterness, resentment, and hatred. I ask that You would bless them. In Jesus' name, amen.

# DAY 118

## IN FOR THE LONG TERM

*Once you were alienated from God and were enemies in your minds because of your evil behavior. But now he has reconciled you by Christ's physical body through death to present you holy in his sight, without blemish and free from accusation.*

COLOSSIANS 1:21-22

Being God's enemy is not a profitable position to hold. God's enemies may appear to be thriving, but their long-term prospects are not good. This passage says that when we place our faith in Jesus as God's Son, and we choose Him as Lord of our lives, we are no longer alienated from God and no longer His enemy. God sees us without blemish, free from accusation. It doesn't say that we will never stumble, that we will never fail, that we won't make mistakes. It says that those sins were addressed by Christ's death and that the curse of our ungodliness was fully paid. That is an amazing gift.

## PRAYER

Heavenly Father, thank You that I am no longer Your enemy but instead one of Your children. I praise You for the blood of Jesus Christ that cleanses me. I want to serve You all the days of my life. I thank You that You've given me everything I need to serve You faithfully. In the name of Jesus, our Savior, amen.

# DAY 119

## A FEW WORDS

*At Caesarea there was a man named Cornelius, a centurion in what was known as the Italian Regiment. He and all his family were devout and God-fearing; he gave generously to those in need and prayed to God regularly.*

ACTS 10:1-2

Acts 10 describes a pivotal moment in the Jesus-story, and one of the important participants is a Roman soldier named Cornelius. Cornelius was not a Jew—he had not studied the Torah or kept the law as most of Jesus' early followers had. Yet this passage tells us he was devout, God-fearing, generous to those in need, and a man of prayer. If someone asked your family, friends, and coworkers to describe you in a few words, which words do you think they would choose? What are the characteristics you encourage in your children and grandchildren? We should always try to align ourselves with Scripture, and sometimes that means adjusting our goals and aspirations.

## PRAYER

Heavenly Father, I am grateful that You have extended Your Kingdom invitation to all who will call on Your name and trust You for salvation. Thank You that You are not interested in my heritage, my IQ, or my income. My greatest desire is to be known as a person who places You above all else. Help me to make that the reality of my life today. In Jesus' name, amen.

## MEASURED BACK

*"Do not judge, and you will not be judged. Do not condemn, and you will not be condemned. Forgive, and you will be forgiven. Give, and it will be given to you. A good measure, pressed down, shaken together and running over, will be poured into your lap. For with the measure you use, it will be measured to you."*

LUKE 6:37-38

We've often heard Luke 6:38 read in the context of giving our money, but that verse is about much more than money. It follows Jesus' reminder about the dangers of judgment and condemnation and the positive consequences of forgiveness. If we will give understanding, if we will give mercy, if we will give forgiveness and give our resources, God will give back to us more abundantly than we give to others. In fact, it says that He takes note of the measure we use in showing understanding and mercy and forgiveness and generosity and considers that when He gives to us. A generous spirit is a sign of spiritual maturity and something we should cultivate.

## PRAYER

Heavenly Father, forgive me for the many times I have stood in judgment or condemnation of others. Show me how to extend mercy to others as You have extended it to me. Show me how to forgive as You have forgiven me. May I always build others up rather than tear them down. Deliver me from any attitudes or actions that do not please You, Lord. In Jesus' name, amen.

# DAY 121

## A PROPER PERSPECTIVE

*You may say to yourself, "My power and the strength of my hands have produced this wealth for me." But remember the LORD your God, for it is he who gives you the ability to produce wealth.*

### DEUTERONOMY 8:17-18

God had just delivered the children of Israel from slavery in Egypt, and Moses was preparing them for their new life in the freedom God had provided. He's warning them about the inclination to look at all you have and say, "Look at what I have done!" We all are tempted to look at the blessings of our lives and say, "Look at what I have accomplished. Look at what I have made happen." We all are tempted to forget that the Lord is the one who has given us those opportunities. Let's guard our hearts so that we will keep a proper perspective of God at work in our lives, and give Him thanks for it.

## PRAYER

Heavenly Father, thank You for the abilities and gifts You've given me. The strength of my hands and any other ability I may have is a blessing from You. May my heart and my words always acknowledge Your provision for me. And may I always be quick to give You thanks for all the ways You are at work in my life. In Jesus' name, amen.

# DAY 122

## TRUE FREEDOM

*"Take my yoke upon you and learn from me, for I am gentle and humble in heart, and you will find rest for your souls."*

MATTHEW 11:29

I have a goal: I want you to become a fully devoted follower of Jesus. If you have been a Christ-follower for most of your life and have been in church for years, I want your commitment to Him to become even greater. If you don't think following Jesus is something you're interested in, I hope you'll give that more thought. I understand there is a cultural resistance to following Jesus. The notion that Christianity will limit your life—even your intellect—has gained some real traction in American culture. I want you to know that is a lie. Following Jesus of Nazareth will bring you more freedom, joy, blessing, and wisdom than any other belief system on the planet—in this life and the next.

## PRAYER

Heavenly Father, show me today how I can know You more, and give me the heart to be obedient to what You show me. I make a decision today to invest time in Your Word and prayer so that You can open doors for me to become a more fully devoted follower in any way You want to impart that to me. I choose to pick up Your yoke and learn from You. In Jesus' name, amen.

# DAY 123

## A PURE LIFE

*Jesus Christ ... gave himself for us to redeem us from all wickedness and to purify for himself a people that are his very own, eager to do what is good.*

TITUS 2:13-14

Paul is writing to Titus about the return of the Lord, and verse 14 gives us an objective of God: to purify a people for Himself. So, if you're ever wondering what God is up to in your life, it is stated very plainly: to purify you. Sometimes we think that God's objective should be to make us happy or successful or fulfilled, but that doesn't seem to be His primary concern. Certainly, purity is difficult to achieve, and none of us will ever be completely successful during our days in the earth. But if purity is something that God is committed to, then I want to try to cooperate with that. Ask the Lord to show you what a more pure life would look like for you today.

## PRAYER

Heavenly Father, I want to live a life that is pure before You—the words I say, the thoughts I think, the attitudes I hold. Help me to think and act in a way that pleases You so that my life will bring honor and glory to You. In Jesus' name, amen.

# DAY 124

## PRIORITIES

*"Call upon me in the day of trouble; I will deliver you,
and you will honor me."*

PSALM 50:15

I have found that I usually receive from God when I am crying out to Him in desperation. Sometimes we try to be coy with God. "God, if You want to do something for me, I'll take it. But it's no big deal; I have a plan." Imagine if I invited you to my house that way. "If you want to come by, it's okay. I'm not sure when I'll be there, but I'd be happy to see you… sometime… if I'm there." You probably wouldn't take me up on that offer. Why would we think that Almighty God would respond to us when we are being so coy? Being desperate before the Lord is not a bad thing. He wants to hear us call on Him. Begin by saying yes to the Lord. Make your time with Him a priority. He wants us to be free. We are learning to be more fully devoted to Him than ever before.

## PRAYER

Heavenly Father, I repent for the times I have been coy with You—not making You a priority—and ask that You forgive me. I want You to be Lord of my whole life. Lord, I thank You that there is a power at work on my behalf, far beyond my strength, far beyond my reason, far beyond my behavior, that the power of the shed blood of Jesus is at work on my behalf today to bring liberty and freedom and wholeness in my life. I praise You for it. For it's in Jesus' name that I pray and believe. Amen.

## PRECIOUS GIFTS

*You were bought at a price. Therefore honor God with your bodies.*

### 1 CORINTHIANS 6:20

The redemptive work of Jesus on the cross was intended to transform us body, soul, and spirit. Honoring God, then, is also an expression of our total person: body, soul, and spirit. So often I think we have tried to reduce the redemptive work of Jesus to something that has benefits just in eternity. "My sins are forgiven, so my ticket is punched and I get into heaven when I'm done here under the sun." That's not what Scripture teaches us. The redemptive work of Jesus was for our whole person, and it was for our lives under the sun as well as our lives in eternity. We will have glorious, perfect bodies in eternity, but we should treat our current ones, as imperfect as they are, as precious gifts that Jesus bought at a price. That means giving attention not only to food and exercise but things like sleep, and stress, and what we put before our eyes and into our ears.

## PRAYER

Heavenly Father, sometimes life in the earth seems limited and bound by the chains of a human body. You have said that I am created in Your image, and everything about me is Yours. Show me how to honor You with my physical self, that my days here would be fruitful for You. In Jesus' name, amen.

# DAY 126

## JUST AN ORDINARY DAY

*"Just as it was in the days of Noah, so also will it be in the days of the Son of Man. People were eating, drinking, marrying and being given in marriage up to the day Noah entered the ark. Then the flood came and destroyed them all. It was the same in the days of Lot. People were eating and drinking, buying and selling, planting and building. But the day Lot left Sodom, fire and sulfur rained down from heaven and destroyed them all. It will be just like this on the day the Son of Man is revealed."*

LUKE 17:26-30

Jesus, speaking prophetically, chooses two previous generations and draws a parallel to the season prior to His coming back to the earth. He says that before He returns it will be like the days of Noah and the days of Lot. While those were both exceedingly wicked generations, Jesus doesn't mention the ungodliness and the wickedness. He says the people were engaged in the normal, everyday pursuit of their own lives and completely unconcerned about the things of God. This is a cautionary note for our generation: Don't be so consumed by the busyness of your daily life that you aren't pausing to ask, "God, what are Your purposes in my generation? I would like to participate with You."

## PRAYER

Heavenly Father, You have said no man will know the day of Jesus' return, but Scripture gives us signs of the end times that we see around us. Make me expectant and hopeful for Jesus' coming, living as though the hour were near. Help me to know Your purposes for me, that I might fulfill my role in extending Your Kingdom in the earth. In the name of Jesus, the coming King, amen.

# DAY 127

## NOT LESS BUT MORE

*"I know that you can do all things; no plan of yours can be thwarted."*

JOB 42:2

Job is one of the Bible's best examples of "Things would have gone a lot better if I'd just cooperated with God." Here, in the last chapter of his story, he finally admits that no purpose of God's can be thwarted. I've been a Christ-follower for over forty years and have been in ministry for a long time. I've had some incredible spiritual mentors. But my reality is there are still times when I struggle to cooperate with God. We want to imagine that if we walk with God for a while, we'll be ready to say, "Yes! Absolutely! Let's go!" at any invitation. But that isn't my experience, and I don't think I'm unique. I think all of us sometimes struggle with the invitations God puts before us because we believe that if we fully yield, if we fully cooperate with God, our lives will be less than we can do on our own. In reality, the more we cooperate with God, the more freedom and blessing we will experience.

## PRAYER

Heavenly Father, I want to cooperate with You! I want to say yes to Your every invitation. Help me to submit my will to Yours, Lord, that Your purposes will be accomplished in my life. And I will give You all the praise and honor. In Jesus' name, amen.

# DAY 128

## MAJESTIC PEACE

*God is not a God of confusion but of peace.*

1 CORINTHIANS 14:33 • NASB®

We live in a remarkably ordered universe. The precision of the natural world is astounding. And the better our ability to observe and measure that precision, the more obvious it is. That is equally true in the spiritual world. Sometimes when we come to the topic of the Spirit of God, we ignore it or avoid it or are frightened of it because we imagine it to be chaotic. If you have seen it expressed in a chaotic way, that chaos did not come from God. He's not a God of confusion; He's a God of peace. And the more we understand the Spirit of God and how to cooperate with Him, the more the peace of God, and the order of God, and the precision of God will be made evident and apparent in our lives.

## PRAYER

Heavenly Father, how it thrills me to see Your mighty hand at work in the physical world! From the diligence of the ants to the orbits of the planets around the sun, Your world is majestic to behold. Lord, reveal to me the working of the Spirit in my life and around me, that I might give You glory for all the ways You are at work in the spiritual realm. Holy Spirit, I want to cooperate with You—that Your work in me will be apparent. May my life reflect Your presence. In Jesus' name, amen.

# DAY 129

## OUT OF TIME

*The world is passing away, and also its lusts; but the one who does the will of God lives forever.*

1 JOHN 2:17 • NASB®

This verse brings to mind a reality that we need to be conscious of, and that is the difference between time and eternity. Right now we are creatures of time. We live in temporary bodies of flesh and blood, and they simply indicate that we have been invited into the game. But when our physical bodies cease to function and we step out of time, we will continue in eternity. The invitation of Scripture is to utilize this brief season in time to prepare for eternity. So often, we only consider our identity in the context of now. I'm a teenager, or I'm a senior. I don't have kids yet, or my kids are grown. Our self-description and self-awareness is almost entirely focused on who we are in time. The prophetic Word of God is a powerful reminder that we need to live with a very significant awareness of eternity because our entire story, the total evaluation of our lives, will not be told in time.

## PRAYER

Heavenly Father, how I long for and look forward to eternity with You! My imaginings of it surely pale in comparison to the glory it holds. Make my days fruitful for Your Kingdom purposes while I am alive in the earth, but keep my vision focused on eternity. Come, Lord Jesus! In His name I pray, amen.

# DAY 130

## IF THEN

*"If you are willing and obedient, you will eat the best from the land; but if you resist and rebel, you will be devoured by the sword."*

### ISAIAH 1:19-20

Hebrew poetry often comes with parallel if/then statements, and these two are pretty straightforward. If you are willing and obedient toward God, then you will get the best. But if you resist Him and rebel, then you will be devoured by the sword. Being willing isn't enough. Being obedient isn't enough. We have to be both willing and obedient. Have you ever been willing, but you haven't been very obedient? Or you may have been outwardly obedient, but inwardly your heels were dug in and you were grinding your teeth. The opposite of willingness and obedience is resistance and rebellion, and that is not a good place to be. We can be passive and rebellious or even compliant and rebellious, but being "devoured by the sword" is surely an outcome to be avoided. We have authority over our will, so let's choose to be willing and obedient.

## PRAYER

Heavenly Father, I am sorry for the times I have been disinterested in Your plans and purposes for me. I ask forgiveness for the times I have turned my back on You and chosen my own way. I acknowledge today that You are Lord of all that I am and all that I have, the Sovereign God who will lead me on a path of Kingdom service and blessing if I will allow You. Give me a willing and obedient heart. In Jesus' name, amen.

# DAY 131

## ACCEPTED AND HIGHLY FAVORED

*To the praise of the glory of His grace, by which He made us accepted in the Beloved.*

EPHESIANS 1:6 • NKJV®

Do you know that God has accepted you? The Bible says He has chosen us. When God created you, He said, "That's good." He didn't look at you and say, "Oops. Do over." God has accepted you, chosen you, and commissioned you as His ambassador. There is an epidemic of rejection in our nation, however, and it has many expressions— racism, unemployment, divorce, abortion, abuse, neglect—the list could go on. Rejection may be the defining characteristic of our nation these days, and we need to know the power of God's acceptance. On the cross, and in that empty tomb, God expressed for time and all eternity His acceptance of you and me.

## PRAYER

Heavenly Father, I thank You that I am accepted in the Beloved. I believe that Your Word is true and that You accept me. I forgive all who have rejected me. I choose to lay down any bitterness, anger, or resentment that rejection has produced in my life. I thank You that I am highly favored and the object of Your special care. Lord, I accept myself. I am Your workmanship, and I believe You have begun a good work in me and will finish what You have started. Thank You. In Jesus' name, amen.

## DAY 132

## THROUGH YOU

*At my first defense, no one came to my support, but everyone deserted me. May it not be held against them. But the Lord stood at my side and gave me strength, so that through me the message might be fully proclaimed and all the Gentiles might hear it.*

### 2 TIMOTHY 4:16-17

Paul is imprisoned in a foreign city and on trial for his life. He is writing to his protégé, Timothy, and says, "Through me, God has some things yet to do." He's not calling out his friends for abandoning him. He's not accusing God of being unfair. He simply tells Timothy that through him, there is a God-story yet to emerge. And the same is true for you. Through you, God has plans. Through you, there is a God-story to be told. Your life, as complicated as it may seem, is no more complicated than Paul's was that day. He said, "Through me the message might be fully proclaimed." That's pretty bold when you are in a Roman prison without Facebook or Twitter. It is staggering that two thousand years later, what Paul said in that letter has come to pass. No human has had more impact for the cause of Jesus Christ than Paul. God can use you, too. Don't ever lose sight of that.

## PRAYER

Heavenly Father, thank You for loving me in spite of the complications in my life. Thank You for allowing me to participate in Your purposes in the earth. May I be as steadfast as Paul when facing life here on earth. In Jesus' name, amen.

# DAY 133

## EVERYTHING WE NEED

*The acts of the sinful nature are obvious.*

GALATIANS 5:19

This is a rather direct statement. In our culture the acts of the sinful nature may be apparent, but we are told repeatedly they're not obvious. In fact, the great clashes in our culture these days are over saying something is sinful. If you say there is such a thing as sin, there is a group of people ready to respond with, "Who says?" And our answer is, "God says." Scripture says that all of us—even Bible-carrying, church-attending, prayer-praying people—have a tendency toward ungodliness. But the tendency is no excuse to indulge those desires because we have everything we need to live a life that pleases God—His Word to instruct us, His Son's example to follow, and His Spirit to guide us.

## PRAYER

Heavenly Father, I come before You acknowledging my sinful nature and my struggles with ungodliness. Thank You for all the ways You have provided a way for me. Thank You for the salvation You have provided for me through Your Son. Thank You for sending Him as a man to live among us, so that we would have His example to follow. Thank You for Your Word that lights my path. Thank You for Your Spirit, who guides my steps. You are a great God and greatly to be praised! In Jesus' name, amen.

# DAY 134

## TOTAL PROVISION

*Let those who love the LORD hate evil, for he guards the lives of his faithful ones and delivers them from the hand of the wicked.*

PSALM 97:10

There is a battle in the earth between the Kingdom of God and the kingdom of darkness, and this is a battle we cannot win on our own. It we were left to our own devices to outsmart or outtalk evil, we could not do it. We need the power of God to help us break the spiritual influences that stand opposed to God's purposes in our lives because the only thing evil will yield to is a power greater than itself. On the cross, God made complete and total provision for your well-being and mine. You and I, through our beliefs and our choices, either reject His provision or we claim it for our own and cooperate with it. The wicked are powerful in our world, but we can rely on His greater power and His promise to guard and deliver us.

## PRAYER

Heavenly Father, thank You for the sufficiency of Your power demonstrated on the cross. Thank You that it is not up to me to define it or defend it, for it is a power beyond my comprehension. Again I claim Your provision for me and Your power over anything or anyone who would oppose Your purposes in my life. I praise You for all You will accomplish in and through me. In Jesus' name, amen.

# DAY 135

## GOOD FRUIT

*The fruit of the Spirit is love, joy, peace, patience, kindness, goodness, faithfulness, gentleness and self-control. Against such things there is no law.*

### GALATIANS 5:22-23

This passage begins by listing nine separate expressions of the Spirit of God that will be made evident in our character when we choose to cooperate with Him. The next statement is truly astounding: "Against such things there is no law." When you and I choose to cooperate with the Spirit of God, to allow the fruit of the Spirit to emerge in our character, there is no law—no physical law, no spiritual law—that supersedes those things. We are not by nature gentle, patient, self-controlled, faithful, good, kind folk. The greatest demonstration of the power of God on your behalf or mine is to see the fruit of the Spirit emerge within us.

## PRAYER

Heavenly Father, I desire to see the fruit of Your Spirit in my life. Thank You that Your power to accomplish Your plans and purposes for my life supersedes every other power in the earth. Holy Spirit, guide my thoughts and my words and my behavior as I seek to live in a way that demonstrates Your work in me. May Your fruits be evident so that the world would see them and marvel at Your power in those who call themselves followers of Jesus. In His name I pray, amen.

# DAY 136

## FREEDOM TO FLOURISH

*"If the Son sets you free, you will be free indeed."*

JOHN 8:36

Would you like to know God's agenda? It's freedom in your life. It's not bondage. He doesn't want to limit your happiness or your joy or your pleasure. If there is a place in Scripture where God says, "Don't do that," or times when the Holy Spirit has made it clear to you that a choice is wrong, it's because if you go forward with it, things are not going to work out well. If we are willing to be really honest, most of us have tried some of those things and regretted it. So we came back and said, "God, I will try Your way after all." God's way will always be the best way to live.

## PRAYER

Heavenly Father, thank You for the freedom You offer through life in Your Son. Thank You for the hedges of protection You have set around my life. Forgive me for the times I have not appreciated Your watchful care over me and have ignored Your boundaries. Thank You for the blessings of love and assurance You pour over me when I am living Your way. May my life be a reflection of You. In Jesus' name, amen.

# DAY 137

## HIS MIGHTY HAND

*Come and see what God has done, how awesome his works in man's behalf!*

PSALM 66:5

The ability to see and acknowledge what God has done is essential if we are going to recognize and participate in His purposes. Don't sit in the seat of the skeptic and think, "I am not going to give God credit unless there's absolutely no other way to explain it." Let me invite you to this perspective: "I am going to give God glory and thanks and honor for everything that has happened in my life." I have decided if there is any possible reason to say, "Yay, God," I am going to. And I love the change that has brought to my heart.

## PRAYER

Heavenly Father, Your works on my behalf are truly awesome! Scripture reminds me of Your mighty hand that moves in my life and blesses me in so many ways. Thank You for all that You do—the large miracles and the small ways You step into my life each day. Thank You that You care for me. Thank You for the new perspective that gives You the credit for the good things in my life. May Your name be lifted up through my life. In Jesus' name, amen.

## TRUST IN THE SPIRIT

*"All this I have spoken while still with you. But the Counselor, the Holy Spirit, whom the Father will send in my name, will teach you all things and will remind you of everything I have said to you."*

JOHN 14:25-26

When Jesus told His disciples, "I'm leaving you, and you can't come with Me," they were understandably alarmed. But then He said, "Don't be afraid. When I'm gone, the Father will send the Holy Spirit to you, and He will remind you of everything I've said." If God had put me in charge of the Jesus-initiative, I would have had Jesus make a list of His twenty most significant teachings and sign it "Jesus of Nazareth." But Jesus never wrote a word, and the New Testament was fueled, guided, and directed by the Spirit of God. The accuracy of the New Testament depends on this very notion: To the extent that I trust Jesus, I can trust the Spirit of God to have given me, with integrity, the lessons I need.

## PRAYER

Heavenly Father, Your Word is a gift in my life. Thank You that it is trustworthy and that its message never changes. Thank You for sending the Holy Spirit to guide us in the truth of Your Word and Your ways. Holy Spirit, give me increased knowledge of the Word and awareness of how I should apply it to my life. May I always be known as a person of the Word. In Jesus' name, amen.

# DAY 139

## POWER DEMONSTRATED

*My message and my preaching were not with wise and persuasive words, but with a demonstration of the Spirit's power, so that your faith might not rest on men's wisdom, but on God's power.*

### 1 CORINTHIANS 2:4-5

Paul says something that is counterintuitive to a preacher like me: His preaching was not with "wise and persuasive words." I spend a lot of time speaking to people, and I don't particularly want to sound dumb when I do. But there has to be an agenda, an objective beyond appearing to be wise, or even being persuasive. Paul said, "I want to demonstrate the power of God." If God is doing something through you, it's not because of your intellect or your clever conversation. It's because you believe something remarkable happened for you at the cross. And to the degree that you are willing to believe that, you will benefit from the power of God at work on your behalf. Every blessing that is attached to being a Christ-follower extends from the power demonstrated in the crucifixion and the resurrection of Jesus. That's remarkable.

## PRAYER

Heavenly Father, I want to demonstrate Your power to a watching world. I pray that the Holy Spirit would completely cover my words and overtake any agenda I might have other than the power of the cross. I present myself a living sacrifice to Your purposes that Your Kingdom might be established in the earth. In the powerful name of Jesus, amen.

# DAY 140

## IT'S ABOUT THE PEOPLE

*Know that the LORD is God. It is he who made us, and we are his; we are his people, the sheep of his pasture.*

PSALM 100:3

God's intention in the earth is directed first and foremost to His people. That is the story from Genesis to Revelation, and it has not changed. God made the earth and everything in it for His people, so we certainly have a stewardship responsibility. But when Jesus appears on this planet the second time, He is not coming back to see Mount Everest or a whale—He is coming back for His people. We hear messages from various groups that people are no more important than other creatures or even the earth itself. That is not true—we are the ones created in His image and for relationship with Him. Don't ever lose sight of the fact that God's people are at the center of His story and His purposes in the earth.

## PRAYER

Heavenly Father, thank You for the unimaginable blessing of being created in Your image. I do not fully understand that, but You say it is so and I trust You. You love me with a love beyond what any human can feel or even comprehend, even sending Your Son to die for me. Help me to love others as You do and to always keep people at the center of my plans and purposes. In Jesus' name, amen.

# DAY 141

## GUIDE AND PROVIDE

*"I have much more to say to you, more than you can now bear. But when he, the Spirit of truth, comes, he will guide you into all truth. He will not speak on his own; he will speak only what he hears, and he will tell you what is yet to come."*

### JOHN 16:12-13

Jesus has just told the disciples that His time on earth is coming to an end. He pours His love and instruction into them and then says, "I have so much I would like to tell you, but right now you just can't hear it all." Haven't we all been there? Maybe the preacher has overloaded you with information or said things you weren't ready to hear. But Jesus said the Holy Spirit will do two specific things for us: He will guide us into truth, and He will provide revelation—all in God's good timing. The secrets of the Kingdom of God will be made known to men and women on the earth through our cooperation and participation with the Spirit of God. When I am frustrated or discouraged by my lack of understanding of His plan and purposes, this brings me great comfort.

## PRAYER

Heavenly Father, thank You for the gift of Your Holy Spirit. Holy Spirit, You are welcome in my life. Guide me into all truth, provide revelation, and teach me in Your perfect timing. I thank You that You oversee my life in a way that is so much better than what I could do myself. Help me to always see Your hand and acknowledge Your watchful care over me. In Jesus' name, amen.

# DAY 142

## WITH ALL OF YOU

*One of the teachers of the law came and heard them debating. Noticing that Jesus had given them a good answer, he asked him, "Of all the commandments, which is the most important?" "The most important one," answered Jesus, "is this: 'Hear, O Israel: the Lord our God, the Lord is one. Love the Lord your God with all your heart and with all your soul and with all your mind and with all your strength.'"*

MARK 12:28-30

If contemporary American Christians were asked this question, many people would answer, "Love God with all of your mind." We think discipleship is about intellect and learning. Get the facts right, study a little more, read a little more, learn a little more. But that's not all of what Jesus said. He said to love God with your heart, your soul, your mind, and your strength. You should worship God physically as much as you worship Him intellectually and emotionally. It requires your entire person. The totality of how you live your life is an expression of your worship to God. It's a remarkable notion.

## PRAYER

Heavenly Father, I want to worship You with everything I have. Show me how to love You in all the areas of my life. Strengthen me in mind and spirit and body so that I will bring You glory in everything I think and say and do. In Jesus' name, amen.

# DAY 143

## CULTIVATE REPENTANCE

*Have mercy on me, O God, according to your unfailing love; according to your great compassion blot out my transgressions. Wash away all my iniquity and cleanse me from my sin. For I know my transgressions, and my sin is always before me.*

### PSALM 51:1-3

One of the reasons the Church in our culture has been so ineffective and has forfeited so much influence is that we imagine everyone else is in the wrong and needs to repent. We are reluctant to say, "I've done wrong. I'm a sinner. Have mercy on me." Repentance needs to start in the Church. A good place to begin is by reading Psalm 51. It's David's prayer of repentance after his sin was exposed, and it will give us some lines, phrases, and simple expressions of repentance. Let's begin today making repentance a part of our routine.

## PRAYER

Heavenly Father, I choose to be like David and make repentance a familiar practice in my life. I repent now for all of the places I've fallen short of Your purposes for my life. Specifically, I repent for _____. I ask You to forgive me, and I receive Your forgiveness. Thank You. Help me to turn from it and choose Your path for my life. In Jesus' name, amen.

# DAY 144

## AN ACTIVE RESPONSE

*All these are the work of one and the same Spirit, and he gives them to each one, just as he determines.*

1 CORINTHIANS 12:11

The Holy Spirit decides which spiritual gifts each of us is given. We don't choose them, but they do require our cooperation. Sometimes I believe Christians are somewhat insincere about this topic. It's not uncommon for me to hear people say, "I'm open to any gift God has for me," as if that fully expresses their responsibility. For what God has done to be effective in my life, I have to respond with something other than, "God, if You want me, come get me." The Bible says we are to eagerly desire spiritual gifts. Think about the effort you give for something you eagerly desire. It invades your calendar, your spending, and your thoughts. I am inviting you to purposefully and intentionally move beyond saying, "God, whatever You have, I'll receive it," to the pursuit of all that God would make available to you and through you.

## PRAYER

Heavenly Father, I thank You that You determine the gifts You want to impart to me. I choose to seek after You to understand the purpose of each one and to cultivate a new desire for the gifts You have planned to give me. Give me a hunger for Your Word and a determination to set aside time to spend in Your presence. Help me today to use the gifts You have given me, that Your love and power will be evident in my life and Your purposes fulfilled in the earth. In Jesus' name, amen.

# DAY 145

## VALUABLE CONTENTMENT

*Keep your lives free from the love of money and be content with what you have, because God has said, "Never will I leave you; never will I forsake you."*

### HEBREWS 13:5

Wouldn't it be nice if we could decide just once to have a proper relationship with money and be done with it? Evidently that's not humanly possible. The wording of this verse suggests that we must make the decision over and over to keep our lives free of the love of money, in the same way we decide daily to make our beds or wash our faces. Money is not evil, and the Bible doesn't condemn wealth. In fact, the Bible says that God gives us the ability to accumulate wealth. It's our attitude about money that we should keep a careful watch over.

## PRAYER

Heavenly Father, I choose to seek Your perspective on money and all the things money can do. I pray for contentment with the blessings You have poured over my life. Give me a generous spirit in all things, that I would reflect Your generosity. Thank You for the promise that You will never leave me or forsake me, for that is worth more than all the world's riches. In the name of Jesus, amen.

# DAY 146

## KEEP IT SIMPLE

*My son, do not forget my teaching, but keep my commands in your heart,*
*for they will prolong your life many years and bring you prosperity.*

### PROVERBS 3:1-2

A good rule of thumb is that the best way to interpret the Bible is to take the simplest possible reading whenever you can. There are some places that obviously won't work, but it should be your first response to God's Word. I believe this passage means precisely what it says—that if we won't forget God's teaching, but if we will keep it in our hearts, that it will prolong our lives many years, and it will bring us prosperity. What an interesting notion! Don't spend your life chasing the blessings of God. If you'll meet the conditions, God will see to it that His blessings flow over you.

## PRAYER

Heavenly Father, I am grateful for the many times Your Word speaks so plainly. Thank You for this simple instruction. Help me to understand and remember Your teachings, Lord, so my days in the earth will be blessed. And I will give You the praise. In Jesus' name, amen.

# DAY 147

## ON THE BATTLEFIELD

*We demolish arguments and every pretension that sets itself up against the knowledge of God, and we take captive every thought to make it obedient to Christ.*

### 2 CORINTHIANS 10:5

"Demolish." "Take captive." This is very assertive language from Paul. I believe he's using himself as an example, that he intends to demolish any thoughts and ideas that set themselves up against his knowledge of God. The only thoughts I can control are my own, and I have to ask myself, "If every thought I have was displayed on a screen for everyone to see and reviewed by the Lord Himself, would I be okay with that?" Guard your mind, the Bible says, because it is a battlefield. Be careful what you watch, what you listen to, and what you let people feed into your mind because it is the well-spring of life. We must acknowledge the fact that there is a constant assault on our minds and that ungodly thinking has to be defeated or it will dominate our lives. Thankfully, we are more than able to do that through the power of the Holy Spirit.

## PRAYER

Heavenly Father, help me to demolish any thought or idea that is contrary to my knowledge of You. Thank You for the Holy Spirit, who leads me as I live my days on the earth with eternity in view. Purify my mind, Lord, so every word and image that passes through it is worthy of a child of the King. In the cleansing name of Jesus, amen.

## AT THE CROSS

*For the message of the cross is foolishness to those who are perishing, but to us who are being saved it is the power of God.*

### 1 CORINTHIANS 1:18

At the heart of the apostle Paul's theology is the cross of Jesus Christ. He consistently asserts that the cross is the demonstration of the power of God, and to deny the cross is to deny the power of God. Something remarkable happened on the cross—an exchange took place. The perfect, obedient, sinless Son of God took upon Himself all of the punishment that was due by divine justice to me for my godlessness and my rebellion. In turn, I received all of the blessings and benefits that were due to Him for His perfect obedience. We don't deserve it, and we can't earn it. The power of God was demonstrated at that cross on Golgotha more than two thousand years ago. What you and I are asked to do is believe that, trust that, and appropriate that power in our lives.

## PRAYER

Heavenly Father, how can I thank You for the Divine Exchange that took place on the cross? Your mercy and grace displayed there are beyond any words that my mind can summon or my tongue can express. With all my heart I believe in Your power, trust in it, and claim it in my life. In the precious name of Jesus, amen.

## DAY 149

### TREASURE HELD CLOSE

*So they hurried off and found Mary and Joseph, and the baby, who was lying in the manger. When they had seen him, they spread the word concerning what had been told them about this child, and all who heard it were amazed at what the shepherds said to them. But Mary treasured up all these things and pondered them in her heart.*

LUKE 2:16-19

There is a romanticized version of the manger scene—the Christmas Nativity display—the animals and the cast of characters gazing at the baby, all looking very peaceful. The truth is Joseph and Mary went through a surprise pregnancy in a small village. Joseph put his pregnant wife on the back of a donkey and her baby was born in a barn. She endured all of that, yet Scripture says, "Mary treasured up all these things and pondered them in her heart." Mary made a decision to pull the God-pieces of her life together and hold them close. What are you holding close today? Are you keeping the promises of God in your heart and pondering them as you wait for His purposes to be fulfilled in your life?

### PRAYER

Heavenly Father, I am humbled as I think about the two young people who endured so much to trust You and allow Your plan to unfold through their lives. Give me the same resolve when following You doesn't fit with my plans and my preconceived notions of what Your plans should be. Fulfill Your purposes in me, Lord. In the name of Jesus, the very Son of God born in a manger, amen.

## A LIGHT ON THE NARROW PATH

*"Enter through the narrow gate. For wide is the gate and broad is the road that leads to destruction, and many enter through it. But small is the gate and narrow the road that leads to life, and only a few find it."*

MATTHEW 7:13-14

Jesus identifies two possible outcomes: "destruction" and "life." He describes the pathways: a broad gate and a broad path that many will take to their destruction, and a narrow gate and a less-traveled path that only a few will find. Did you know that being a Christ-follower is a minority position? Jesus said we're laboring in the fields of humanity, saying to people, "There is a God. He's alive. His Son's name is Jesus, and He will change your life. There is a doorway, a gate over here, which leads to Him. It's a bit narrower. Not everyone is walking that way, but I've been on the journey awhile and can tell you it's been the most rewarding, the most liberating thing I've ever found. Why don't you walk that way with me?" Share your Jesus-story. It's a privilege to be a difference-maker in the lives of people.

## PRAYER

Heavenly Father, thank You that You have provided a way of salvation—a narrow gate and path, yes, but there for all who seek it. Thank You for the glorious blessing and eternal reward You promise to all who decide to walk that way. May many choose You and the narrow path, Lord, and may Your Kingdom be extended. In Jesus' name, amen.

# DAY 151

## CULTIVATE HOPE

*Be strong and take heart, all you who hope in the Lord.*

PSALM 31:24

I never thought about hope requiring strength and courage, but this verse says to be a person of hope will require both of those things. The Hebrew word that's translated "hope" in this verse is translated "wait" elsewhere in the Old Testament, so there's a connection between hoping in the Lord and waiting on the Lord. Hope has fallen on hard times in many segments of Christianity because it's seen as an expression of weakness and uncertainty. But I believe hope is the insulation that protects and strengthens our faith. Faith is about now, and hope is about what we anticipate coming. Sometimes hope will require a lot of focus and determination from us, but it is worth the effort to cultivate it in our lives.

## PRAYER

Heavenly Father, I thank You that You watch over my future. I am sorry for the times I have put my hope in places other than You. May my hope in You be more real to me than the anxiety and stress that are a part of life in the earth. Today I choose to be strong and take heart and hope in You. In Jesus' name, amen.

# DAY 152

## INVEST YOURSELF

*I turned around to see the voice that was speaking to me. And when I turned I saw seven golden lampstands, and among the lampstands was someone "like a son of man," dressed in a robe reaching down to his feet and with a golden sash around his chest.*

### REVELATION 1:12-13

In this opening chapter of Revelation, the seven lampstands symbolize seven churches. Not surprisingly, that's where we find Jesus: standing in the midst of His churches. "Church" is not about a denomination, tradition, label, or location; it is every person who believes in Jesus Christ. Jesus said He would build His Church and Hell itself wouldn't be able to withstand it. The New Testament says when He comes to earth again He's coming for His Church. If you want to invest yourself in something of significance in the Kingdom of God, be a person who strengthens the Church. We're an imperfect lot. God loves us and has made provision for our inconsistencies. It is a paradox, but the great weakness of the Church—people—is also its great strength. The Church matters to Jesus, so let's commit ourselves to be about the business of building it until He returns.

## PRAYER

Heavenly Father, how I love Your Church! Thank You for allowing me to work and worship in the midst of Your people. Help me to strengthen those in my circle of influence that the Body of Christ will draw nearer to You as the day approaches when Jesus will return for His Church. I ask for Your grace and mercy and power to press on toward that day. In the name of Jesus, amen.

# DAY 153

## NOT ME, BUT THEE

*So then, just as you received Christ Jesus as Lord, continue to live in him, rooted and built up in him, strengthened in the faith as you were taught, and overflowing with thankfulness.*

### COLOSSIANS 2:6-7

Sometimes cooperating with God will take you to a place that's unexpected and perhaps even unpleasant. But how will you respond to that? If you've been around a newborn, you know that they communicate their unhappiness at maximum volume. They don't care if you're asleep or watching the game, they will make sure you know they are displeased. And that's to be expected because they are young. But if you get to forty and you're still disagreeable until you are satisfied, that's immature. Sometimes we want to say to God, "I don't want to do that. I want my way. If You want me to follow You, You need to make me happy." The next time we're about to make one of those pronouncements to God, we should stop and reconsider what it means to "live in Him." Let's behave like the called people we are and wait on Him. Let's commit our energy and strength and resources to be a part of His purposes.

## PRAYER

Heavenly Father, forgive me for the times when I have wanted my way more than I have wanted Your way. I truly desire to live in You, be rooted in You, and be built up in You. I pray that I will be strengthened in my faith and filled with joy, no matter where my journey leads. I choose to be thankful for the places You bring maturity to me. In Jesus' name, amen.

## DAY 154

### FOUNTAIN OF LIFE

*The mouth of the righteous is a fountain of life.*

PROVERBS 10:11

We all share a common ability: the knack for discerning the weaknesses of others. It doesn't take great wisdom to see other people's flaws. Even the best of us struggle with our inconsistencies. At every defining moment of my life, God has provided a voice of encouragement, a "fountain of life" who helped me stay the course. Sometimes it was a personal friend, and sometimes it was a stranger speaking to me from a stage. Because of that, one of the priorities in my life is to be that for other people. I want to lift people up when they are struggling. It takes effort, and sometimes it can be awkward, but encouragement is an important part of the Christian life. And since Scripture says we will receive by the same measure we give, if we want to be encouraged by others, we should determine to be encouragers for others.

### PRAYER

Heavenly Father, thank You for the body of Christ—Your people, Your hands and feet and voice in the earth. Thank You for every person who has been a fountain of life for me, whether it was a friend in conversation or a stranger on a stage. Help me to be that for others. Give me wisdom to know what to say and when to say it so that I might encourage others and build them up in Christ. In Jesus' name, amen.

# DAY 155

## THE GIFT WITHIN

*"I will ask the Father, and he will give you another Counselor to be with you forever—the Spirit of truth. The world cannot accept him, because it neither sees him nor knows him. But you know him, for he lives with you and will be in you."*

JOHN 14:16-17

Being a Christ-follower is a personal choice you make regarding Jesus of Nazareth. You're willing to say, "God, I'm a sinner. I need a Savior. I believe Jesus is Your son. He died for my sins. I choose Him as Lord of my life. I will live to honor Him." That's how we're birthed into the Kingdom of God. When you become a Christ-follower, the Holy Spirit takes up residence within you. We know this, but many times we ignore Him or dismiss His voice almost entirely. Let's not make light of the Spirit of Almighty God dwelling within us. Let's learn to recognize His voice and His promptings and seek to become aware of His guiding hand and power in our lives.

## PRAYER

Heavenly Father, thank You for the gift of the Holy Spirit who lives within me. Thank You for His constant presence to guide me and lead me into a deeper knowledge of Your truth. Help me to know His presence in a deeper way and follow His leading so that my days in the earth might be blessed and bring glory and honor to You. In Jesus' name, amen.

## DAY 156

### UNCHANGING WORD

*"Heaven and earth will pass away, but my words will never pass away."*
MATTHEW 24:35

It's interesting to think about how technology has changed daily routines in my lifetime. I remember the first time I saw a push button phone. It was right after the last dinosaur died, but it was a big deal because every phone I had seen had a rotary dial. It took forever to call someone, and if you dialed the wrong number you had to start over again—and that was after you looked up the number in the telephone book! You may be too young to remember those ancient artifacts! I remember the first time I saw a fax machine. We'd send something and call to ask, "Did you get it?" "Yeah, I got it. That's unbelievable!" Those events were "Can you believe that?" moments, but all kinds of items that are a part of our lives now will soon make their way into the antique mall because they will be obsolete. Scripture says that all of the "things" of this world—even the heavens and the earth—will pass away, but God's Word, His message to us, never will. In a world with as much change and uncertainty as ours, I'm very grateful for that.

### PRAYER

Heavenly Father, I am so thankful for Your unchanging nature and Your unchanging Word. In days when the earth seems to be shaking from its very core, You are constant, faithful, and true. Your Word is a light for my path during times when the world around me seems dark and full of pitfalls. I choose to hold fast to You today, Lord. In Jesus' name, amen.

# DAY 157

## THE PRIVILEGE OF WORSHIP

*O LORD, you are my God; I will exalt you and praise your name.*

### ISAIAH 25:1

In every era there have been Christians who have made worship a point of controversy. I hear this generation's discussions about worship: "Is your music traditional or contemporary?" "Is your podium acrylic or wood?" "Does your pastor wear a robe or jeans?" All of those may be legitimate questions, but it's easy to confuse preference, style, and tradition for the substance of worship, which is acknowledging the authority of Almighty God. Our priority should be the One we worship, and the privilege we have of honoring the Lord in public. Worship will change you at the most fundamental level and bring God's power to bear in your life. It is critical to our development and maturity as Christ-followers, so I'm not surprised that our adversary has tried to reduce it to a debate. Let me encourage you to take advantage of opportunities to worship the Living God, even if the presentation is not a style you would choose. You will be transformed when you come into His presence!

## PRAYER

Heavenly Father, thank You for the privilege of coming into Your presence in worship. Thank You for the many expressions of worship that honor You. Help me to see through the distractions and focus on You. I want to honor You with my life. In Jesus' name, amen.

# DAY 158

## MERCY FIRST

*Jesus straightened up and asked her, "Woman, where are they? Has no one condemned you?" "No one, sir," she said. "Then neither do I condemn you," Jesus declared. "Go now and leave your life of sin."*

### JOHN 8:10-11

This is the conclusion of one of my favorite Bible stories. Jesus was teaching in the Temple, and some religious leaders brought in a woman who had been caught in adultery. According to the law she should be executed. They didn't care about the woman—they were trying to trap Jesus into defying their rules. Jesus made His famous statement challenging any of them without sin to throw the first stone, and they drifted away until only Jesus and the woman were left. "Neither do I condemn you." He also said, "Go now and leave your life of sin." Jesus is compassionate, and He also wants us to leave a destructive path. It's unfortunate that sometimes those of us who are religious, in our self-righteousness and smugness, forget that we all are people who need mercy—and we need it before we need further instruction. Jesus never forgot that. If you'll come to Him, He'll be compassionate to you and offer you a better way to live.

## PRAYER

Heavenly Father, thank You for the compassion You show even when I am undeserving. Give me a heart like Yours so that I will feel compassion before I feel judgment. Give me a gracious spirit so that I will show mercy before I give advice. Thank You for the people who have extended grace and mercy to me, Lord, and I pray for opportunities to do the same for others. In Jesus' name, amen.

## FIND QUIET

*I will meditate on all your works and consider all your mighty deeds.*

PSALM 77:12

Typically when we think of meditation, we think of somebody lighting incense and getting into a contorted position that would send me to a chiropractor. That's not how I understand meditation. Meditation in Scripture simply means to be quiet and think about the things of the Lord. One of the maladies of our generation is constant noise. With music, podcasts, and streaming everything, we can just keep the ear buds in and we're good to go. We live with so much noise that we don't know what to do with quiet. Let's try to set aside a few minutes every day to sit in silence and meditate on God's works and mighty deeds. Read a psalm out loud and say, "God, I just want to thank You for all You have done." It will change your life.

## PRAYER

Heavenly Father, I am guilty of wanting the distraction of noise. Forgive me for the times when I have given up time meditating on You for the sake of aimless chatter in my ears. Give me a yearning for stillness and quiet, and show me how to seek You in those moments. In Jesus' name, amen.

# DAY 160

## RESISTANCE PLAN

*Be self-controlled and alert. Your enemy the devil prowls around like a roaring lion looking for someone to devour.*

### 1 PETER 5:8

I'm afraid that many of us who think of ourselves as "religious" have a hard time believing in the existence of Satan and demonic influences. Jesus had firsthand experience with the Devil. At a time of great vulnerability in His life, Satan appeared to tempt Him where he thought Jesus might be weakest. And if Satan had the audacity to do that to the Son of God, I can guarantee that he will exploit our weakest spots at the times when we are the most vulnerable. Given that reality—that Satan is prowling about with the objective of devouring us—we need to be prepared for it with an intentional, well-crafted plan that we can articulate. Just as you lock your house when you leave and have insurance on your car, it's prudent to devise and implement a plan to resist the temptations that will surely come. But we are not alone in fighting temptation—the Holy Spirit is with us to remind us of the things of God and give us the power to resist everything else.

## PRAYER

Heavenly Father, I thank You for the power in Your name. I take a stand against every scheme of the Devil. I renounce it and cancel every plan with the authority of Jesus' name. I resist the Devil and submit to God. In Jesus name, amen.

# DAY 161

## CAREFULLY PLACED TRUST

*Some trust in chariots and some in horses, but we trust in the name of the LORD our God.*

### PSALM 20:7

Where do you place your ultimate trust? In your physical abilities? In your capacity to acquire resources? In the psalmist's time, people put their trust in the strength of chariots and horses to protect and defend. But this passage says, instead of bolstering our strength with our abilities and resources, we should put our trust in the name of the Lord. We need that awareness in more than language; we need to live like we believe it. I'm not counseling foolishness. Don't cancel your insurance or stop giving your children their medicine. But let's strive to understand the power of God to deliver us and protect us.

## PRAYER

Heavenly Father, thank You that You are my Protector and Defender. Forgive me for the times I have placed my trust in my own strength and resources. I want to put my trust in You in a new way. In Jesus' name, amen.

# DAY 162

## IT'S A BIG DEAL

*He was delivered over to death for our sins and was raised to life for our justification.*

ROMANS 4:25

The thing that sets Christianity apart from other religious systems is the belief that the One we worship is alive. I'll never forget a lecture I heard in graduate school. We were studying the New Testament; but this class was not a particularly faith-filled environment. I was taking notes as fast as I could, and the professor, almost in passing said, "What separated Christianity? What caused it to emerge? Those first disciples really believed in Easter." It occurred to me he meant they really believed in the Resurrection. People sometimes ask, "Why do we make such a big deal out of Easter?" I'm of the opinion that if God raised His Son from the dead, those of us who have chosen Him as Lord ought to have a full out celebration of that when we're given the opportunity. The Resurrection, the redemptive work of Jesus, is at the heart of the Christian faith. Through the cross God has made complete provision for our lives in time and eternity.

## PRAYER

Heavenly Father, how grateful I am that the God I serve is not a pile of dust in a grave! Lord, the enormity of the Resurrection is beyond my comprehension, but I claim its truth and power in my life. I celebrate today that my God is living and active in the earth and in my life and in the lives of all of Your people. In the name of Jesus, our Risen King, amen.

# DAY 163

## KEEP IN STEP

*Since we live by the Spirit, let us keep in step with the Spirit.*

GALATIANS 5:25

I love the notion that the Spirit of God is making a path before us. I have been in jungles where we had to walk through dense vegetation, and whoever had to go first and break the path had the most difficult job. The Spirit of God is like that, going ahead of us and making a path for our lives. The invitation to you and me is to keep in step with the Spirit and walk with Him so that His fruit will emerge within us. As we mature as Jesus-followers, keeping in step with the Spirit becomes a daily agenda for every aspect of our lives: how we treat our families, how we do business, how we interact with people, and how we see the world. Let's keep in step and anticipate harvests of God's best yet to come!

## PRAYER

Heavenly Father, how great Your love is for Your children that You would send Your Holy Spirit to guide us—each one, individually, day by day, moment by moment—so that Your fruit will emerge in our lives. Holy Spirit, help me to keep in step with You so that my choices and daily interactions will bring a great harvest, and I will give all the glory to God. In Jesus' name, amen.

# DAY 164

## UNDER HIS WINGS

*Have mercy on me, O God, have mercy on me, for in you my soul takes refuge. I will take refuge in the shadow of your wings until the disaster has passed.*

PSALM 57:1

Disasters come to all of our lives, Christians and non-Christians alike. Not everyone suffers the same disasters, but they are a part of the human experience. But in the midst of the disasters, God promises us a place of refuge. Where pain, suffering, heartache, disappointment, and even abuse have touched your life, I would encourage you to not allow those things to define you. Don't build a wall of anger, frustration, or hostility. Don't withdraw into self-pity. Don't withdraw from God. Run to Him. Take refuge in the shadow of His wings until the disaster has passed. God is faithful to bring you through.

## PRAYER

Heavenly Father, You have shown me mercy and delivered me from destruction. You have brought me into Your Kingdom, and I lift my voice in praise and thanksgiving. Lord, lift me above any turmoil in my life and guide me into the shelter of Your wings. Open my eyes to see Your protection and purpose. In Jesus' name, amen.

# DAY 165

## CHOOSE TRUTH

*"You belong to your father, the devil, and you want to carry out your father's desires. He was a murderer from the beginning, not holding to the truth, for there is no truth in him. When he lies, he speaks his native language, for he is a liar and the father of lies."*

JOHN 8:44

This is harsh language, isn't it? It's even more shocking because Jesus is speaking not to recognized public sinners, not to the blatantly immoral people of His day, but to the religious leaders. Jesus was speaking to people with all the trappings of religion—they were making all the right sacrifices, obeying the rules, celebrating the feasts and festivals. Yet Jesus said, "You are of your father, the devil, because you are liars." This very starkly identifies a point of great clarity in Scripture: It doesn't matter where we are sitting on the weekend. When we choose anything less than the truth, we are cooperating with Satan. And when we choose the truth, we are cooperating with the Spirit of God.

## PRAYER

Heavenly Father, I know that You are not only a God of truth, You are Truth. I want to cooperate with the truth. Show me places in my life where I have been skating the truth—in my relationships, business, financing, etc. I yield to Your truth and ask for Your help. In Jesus' name, amen.

# DAY 166

## A PLACE IN THE KINGDOM

*I thank Christ Jesus our Lord, who has given me strength, that he considered me faithful, appointing me to his service. Even though I was once a blasphemer and a persecutor and a violent man, I was shown mercy because I acted in ignorance and unbelief.*

### 1 TIMOTHY 1:12-13

If you think God doesn't want you because of your language, your morals, or your anger issues, I want you to know that He is the very place to begin. The Apostle Paul, perhaps the greatest human advocate for God's Kingdom the world has ever known, said to Timothy, "God called me when I spoke profanely against Him and persecuted His Church and killed His people." The word "gospel" means "good news." And the good news of the Gospel is that God makes it possible for flawed, imperfect, broken people to be transformed and welcomed into His Kingdom. That's my story. That's your story. We've made mistakes, but we are not mistakes. We've failed, but we are not failures. God wants to release His almighty power toward you and me to give us a new future. He has a great plan for our lives!

## PRAYER

Heavenly Father, how grateful I am that You can take each of us, even the most vile and evil of us, and make us Your own beloved children. Thank You that I can be useful in Your Kingdom, no matter my past. I yield my life to You, for Your purposes to emerge. I am trusting Your plan for my life, in spite of my inconsistencies and failures, for You are a great God. In Jesus' name, amen.

## AIM HIGH

*Hezekiah was twenty-five years old when he became king, and he reigned in Jerusalem twenty-nine years. He did what was right in the eyes of the LORD, just as his father David had done.*

### 2 CHRONICLES 29:1-2

What do you want to be said of you when you have stepped into eternity? Do you want people to talk about your bank balance? Awards won? Power gained? Pleasure experienced? None of those things are innately evil, but perhaps the best description of a life lived well is that you "did what was right in the eyes of the Lord." This is an outcome that will not happen on its own—it requires a choice on your part and mine. In the context of your marriage, you've got a good idea of what's "right in the eyes of the Lord." Do that. In the context of business, you know pretty much what's "right in the eyes of the Lord." Do that. If you will take segments of your life and let that statement guide you, you will be amazed at the momentum toward the Lord you will experience.

## PRAYER

Heavenly Father, I want to be known as one who did what was right in the eyes of the Lord. Guide my every decision and conversation so that when my days in the earth are done there will be no doubt that my highest aim was to bring glory to You. In Jesus' name, amen.

## GET WITH HIS PLAN

*As he [Jesus] approached Jerusalem and saw the city, he wept over it and said, "If you . . . had only known on this day what would bring you peace—but now it is hidden from your eyes. The days will come upon you when your enemies will build an embankment against you and encircle you and hem you in on every side. They will dash you to the ground, you and the children within your walls. They will not leave one stone on another, because you did not recognize the time of God's coming to you."*

LUKE 19:41-44

He wasn't weeping because of His own pain or because of the horror about to befall Him. He was weeping because he could see the future of the city. Forty years later the Romans built a siege ramp and destroyed the city of Jerusalem. We often don't recognize that when we push the Lord away, we're choosing the consequences of ungodliness. And when we seek Him and His purposes, we're choosing a life of blessing. Get in line to receive the blessings of the Lord.

## PRAYER

Heavenly Father, thank You for providentially maintaining the embankment around the city wall of Jerusalem—a sign to me of Jesus' words fulfilled. I want to be a person who cooperates with Your plan for my life. Help me to see where I push back or ignore Your promptings, and give me courage to cooperate with You. In Jesus' name, amen.

# DAY 169

## THE MOST IMPORTANT DECISION

*He was in the world, and though the world was made through him, the world did not recognize him. He came to that which was his own, but his own did not receive him. Yet to all who received him, to those who believed in his name, he gave the right to become children of God.*

JOHN 1:10-12

Jesus came into the world, but the world and the religious leaders didn't recognize Him. That seems nearly impossible. They knew the law. But Jesus didn't meet their expectations. Their vision of the Messiah is a political, military deliverer who will drive out the Romans and restore autonomy and independence to Israel. Jesus shows up with a message about the Kingdom of God, and they don't recognize Him. It sobers me, because when we fail to recognize Him, we reject Him. And when we reject God, there's a consequence attached. The good news is that for all who do receive Him, there is a nearly indescribable payoff with eternal rewards: "the right to become children of God." The decision each of us makes about Jesus truly is the most important decision we will ever make.

## PRAYER

Heavenly Father, I thank You for the right to become a child of God. Forgive me for the places I've rejected You. I want to be open to hearing Your voice and being obedient to it. Thank You that You called me to this great inheritance. In Jesus' name, amen.

# DAY 170

## SORROW SHARED

*He was despised and rejected by men, a man of sorrows, and familiar with suffering. Like one from whom men hide their faces he was despised, and we esteemed him not.*

ISAIAH 53:3

One characteristic of Jesus that we don't talk about a great deal is that He was "a man of sorrows." It almost seems irrational to me, illogical, to think about Jesus as a man of sorrow, a man who was rejected. After all, He could turn water into wine, walk on water, and raise the dead. But in spite of all those things, things that should've proved His authority, Jesus still was rejected. Why does that matter to you and me? Because if your heart is broken, if you're suffering disappointment, if you know the bitter taste of rejection, Jesus understands. You can take those things to Him and know that He has suffered too. Ephesians tells us that Jesus has made us accepted in the Beloved. Jesus bore our rejection that we might receive the acceptance due Him.

## PRAYER

Heavenly Father, I believe Jesus is Your Son and the only way to You. I believe He died on the cross for my sins and rose again from the dead. I believe Your Word is true, and I believe that You accept me. I am accepted, highly favored, and the object of Your special care. I thank You for accepting me, and I choose to accept myself. In Jesus' name, amen.

# DAY 171

## INVITATION TO REST

*"Come to me, all you who are weary and burdened, and I will give you rest. Take my yoke upon you and learn from me, for I am gentle and humble in heart, and you will find rest for your souls. For my yoke is easy and my burden is light."*

MATTHEW 11:28-30

You might think Jesus would be looking for people with spotless track records and unfailing faith to be a part of His Kingdom, but those are not the individuals to whom this invitation is extended. He says, "If you are weary and burdened, come with me." And then there is a promise: "I'll give you rest." Notice that He didn't say, "I'll give you criticism," or "I'll show you what you've been doing wrong." He said, "Here is a shelter from the storm. I will provide rest for you." What a remarkable invitation. Those of us who are weary and burdened are not disqualified from membership in His Kingdom. None of us are second-class citizens. Whether you are new to faith or have been a believer for many years, if you are weary or burdened, walk toward Jesus. He is "gentle and humble" and wants to help carry your load.

## PRAYER

Heavenly Father, thank You that we can come to You. Thank You for this promise of rest and renewal for my soul. I'm here, Lord, seeking Your way and the rest that only You can provide. In Jesus' name, amen.

# DAY 172

## OBEDIENCE TO THE TRUTH

*The secret things belong to the LORD our God, but the things revealed belong to us and to our children forever.*

DEUTERONOMY 29:29

This passage says there are two categories of understanding regarding spiritual matters—those things that are unknown to us, that God has held to Himself, and those things that are revealed. We will never know everything. We cannot study enough to discern something that God has said He's not going to make known. One example is the Bible says no person knows the day or the hour when Jesus will return. There are those who refuse to believe that—they are sure they have it figured out—and one group or another makes the news every few years as they sit and watch the clock. There are many things that God has revealed to us, however, and I find that my plate stays pretty full just trying to keep up with those things. The great wisdom in dealing with the Word of God is not in mastering the nuances and the subtleties; it's in being obedient to the truth that you know.

## PRAYER

Heavenly Father, how gracious You are to reveal any of Your plans and purposes to me. As I navigate this life, help me to not be distracted by the things I don't understand. Instead, help me to be obedient to the truth I know. Bring to my mind any place that I need to give attention. In Jesus' name I pray, amen.

# DAY 173

## A DAILY AGENDA

*Then he said to them all: "If anyone would come after me, he must deny himself and take up his cross daily and follow me."*

LUKE 9:23

Jesus said a believer must "deny himself" and give Him first priority. Next, a believer must "take up his cross daily and follow me." Today the cross is a symbol of Christianity, but in the first century the cross was a method of execution. The Romans executed people publicly in order to make an example of them, and crosses sometimes lined the roads outside Roman cities. So the cross was a hated thing for Jesus' audience. When He said you must take up your cross, it was not a casual invitation. He was inviting them to reorient their lives around Him. Being a Christ-follower is a daily set of choices. It's about saying, "Jesus, what does it look like to honor You at home, at work, at school, at the gym, with my time, with my resources?" Living with this Jesus-orientation will not limit your life; it will bring you more blessing, more hope than you ever could have imagined.

## PRAYER

Heavenly Father, thank You for the privilege of being a part of Your family, Your Kingdom. Thank You for allowing Your people to play a part in Your purposes in the earth. I choose to follow You with all of my heart and all of my words and all of my decisions. Thank You for all the ways You have blessed me and given me hope for the future. In Jesus' name, amen.

## TAKE AS PRESCRIBED

*Direct my footsteps according to your word; let no sin rule over me.*

PSALM 119:133

For many years my dad practiced veterinary medicine. If you took your dog to him, he would not only make a diagnosis and prescribe the medication, he would dispense the medication—one-stop shopping. One of the things that amazed me was the difficulty people had in following instructions. He would write the directions down, print them on the label, and then tell the owner exactly what to do. Still, people ignored all that and did whatever seemed like a good idea. We're a little bit like that with God. We think we can deal with Him on our terms and live the way we want to. How could it matter if I do it His way or my way? Actually, it does matter, and He has given us His instruction manual—the Bible. It will be a challenge to follow its instructions, because we are imperfect people. But we should make every effort to follow its commands and principles, because life is much easier when we do.

## PRAYER

Heavenly Father, thank You for giving us the Scriptures—Your Holy Word for us, an absolutely trustworthy guide for how to practice our faith and live our lives. Show me the places where I have my own ideas and follow my own instructions. Give me a hunger and thirst for Your Word. I want Your best for my life. In Jesus' name, amen.

# DAY 175

## TELL YOUR STORY

*"Go home to your family and tell them how much the Lord has done for you, and how he has had mercy on you."*

MARK 5:19

One of the fears I hear when I talk to people about telling their Jesus-story is, "What if somebody asks me a question—a really hard one with no easy answer? What am I going to say?" I'll tell you what to say: "I don't know." There is a God, and we are not Him. Isn't that good to know? I began breathing so much easier when I finally understood I didn't have to know all the answers. Here's what you can say: "I can tell you about my journey and the rough patches in my life. I can tell you about the times God lifted me up and restored me. I can tell you about His grace and His mercy." I've discovered that in places of suffering and searching, people don't need great answers. They need someone who is simply willing to sit with them as they are trying to sort out life and make their way to God. And your gentle insistence that Jesus makes the difference will change everything.

## PRAYER

Heavenly Father, thank You for my story. Thank You for the things You've done in my life. You have lifted me up and dusted me off and restored me. Thank You for Your grace and mercy that sees me through every day and for Your provision for my every need. Give me the courage to tell my story. In Jesus' name, amen.

# DAY 176

## LEAN INTO THE LORD

*Seek the LORD while he may be found; call on him while he is near. Let the wicked forsake his way and the evil man his thoughts. Let him turn to the LORD, and he will have mercy on him, and to our God, for he will freely pardon.*

### ISAIAH 55:6-7

Scripture, from the beginning to the end, tells us again and again to seek the Lord, and when we find Him, to turn to Him and receive His mercy. We are not only given permission to lean into the Lord, we are encouraged to do so. He is the God of the universe, but we don't have to fear Him. Don't stand at a distance and think, "If I get closer to God, He's going to take the best things in my life away." The very opposite it true—He has promised to bring better things to our lives. Sometimes there are things we're reluctant to let God know about, but we're only fooling ourselves because He already knows about them. And whatever we're reluctant to bring into the light of God, whatever we try to hide in the darkness, becomes destructive. Don't be afraid of the Lord. He is waiting to receive you with open arms of mercy and pardon.

## PRAYER

Heavenly Father, what a great and mighty God You are—the Creator of the universe, the Lord of Heaven and earth—yet You still want to have a personal relationship with me. May I never lose sight of the wonder and privilege of that. Thank You for the pardon You so freely give when I turn to You in repentance. Lord, I repent for_____. I receive Your forgiveness. Help me to turn from it and begin a new path with You. In the name of Jesus, amen.

# DAY 177

## ALWAYS FAITHFUL

*Cast all your anxiety on him because he cares for you.*

### 1 PETER 5:7

God cares for you. It's in the Book—the one that has "Holy" on the spine. The eternal, unchanging, authoritative Word of God says that God cares for you. Many of us spend considerable portions of our lives wondering if anyone cares. Perhaps your childhood was less than perfect. Maybe your parents had a difficult time expressing affection or affirmation. Perhaps you invested emotionally in relationships that didn't turn out as you had hoped they would. The next time you're disappointed because someone doesn't care about you in the way you wish they would, and that question explodes in your heart—"Does anyone care for me?"—say out loud, "God cares for me. I matter to Him."

## PRAYER

Heavenly Father, I know that Your love and concern and compassion for me is far beyond what any human can express. The word "care" seems so inadequate. Thank You for Your love that is beyond what I can imagine or understand. Thank You that although the people and things of this world may disappoint me, You will always be faithful. In Jesus' name, amen.

# DAY 178

## WITHOUT RESERVATION

*Therefore the Lord himself will give you a sign: The virgin will be with child and give birth to a son, and will call him Immanuel.*

ISAIAH 7:14

People often say to me, "You mean you believe in the virgin birth thing?" "Uh-huh." "How do you suppose that happened?" "I don't know." We are twenty centuries on the other side of this event, and we still struggle to process and explain the virgin birth. It's not a part of my life experience, so I don't have to answer for it in a personal way. But the truth is that if you follow God long enough there will be parts of His path for your life that will require you to trust Him beyond your rational ability to explain. That can be hard for me because I'm a rational person. I like a logical explanation for most of the things going on in my life. While following God will not require you to check your intellect at the door, it will require you to have complete confidence in His plan, even when you don't understand it. When we learn to follow Him without hesitation or reservation, we will be blessed.

## PRAYER

Heavenly Father, I realize that I will never understand all there is to know about You and Your ways and Your plans. Thank You for the wealth of knowledge and insight You give to us through Your Word and the example of Your Son and the leading of Your Holy Spirit. Give me a willing spirit so that I might follow You wherever Your path leads me. Give me boldness to move forward when I sense Your direction. In the name of Jesus, Immanuel, amen.

# DAY 179

## YOUR JESUS-STORY

*In my former book, Theophilus, I wrote about all that Jesus began to do and to teach.*

ACTS 1:1

When Luke sat down to write the gospel that bears his name and the book of Acts, he probably wasn't writing for a twenty-first-century audience. He had personally witnessed much of Jesus' ministry, or was a friend of those who had. He was a frequent traveling companion of the Apostle Paul, so he had firsthand knowledge of the unfolding narrative of the birth of the Church. His desire was to record the Jesus-story in the context that he knew, for his generation, so that people who hadn't had those personal experiences would understand what had happened. He had no idea that his account would impact the world as it has. Like Luke, we have been placed in a specific place at a specific time to tell others about the ways we have experienced God at work in our lives or seen Him at work in the lives of others. It's a great privilege to tell our Jesus-stories, and only God knows how He will use them to build His Kingdom.

## PRAYER

Heavenly Father, thank You that Your work in the earth did not end in the first century but continues on through every believer until the day of Jesus' return. Thank You for the privilege of sharing my Jesus-story. Give me boldness to tell about the ways You are at work in my life, so that many will seek and know You as Savior. In Jesus' name, amen.

# DAY 180

## COURAGE

*Then Peter, filled with the Holy Spirit, said to them: "Rulers and elders of the people! If we are being called to account today for an act of kindness shown to a cripple and are asked how he was healed, then know this, you and all the people of Israel: It is by the name of Jesus Christ of Nazareth, whom you crucified but whom God raised from the dead, that this man stands before you healed. . . . Salvation is found in no one else, for there is no other name under heaven given to men by which we must be saved."*

ACTS 4:8-10, 12

Peter had watched this group plot Jesus' execution. Now empowered by the Holy Spirit, he stands before the same group, knowing their willingness to eliminate a threat to their authority. Peter declares, "You killed the Messiah. And salvation is found in no other name." That statement makes people just as uncomfortable today as it did in the first century. Do we have the courage to believe it? To say it? In every generation God calls people to speak the truth—not to condemn others, but to invite them to share in the freedom found only in Christ.

## PRAYER

Heavenly Father, thank You for the example of Peter, whose failures did not keep him from coming back to You and serving Your Kingdom in a mighty way. Give me the same boldness he showed as he stood and defended Your name at the risk of his own life. Show me the purposes You have for me, Lord, that I might fulfill them in the earth. In Jesus' name, amen.

# DAY 181

## DOORS OF POSSIBILITY

*Jesus Christ is the same yesterday and today and forever.*

### HEBREWS 13:8

There are many people in academic circles, even in ministry, who consider Jesus to be a first-century teacher of Scripture who had stories of healings and miracles associated with Him. But that is not the complete story of Scripture. The Jesus we meet in the Old Testament, the pre-incarnate Christ, and the Jesus we meet in the gospels is the same Jesus who is interacting with you and me today. He was present at creation described in Genesis, He came to live and die for our salvation, and every knee will bow when He returns to judge the earth as foretold in the book of Revelation. Hebrews 13: 8 says, "Jesus Christ is the same yesterday and today and forever." Hebrews 7:25 says that He "lives to intercede" for us. This opens wide the door of possibility for us and brings Jesus into the moments of our everyday lives. Jesus is not a shadowy, historical figure who lived in the first century. Jesus is alive today, sitting at the right hand of God, waiting to be called on by those of us who love Him.

## PRAYER

Heavenly Father, thank You for sending Your Son, Jesus, as the Savior of the world. Thank You that even now He is sitting at Your right hand, interceding for me and all who will call on Him. Keep me focused on Your purposes that I will be found faithful upon His return to the earth. In the name of Jesus, amen.

# DAY 182

## SIN IS NOT MY MASTER

*For sin shall not be your master, because you are not under law,
but under grace.*

ROMANS 6:14

Christians struggle with sin. Scripture says even Jesus was tempted. We live in a sin-filled world, and it tempts us because it looks good. But this verse says sin isn't our master. We live in a sinful world, and the ungodliness in others touches our lives. Jesus certainly suffered because of the sinful actions of others. We too suffer unjustly and inappropriately because sin flourished and still flourishes in our world. It may influence your life or even feel like it has directed your life, but it can't master your life because there's an authority at work on your behalf. You will not defeat sin in your life with your own self-discipline, with your self-will, or with your strength of character. That's why it's important to know the authority over sin that God has made available to you and claim the promise that sin will not be your master.

## PRAYER

Heavenly Father, Your power is greater than any power on the earth. Thank You that sin is not my master. Thank You for the authority You have given me over it in Jesus' name. Thank You that it may touch my life, but it does not rule my life. You are a great Deliverer, and greatly to be praised. In Jesus' name, amen.

# DAY 183

## GOD IS FOR YOU

*"Now for a brief moment, the LORD our God has been gracious in leaving us a remnant and giving us a firm place in his sanctuary, and so our God gives light to our eyes and a little relief in our bondage."*

### EZRA 9:8

Ezra's generation is suffering because of their rebellion, their stubbornness, the hardness of their hearts, and their unwillingness to cooperate with God. They have endured much. They've seen Jerusalem and the Temple destroyed. Much of the population has suffered greatly, yet Ezra says, "We are not alone. God has not deserted us." I want to be absolutely certain you're aware of that: God is with us. We aren't just the people of God by default, because of a prayer we prayed or a building we sit in on the weekends. Our stories are imperfect. Our family legacies are often less than ideal. Our circumstances typically are not wonderful. You may be enduring a difficult season—physically, emotionally, relationally, or financially. There may be places in your heart where disappointment and brokenness have invaded. But you are not alone. We are God's people, and He watches over our lives. It changes everything.

## PRAYER

Heavenly Father, what a joy it is to know that You are watching over my life, even when I am in a difficult season. Thank You that Your love for me is not determined by my circumstances or my attitudes. Thank You that You are a gracious and forgiving God who sees me as a beloved child. Help me to always see Your love as constant and secure, even when things around me seem as shifting sand. In Jesus' name, amen.

# DAY 184

## SOWING SEEDS

*A man reaps what he sows. The one who sows to please his sinful nature, from that nature will reap destruction; the one who sows to please the Spirit, from the Spirit will reap eternal life.*

### GALATIANS 6:7-8

Sin looks good in the short run, but it is deceptive. It can never deliver what it promises and always leaves us dissatisfied and unfulfilled. Every time you and I make a choice toward godliness or ungodliness, we sow a seed. Your life and mine are surrounded by harvest fields that we have planted, and some of us are desperately praying for crop failure. Let's say no to ungodliness and make decisions that will "please the Spirit" so that we can anticipate a harvest that we are excited about both in time and for eternity.

## PRAYER

Heavenly Father, thank You that Your Spirit is present among Your people to make Your wisdom known to us. Today I choose to cooperate with Him as never before, to say yes to godliness and no to ungodliness. We live in a world that desperately needs to see Jesus, and today I choose to glorify Him with my words, my actions, and my resources. Father, we thank You for the harvest You have promised. It's in Jesus' name that I pray, amen.

# DAY 185

## THE PEOPLE OF GOD

*Once you were not a people, but now you are the people of God; once you had not received mercy, but now you have received mercy.*

### 1 PETER 2:10

Though we are scorned by many, Christ-followers are important. We are "the people of God." We bring the truth of Almighty God to all humanity. We are fallible and inconsistent, yet He said we are salt and light. We struggle and stumble, yet we are at the center of God's purposes. Be grateful for every person who bears the name of Jesus. We are not perfect, and we don't always get it right. When you see a Christian stumble or fall, don't mock or celebrate. Weep for them and extend a hand of mercy as God has extended a hand of mercy to you. Don't join in when others diminish Christianity, ridicule Christ-followers, or give our faith as a reason for the weaknesses of our lives. In spite of our imperfections, we are the light of the world. Following Jesus is the very best way to live, and we should celebrate it.

## PRAYER

Heavenly Father, I am so grateful that I belong to You, that I am one of Your own beloved children. Thank You for the mercy I have received from Your hand. May I be faithful in extending grace and mercy to others as You have extended it to me. May Your Church be expanded during this generation, Lord, so we would be found faithful upon Your return. In Jesus'

# DAY 186

## CHOOSING THE TRUTH

*The time will come when men will not put up with sound doctrine. Instead, to suit their own desires, they will gather around them a great number of teachers to say what their itching ears want to hear.*

2 TIMOTHY 4:3

We are living in a time when good is called evil and evil is called good. We only have to tune into the day's news to see it. Accomplished people, successful people, powerful people, educated people, affluent people give their opinion on things that, from a God-perspective, are evil, yet they say they are good. And they look at things God says are good and call them evil. God told us this would happen, not to frighten us but so that we would be prepared. This knowledge has significant implications for us individually, because when there is cultural encouragement that good is evil and evil is good, our choices become very important. There will be momentum for us to ignore God's invitations and choose evil. Let's ignore the voices around us that mock Almighty God and stand firmly on sound doctrine. Let's choose Jesus.

## PRAYER

Heavenly Father, thank You that You have prepared us through Your Word for the things to come. I want to be a light in the darkness. Give me strength to stand strong in Your Word and share it with all who will hear. Help me to proclaim Jesus Christ as Lord and King in a way that will draw people to Your Kingdom, in the powerful name of Jesus. Amen.

# DAY 187

## CHOOSING A GOD-PATH

*What shall we say, then? Shall we go on sinning so that grace may increase? By no means! We died to sin; how can we live in it any longer?*

ROMANS 6:1-2

I'm an advocate for the grace of God. I have needed it. I have experienced failure, publicly. I know what it is to be desperate and find the grace of God. I am very grateful for that, and I promised the Lord I would give my life to extending His grace to other people. Don't take His grace for granted, however. Don't willingly choose to sin and think you'll repent when you're in the mood. That is a very dangerous choice to make because sin always destroys. When God placed our sin on Jesus, it destroyed Him. Christians are not perfect people, and we all struggle with temptation. We all battle sin's encroachment in our lives. There is a difference between that and choosing to sin. Life is made up of one choice after another. Choose godliness . . . one choice at a time.

## PRAYER

Heavenly Father, thank You for the grace You have extended to me time and time again. Give me the willingness to choose your path. Grant me the wisdom, discernment, and compassion to extend grace in Your name to others, so that lives may be renewed and restored and Your Kingdom extended. In Jesus' name, amen.

# DAY 188

## SEARCHING FOR UNDERSTANDING

*If you call out for insight and cry aloud for understanding, and if you look for it as for silver and search for it as for hidden treasure, then you will understand the fear of the LORD and find the knowledge of God.*

### PROVERBS 2:3-5

Sometimes, particularly in the Christian Church, we have this notion that if we don't know something, somehow we will be delivered from its consequences. It's true in other parts of our lives too. People had been smoking tobacco for centuries before a report came out in 1964 saying it was harmful. Smokers had always suffered the health consequences of it, whether they knew the cause or not. Their ignorance did not prevent their disease. The same is true of spiritual ignorance. We are unwise as believers if we choose to remain unaware of the things of God. This passage tells us to search for understanding as if it were hidden treasure of gold or silver, so that we will find the knowledge of God. Invest yourself in securing it. It will make a difference in your life, in your family, in your future.

## PRAYER

Heavenly Father, thank You for Your promises. Your Word says in James 1:5 that if I ask for wisdom You are generous to give it—and I need Your wisdom and insight. I thank You in advance for what You will do. In Jesus' name, amen.

# DAY 189

## JESUS' CHARACTER

*Now he commands all people everywhere to repent. For he has set a day when he will judge the world with justice by the man he has appointed.*

ACTS 17:30-31

I have studied in some very diverse academic settings. In all of them, when the topic of Jesus comes up, there is a healthy discussion about His life. I've heard some interesting debates! Scholars apply the criteria of historical authenticity to the Jesus-story, to try to decide how much of it is really true. I believe the Bible's assertion that Jesus is the Son of God and that He is coming back to the earth a second time. And when He comes back, He's not coming as a baby in a manger or the Lamb of God to take away the sin of the world. When He comes the second time, He's coming as Judge of all the earth. It's very important that we grasp this aspect of Jesus' character. We hear a lot about being "on the right side of history," and this is one event you will want to be on the right side of.

## PRAYER

Heavenly Father, thank You for sending Your Son, Jesus the Christ, as the Savior of the world. I believe Jesus is the Son of God and is coming back to the earth a second time. I yield to Your purposes. Use my life to help others be ready for His return. In His name I pray, amen.

## STANDING FOR THE CHURCH

*He is the head of the body, the church; he is the beginning and the firstborn from among the dead, so that in everything he might have the supremacy.*

COLOSSIANS 1:18

Have you ever wondered why I sometimes write "church" and at other times "Church"? A "church" is a particular Christian group or the religious services they hold or the building where they meet. "Church" with a capital C is the universal Church made up of every individual who has a relationship with Jesus of Nazareth as Lord and Christ. It's not about architecture, music, or style of the presenter, or translation of the Bible. The Church is about the Body of Christ helping people have a relationship with Jesus. If a group is not endeavoring to help people have a relationship with Jesus as Lord and Christ, it's not Church. From a biblical perspective, the truth about Jesus is the defining characteristic of Church. Jesus is the head of the Church, and every local body of believers should want to give Him supremacy in everything they do. Make a decision today to support and pray for the Church. It will bring good things to you!

## PRAYER

Heavenly Father, thank You for the Church, the Body of Christ in every generation. Thank You for the men and women who have gone before me, preaching and teaching and extending Your Kingdom one person at a time. Strengthen my brothers and sisters in Christ around the world who are facing persecution for Your name. Come soon, Lord Jesus! It's in His name I pray, amen.

# DAY 191

## A GIFT GIVEN

*He also bypassed the sacrifices consisting of goat and calf blood, instead using his own blood as the price to set us free once and for all. If that animal blood and the other rituals of purification were effective in cleaning up certain matters of our religion and behavior, think how much more the blood of Christ cleans up our whole lives, inside and out. Through the Spirit, Christ offered himself as an unblemished sacrifice, freeing us from all those dead-end efforts to make ourselves respectable, so that we can live all out for God.*

HEBREWS 9:12-14 • THE MESSAGE®

Jesus has accomplished something on our behalf that gives us peace with God and therefore peace with all of creation, and imparts to us a value and a meaning and a purpose that transcends everything else. The basis of that transaction is the blood of Jesus Christ. When we understand the extravagance of that gift and the authority it confers on us, we are set free to reorder our priorities and serve the Living God with a whole heart.

## PRAYER

Heavenly Father, thank You for the blood of Jesus. Lord, forgive me for the times I've worked to find fulfillment outside of Your provision. I want to know Your peace, contentment, and all that You have for me. In Jesus' name, amen.

# DAY 192

## POINT OF DESPERATION

*While Jesus was in one of the towns, a man came along who was covered with leprosy. When he saw Jesus, he fell with his face to the ground and begged him, "Lord, if you are willing, you can make me clean." Jesus reached out his hand and touched the man. "I am willing," he said. "Be clean!" And immediately the leprosy left him.*

LUKE 5:12-13

Leprosy is an incurable skin disease. In the first century, it meant you were a social outcast. It meant a tremendous amount of rejection, yet this man who was "covered with leprosy" recognized Jesus' authority and power to make him well. He approached Jesus, fell to the ground, and begged Him for healing, "if you are willing." You can hear his desperation. Jesus reached out and touched him, and he was healed—immediately. No reminders of the man's past, no hoops to jump through. I've learned something about freedom in our lives: True breakthroughs come from a sense of desperation, not casual concern. Jesus' response was a game-changer. Hear Him say it again: "I am willing. Be clean."

## PRAYER

Heavenly Father, give me courage to trust You for the impossible. Give me the boldness to step out and place my life in Your care. Forgive me for my desperate attempts to remain in control. I need You to break into my life with Your miraculous power. As I choose You, I expectantly look forward to Your interaction in my life. I rejoice today in Your strength, concern, and watchfulness. In Jesus' name, amen.

# DAY 193

## AMBASSADORS IN THE EARTH

*"He has granted us new life to rebuild the house of our God and repair its ruins, and he has given us a wall of protection in Judah and Jerusalem."*

EZRA 9:9

The Temple in Jerusalem has been destroyed, but Ezra says God will "rebuild the house." God is in the business of rebuilding. He can rebuild your life, your hopes, your dreams, and your relationships. Our God is able. Then comes a wonderful declaration: "God has given us a wall of protection in Judah and Jerusalem." Ezra knew he was going into a difficult place. But he said, "God has given us a wall of protection." It is so important that we shake ourselves from the doldrums of thinking that we're just good, polite folks who gather on the weekend. That's not it at all. The power of God is at work in the midst of His people as a demonstration that our God is mighty. We are God's ambassadors in the earth. The Jesus-story is being displayed through us, and He will put His wall of protection around us. He is faithful!

## PRAYER

Heavenly Father, thank You that You are in the business of rebuilding—lives, hopes, dreams, relationships—even things that seem impossible in our eyes. Thank You for the wall of protection You have placed around us, even holding back things that we will never see. Use me to tell the story of Your love and protection, Lord, so Your Kingdom may be extended in the earth. In Jesus' name, amen.

# DAY 194

## CITIZENSHIP IN HEAVEN

*Our citizenship is in heaven. And we eagerly await a Savior from there,
the Lord Jesus Christ.*

PHILIPPIANS 3:20

I have a little blue passport that says I am a citizen of the United States. And with that citizenship come certain rights and privileges. I am very grateful for that. But I am far more grateful that I am a citizen of the Kingdom of God. The Bible refers to the fact that our names are written in the Lamb's Book of Life, and that ultimately, when we stand before the King of all kings and the Lord of all lords, we will be judged by whether or not our name is there. Citizenship in the Kingdom of God is more than being a church member, a religious person, a moralist, or even a person with high ethical values. Citizenship in the Kingdom of God comes when we trust in Jesus of Nazareth as our Savior and our Lord. And the rights and privileges that come with that citizenship are beyond compare.

## PRAYER

Heavenly Father, thank You for the privilege of being a citizen of Your Kingdom, with all the rights and privileges that conveys. Thank You for what that means in my life. Help me to share with others the blessing they will receive when they choose to follow You. May Your Kingdom be extended in my generation. In Jesus' name, amen.

## CATALYST FOR FAITH

*After John was put in prison, Jesus went into Galilee, proclaiming the good news of God. "The time has come," he said. "The kingdom of God is near. Repent and believe the good news!"*

MARK 1:14

Jesus said, "The kingdom of God is near." I'd say so—Jesus was in town! And He said to the people, "The process for believing begins with repenting." All of us struggle to believe God. There are battles in our minds about what we believe. Even pastors process those struggles. And the catalyst to help you grow in your belief, to implement God's truth in your life, is repentance. I like the imagery of repentance as a catalyst. In chemistry, if you're trying to make a chemical reaction happen more quickly you add a catalyst. Repentance is the catalyst for faith, for belief, growing in your life. Repentance opens the doorway to believing God in greater ways. Let's make a practice of repentance and look forward to a greater faith in God.

## PRAYER

Heavenly Father, thank You for Your Word and the truth it brings to my life. Lord, I choose repentance. Forgive me for choosing my own path. I want to live my life for Your purposes, not my own. I receive Your forgiveness. In the name of Jesus, amen.

# DAY 196

## POWER OF GOD

*Now Stephen, a man full of God's grace and power, did great wonders and miraculous signs among the people.*

### ACTS 6:8

Stephen was a second-generation Christ-follower, and Luke seems to imply that he had come to faith through the events he had witnessed in Jerusalem. Perhaps he had seen Jesus' triumphal entry into the city— we don't know. We are simply told that at this point he had become a man full of God's grace and power, able to do "great wonders and miraculous signs." Some people suggest that miracles and supernatural events subsided with the passing of the original twelve disciples. But Luke is saying, "Oh, no. Every generation of believers will demonstrate the power of God." Certainly there are miracles happening all around us, but in our generation perhaps we have become too quick to give the credit to good luck or someone's intelligence or a feat of ingenuity. Let's look for the hand of God at work around us and be quick to give Him praise and glory for the things He is doing.

## PRAYER

Heavenly Father, I praise You for the many ways You supernaturally intervene in the earth. Help me to see You at work in my life and the lives of the people around me and in the world. May I be quick to give You glory for all of Your acts, big and small, that bless and protect us. In the name of Jesus, amen.

# DAY 197

## SPIRITUAL STRENGTH

*May our Lord Jesus Christ himself and God our Father, who loved us and by his grace gave us eternal encouragement and good hope, encourage your hearts and strengthen you in every good deed and word.*

2 THESSALONIANS 2:16-17

The only way to gain strength is to exercise to the point of fatigue. You can't get stronger unless you get exhausted. I would like to believe that I can stretch out on the couch with a bag of cheese doodles and three liters of soda and get fit while I watch a football game. Sadly, we know that will not happen. What's true physically is also true spiritually: We gain spiritual strength at those places where we are fatigued. We have brought that "watch the football game" model to Christianity. We think we gain spiritual strength by coming to church and watching somebody talk to us about the Bible. It's a nice idea, but it's wrong. In the places where the challenges of life bump up against you, where you get tired of doing good, where you don't want to forgive one more time—it's in those places of weariness and fatigue that we have opportunities to gain strength.

## PRAYER

Heavenly Father, give me strength to push on when I am in a place of weariness. Give me perseverance and patience to take another step, knowing that greater strength is on the other side. Remind me when I have an opportunity to encourage others, Lord, so Your people may be built up and Your Kingdom extended. In Jesus' name, amen.

# DAY 198

## BELIEF IN GOD

*"I looked for a man among them who would build up the wall and stand before me in the gap on behalf of the land so I would not have to destroy it, but I found none.*

### EZEKIEL 22:30

Ezekiel was one of the Old Testament prophets who delivered God's perspective to the people. God is saying through Ezekiel, "I looked for someone in the nation who would stand up on my behalf." God has always searched the earth for men and women who will believe in Him. Not believe about Him—believe in Him, stand up for Him. And the wonderful story of Scripture is that, in the overwhelming majority of the generations, those people emerged. But in Ezekiel's generation, God says, "I couldn't find anyone." God is still searching for people who will trust Him. What are you aspiring to be? What are you striving to accumulate? I want to invite you to make a decision in your heart to be one of God's people—not a churched person, not a polite one. When somebody thinks of you, let it be said, "That person really stands up for their belief in God."

## PRAYER

Heavenly Father, I want to live in a way that honors You. I choose to turn away from anything that hinders or diminishes my faith. May Jesus become a greater reality in my heart than ever before. Grant me a willing spirit and the humility to follow Your plan for me, even when it seems unclear. In Jesus' name, amen.

## USING YOUR INFLUENCE

*To them God has chosen to make known among the Gentiles the glorious riches of this mystery, which is Christ in you, the hope of glory.*

COLOSSIANS 1:27

I don't think we can fully understand or even imagine the power of our Jesus-story. God gives every one of us a sphere of influence—in our neighborhoods, in our homes, in our workplaces, among our friends—and wherever that may be, there are people who trust and respect you. If you're willing to share your Jesus-story in that arena, it becomes a powerful invitation of hope. We've become so acclimated to religious activity that I think in some ways it has diminished our imagination of the power of God to deliver people from sin and darkness. God isn't just an organized expression of doctrine—He's a delivering God. It's the essence of the Bible's story, from Genesis all the way through the book of Revelation. People apart from God are awaiting a hellish eternity, and your Jesus-story can lead them away from that. Remember: Christ in you is the hope of glory.

## PRAYER

Heavenly Father, thank You for the deliverance You have brought to my life and for the privilege of sharing with others what You have done for me. Thank You that You use our Jesus-stories to bring people into Your Kingdom. Thank You for Your Word—for its truth, its power, and its authority. In Jesus' name, amen.

# DAY 200

## PROCESSING CONVICTION

*With many other words he warned them; and he pleaded with them, "Save yourselves from this corrupt generation."*

ACTS 2:40

Peter's message, delivered in the first century, is just as current as today's headlines and just as relevant to you and me. But we cannot save ourselves on our own. We need the power of God to set us free. If the Spirit of God is dealing with you—"conviction" is what we call that in church language—if you're uneasy with some attitude, practice, habit, or some thought you're holding, give it to God. If there's a place you just can't get comfortable with the Lord, don't just live with it—repent. Say, "God, I'm sorry. I want to turn away from this." And He will help you. Don't keep looking around for a messenger who will give you a pass or one with a softer message, or you will miss God's invitation to freedom. And that is exactly what God wants to do: set you free.

## PRAYER

Heavenly Father, please forgive me for the times I have chosen ungodliness. I am grateful for the conviction of Your Holy Spirit. Specifically, I choose to turn from _____. Thank You for the freedom You offer to all who call on Your name. In Jesus' name, amen.

## YOU ARE ACCEPTED

*He chose us in him before the creation of the world.*

EPHESIANS 1:4

Did you know that God chose you? He knows what we've done, what we've thought about doing, and what we wish we'd done. And in spite of knowing that—this is remarkable to me—God said, "I choose you." If you're afraid for anyone to ever know who you are, if you're hoping people won't see past the shiny façade you present to the world, this one might be hard to believe. He didn't take you pending future negotiation, for "a player to be named later" so He can get some A-list star when one becomes available. God looked across the planet and said, "I want that one." And when that really takes root in your heart, it's a game-changing notion. You may have faced rejection by other people and the hurt that comes with it, but Almighty God says, "I'll take you."

## PRAYER

Heavenly Father, thank You for choosing me. What a remarkable privilege it is to be fully known and yet still claimed by Almighty God. What a blessing it is to live as one of Your children. Help me to understand and appreciate that more each day. In Jesus' name, amen.

# DAY 202

## KEEPING ETERNITY IN MIND

*Do not conform any longer to the pattern of this world, but be transformed by the renewing of your mind. Then you will be able to test and approve what God's will is—his good, pleasing and perfect will.*

ROMANS 12:2

Spiritually, you and I are in one of two categories: We are either being conformed to the standards of this current age, or we are being changed by adapting to a standard of another age. One of those two things is being made evident in your life, and it has to do predominantly with your will. One of the unique attributes of a human being is that God created us with a free will, and He will not violate it. We have to choose which age will predominate our thoughts, our values, our hopes, our dreams. Will we be fully invested in this age, which is coming to a conclusion? Or will we invest ourselves in the eternal things of God? Are you being conformed to this age, or being transformed more completely into the image of Jesus? Let's live so that there will be no doubt in our minds.

## PRAYER

Heavenly Father, I want to live with an eternal focus. I pray that You and Your purposes will predominate my thoughts. I pray that my actions would draw more attention to You than to me. May I live in such a way that all would know You are my priority in this life and the next. In Jesus' name, amen.

# DAY 203

## DAVID-LIKE COURAGE

*David said to the Philistine, "You come against me with sword and spear and javelin, but I come against you in the name of the Lord Almighty, the God of the armies of Israel, whom you have defied. This day the Lord will deliver you into my hands."*

1 SAMUEL 17:45-46

About a thousand years before Jesus, the Philistine armies marched toward Israel and stopped on a ridge on one side of the Elah Valley. On the opposite side was the Israelite army. Every day, morning and evening, the champion of the Philistines would come into the valley and say, "It's senseless to have a slaughter of all the armies. Let the champions fight, and whoever is victorious will be lord over the other." For forty days the Israelites heard that challenge, and the bravest men in the Israelite camp hid in their tents. Then God sent a shepherd boy into the midst of that, and he heard that challenge differently. David said, "He isn't challenging the armies of Israel. He's challenging the Living God." And with a rock and a sling, God used a boy who believed in Him to impact the destiny of his own nation and the course of history.

## PRAYER

Heavenly Father, give me the courage of David to stand up for You. Give me endurance to be faithful when others oppose You and my morale is low. Reveal to me the things that are in my hand and how to use them to demonstrate Your power. And show me how to be useful in Your Kingdom. In Jesus' name, amen.

# DAY 204

## IT'S NOT ABOUT ME

*Do not repay evil with evil or insult with insult, but with blessing, because to this you were called so that you may inherit a blessing.*

### 1 PETER 3:9

I'll tell you what I've discovered as a born-again, Spirit-filled, Bible-reading, prayer-offering Christ-follower: Self will never cease its demands. Even as Christians, our selfish natures continue to scream, "I'm important! Look at me!" We're all hard-wired that way. It's possible to sit in church week after week after week, read our Bibles, pray, serve, and still be occupied with self. That's why biblical concepts like forgiveness and mercy and grace are so profound when the injustices and the sufferings of life touch us. Without the help of the God-perspective, we're filled with anger, bitterness, and resentment. And those things hold us captive, not the person who has wronged us. When we are able to forgive, when we make a conscious, selfless decision to say, "It isn't all about me. I forgive you," we are set free to receive God's blessing.

## PRAYER

Heavenly Father, I want to make daily decisions to crucify my selfish nature. I'm sorry for being focused on my own self and not others. Remind me when I have an opportunity to put others first. I thank You that You are faithful to help me. In Jesus' name, amen.

# DAY 205

## MATURING IN THE LORD

*Then Jesus said to his disciples, "If anyone would come after me, he must deny himself and take up his cross and follow me. For whoever wants to save his life will lose it, but whoever loses his life for me will find it."*

MATTHEW 16:24-25

Jesus said there are two things required of His followers: Deny yourself and take up your cross. I have an internal messaging system that fills my head with "I want" statements. "I want to do this. I want it to happen this way." I also have the "I feel" statements. Feelings are real, but feelings aren't always right. I am also hard-wired with another set of messages: "I think." The challenge isn't to know what I think; the challenge is to know what God wants. What does God's Word say? As we cooperate with the Spirit of God, we begin to choose the Lord with our whole heart. We will say no to our own desires, and our own willful intention, and sometimes even our preferences, to let God's way emerge within us. It's not an easy thing, but it's an important part of maturing in the Lord.

## PRAYER

Heavenly Father, I truly do want to put You first, but I battle "I want" and "I feel" and "I think." Help me to deny myself and cooperate with the Holy Spirit as He works in my life so that Your purposes can emerge within me. In Jesus' name, amen.

# DAY 206

## EXTRAVAGANT PROVISION

*For if, by the trespass of the one man, death reigned through that one man,*
*how much more will those who receive God's abundant provision of grace*
*and of the gift of righteousness reign in life through the one man,*
*Jesus Christ.*

ROMANS 5:17

God's provision for you and for me, through Jesus, is not merely adequate—it is extravagant, beyond anything we could have imagined. We are rebellious creatures who were separated from God. God saw there was only one way to deliver us from that condition: the life of His Son. Through the death of God's Son, the Kingdom of God was opened to you and me. If you don't believe you can trust God—that He will deal with you extravagantly, and He will improve the quality of your life— you'll never fully trust Him or serve Him with a full heart. You'll always withhold a part of yourself and imagine that you are a more faithful protector of your interests than Almighty God. His provision is a gift that any person can freely receive. It doesn't belong to any tradition, to any denomination, to any race or nationality. The Kingdom of God is open to all of humanity.

## PRAYER

Heavenly Father, thank You for Your extravagant provision through the blood of Jesus Christ. Thank You that You've forgiven my sins, cleansed me, and set me free. Thank You that I am sanctified, made holy, set apart to God. Thank You that I am redeemed out of the hand of Satan. What a privilege You have bestowed upon me! In the name of Jesus, amen.

# DAY 207

## OVERCOMING

*"I have given you authority to trample on snakes and scorpions and to overcome all the power of the enemy; nothing will harm you."*

LUKE 10:19

On the cross, Jesus defeated Satan and his kingdom for time and eternity. It's an irreversible, complete, and total victory. But Satan hasn't been banished from our world yet, and you and I are left to bring about that enforcement. We are still in the midst of that task, but we're not left without authority and power. The greatest tool our adversary has against us is deception. I have a friend who was a missionary in Kenya for many years and lived in the midst of the wildlife of that nation. She said when the lions become too old to hunt effectively they simply roar to intimidate their prey. You know that the lions who roar are too old to be truly dangerous. 1 Peter 5:8 says that our adversary is "like a roaring lion." He may be scary, but we've been given the resources to overcome the power of our enemy.

## PRAYER

Heavenly Father, thank You for the victory on the cross. Thank You for the authority You've given in the name of Jesus. I stand against Satan and every plan he may have today to disrupt Your purposes in my life. Thank You that You have given me everything I need to be an overcomer. In Jesus' name, amen.

# DAY 208

## THE POWER OF GOD UNLEASHED

*Therefore leaving the elementary teaching about the Christ, let us press on to maturity, not laying again a foundation of repentance from dead works [useless rituals] and of faith toward God.*

HEBREWS 6:1 • NASB®

I have observed that newer Christians often have a greater capacity to make strides in belief while those of us who are churched and religious are more resistant to believing in new ways. Why? Because we're resistant to repent. Most of us have an awareness of godliness and ungodliness. We think, "Well, I'm not doing anything really immoral. That repentance thing is for other people." We miss the idea that repentance isn't about just gross sin, but anything in our lives that obstructs our ability to believe God and to grow in faith. If you are in a place where you need the power of God unleashed in your life in a more significant way—and who among us isn't—then repentance is for you. The power of the Living God is at work in you and through you, and repentance is a powerful tool for allowing God's purposes to emerge in your life.

## PRAYER

Heavenly Father, I repent for all things in my life that distract me from Your purposes. Forgive me for being stagnant. I want Your best for my life. If there is any thought or behavior that hinders me, help me to recognize it. I want to follow You more fully. In Jesus' name, amen.

# DAY 209

## GOD-SPACE

*"Remember the sabbath day, to keep it holy. Six days you shall labor and do all your work, but the seventh day is a sabbath of the LORD your God; in it you shall not do any work . . . For in six days the LORD made the heavens and the earth, the sea and all that is in them, and rested on the seventh day; therefore the LORD blessed the sabbath day and made it holy.*

### EXODUS 20:8-11 • NASB®

I want to encourage you to purposefully, intentionally practice the Sabbath on a weekly basis. The notion of the Sabbath begins in the book of Genesis and is carried right on through Scripture. It's included in the Ten Commandments. I don't know that there is a day that is more holy, but I do know that God says we should take a day and yield it to Him. This is not an attempt to recruit you for more routine church attendance, but I would encourage you to routinely make space in your life for God. As you think about your schedule, plan a time on a weekly basis where you can turn your heart to the Lord. It will make a difference.

## PRAYER

Heavenly Father, thank You for rest. As I prepare to adjust my calendar to include a day of rest, I ask for Your Holy Spirit to meet me and teach me Your truths. In Jesus' name, amen.

# DAY 210

## ON GUARD AND ALERT

*"When an evil spirit comes out of a man, it goes through arid places seeking rest and does not find it. Then it says, 'I will return to the house I left.' When it arrives, it finds the house swept clean and put in order. Then it goes and takes seven other spirits more wicked than itself, and they go in and live there. And the final condition of that man is worse than the first."*

LUKE 11:24-26

Jesus isn't speaking metaphorically—He's describing our thoughts and emotions and physical bodies being negatively impacted by spiritual forces. Do you know how to defend yourself spiritually? The Bible's counsel is to not seek direction from any spiritual influence other than the Spirit of God. My personal choice is to avoid all kinds of fortune telling, including reading horoscopes. If God thinks I need to know, He'll tell me. I don't watch movies or read books that glorify dark spiritual forces. I know I forfeit some "cool" points, but the spiritual risk is too high. Just as we are physical beings, we are spiritual beings. We must learn how to guard and protect our spiritual life and well-being.

## PRAYER

Heavenly Father, thank You. Thank You for Your Word. Thank You for the Spirit of the Living God that lives within me. Open my eyes to see the places in my life where darkness may reside. I repent for any place where I have sought direction or insight from any spiritual influences other than You. I want to cooperate with You. In Jesus' name, amen.

# DAY 211

## COURAGEOUS BELIEF

*Someone came from the house of Jairus, the synagogue ruler. "Your daughter is dead," he said. "Don't bother the teacher any more." Hearing this, Jesus said to Jairus, "Don't be afraid; just believe, and she will be healed."*

LUKE 8:49-50

A synagogue ruler named Jairus has come to Jesus and asked for help because his daughter is sick, and it's quite an expression of humility on Jairus' part. He's a part of the religious establishment, and Jesus is just a traveling rabbi with no authority in the official religious system of the nation. They're headed to Jairus' home, and a messenger comes to tell him his daughter is dead. Jesus' response must've seemed odd: "Don't be afraid; just believe, and she will be healed." There will be times in your life when believing in God will take tremendous courage. In retrospect I can see that my most challenging seasons were my most fruitful seasons, but at the time it took every ounce of strength I had to say to the Lord, "I believe in You. I'm going to walk with You on this one." Belief in God is a lifelong journey, not something you will achieve and put on the shelf to admire. It's an ongoing process in my life, but it has brought security in God's faithfulness that I couldn't have obtained any other way.

## PRAYER

Heavenly Father, I'm choosing to walk out my circumstances with You. My situation may not be what I would prefer, but I wait in anticipation for the things I will learn through it. I thank You in advance for how we will walk through this season together. In Jesus' name, amen.

## A VALUABLE COMMODITY

*Buy the truth and do not sell it.*

PROVERBS 23:23

We live in an age where truthfulness is on the decline. In almost every aspect of our lives, from personal relationships to business to politics to religion, there is a vocabulary to describe avoiding the truth: We tell a little white lie, spin the news, craft a message, and accept all viewpoints. However, Scripture says that there is truth; and if we really are Jesus-followers, we will know the truth, and it will set us free (John 8:31-32). The only way to grow in the Lord is to ask God to show us the truth, open our hearts to the truth, face the truth, and cooperate with the truth. Truth is a valuable commodity that will change your life. Secure the truth—and when you get it, use everything you have to protect it. Practice it, cultivate it, and never let it go.

## PRAYER

Heavenly Father, You are true in all Your ways—all-knowing and unchanging. In a world where truth isn't held in high esteem, give me a hunger and thirst for the truth in my life. May I always speak Your truth, Lord, and bring honor to You. In Jesus' name I thank You, amen.

# DAY 213

## STRONGER TOGETHER

*From him the whole body, joined and held together by every supporting ligament, grows and builds itself up in love, as each part does its work.*

### EPHESIANS 4:16

Paul is writing to the church at Ephesus about growing in the Lord as the Church, the Body of Christ. Growing in Christ is a whole-body event. We are interdependent. We need one another. This can be tough for Americans. We've got that John Wayne thing in our DNA, toughing it out and doing it on our own. But there's an aspect of our growth and maturity in the Lord that only comes in community. People say to me, "I don't need church to be a Christ-follower. I've got my Bible and the Holy Spirit." You're right. You don't need a pulpit or a building in order to find your way into the Kingdom of God. But you'll never reach maturity by yourself. Alone, you will never find the fullness of what God created you to be. We're a body. When every part is healthy, it's just better! You have parts you don't even know about, but if one of them stops functioning, you'll become aware of it. And that's true in the Body of Christ as well. We need one another.

## PRAYER

Heavenly Father, Your wisdom in creating us as connected, interdependent beings is amazing to me. Thank You that You did not design us to live and grow in isolation but in community. Thank You for the love and wisdom we can find in the Body of Christ. I pray for a great increase in churches of faithful Jesus-followers where Your people can find fellowship and support and accountability. In the name of Jesus, the Head of the Church, amen.

## DAY 214

## JOY IN PERSEVERANCE

*Consider it pure joy, my brothers, whenever you face trials of many kinds, because you know that the testing of your faith develops perseverance. Perseverance must finish its work so that you may be mature and complete, not lacking anything.*

### JAMES 1:2-4

Pure joy . . . trials . . . testing . . . perseverance. Left to my own thinking, I probably wouldn't mention joy with those other things. Perseverance can be a challenge for me because it involves patience, and I'm not very patient. I like the microwave, and even the microwave is a little slow for me. But there have been times in my life when God has said, "You're going to have to wait on this one a little bit." Maturity gained is always a good thing; maturity in process is always uncomfortable. If you're in a place where you're being asked to persevere, don't grumble—celebrate, because joy and perseverance go together, and God is allowing you to mature. Even though they may have been—and may still be—uncomfortable, let's be grateful for all the places in life where we have shown the maturity to respond well.

## PRAYER

Heavenly Father, help me to see the circumstances and events of my life through Your eyes. Give me wisdom to see Your plan and Your purposes for my life. Thank You for the times of testing You have given me, for I want to be mature and pleasing to You. I choose today to be an overcomer. Give me the strength I need to persevere. I'm trusting You. In Jesus' name, amen.

# DAY 215

## NEW THINKING

*As he thinks within himself, so he is.*

PROVERBS 23:7 • NASB®

Our thoughts have an enormous influence on the outcome of our lives. We've all been encouraged and motivated and calmed by positive thoughts. And we've all been physically upset and agitated and tormented by negative thoughts. Some of the thoughts that enter our minds don't come from the Lord, and the fact that a thought comes across the screen of my mind doesn't mean I want to entertain it or reflect on it or let it describe me. There are some thoughts that come and I say, "Get out of here! You have no place in me!" Each one of us is responsible for the thoughts that we allow to fill our mind, so we should ask the Holy Spirit to help us think in a way that honors the Lord.

## PRAYER

Heavenly Father, thank You that You are aware of my every thought. Give me discernment to know which thoughts should be entertained and which thoughts should be banished. Your Word teaches me to hold every thought captive to the obedience of Jesus Christ (2 Cor. 10:5). I want my thoughts to honor You, Lord, so my life will honor You. In Jesus' name, amen.

# DAY 216

## THE LIVING TEMPLE

*Don't you know that you yourselves are God's temple and that God's Spirit lives in you?*

1 CORINTHIANS 3:16

One of the ground-shaking messages of the New Testament is that God no longer dwells in a building constructed by human hands; the Spirit of God literally dwells in each one of His people. Therefore, how we treat our bodies is an expression of worship. We can get the "amen corners" in almost any church fired up if we preach on drunkenness, but the Bible says far more about gluttony than it does drunkenness. You can dishonor God with a fork, because how we treat ourselves is a reflection of worship. I don't think it's appropriate to spray graffiti on the walls of the sanctuary, and I wouldn't put it on a living temple either. Because our bodies are His dwelling place, we have a responsibility to God for how we treat them.

## PRAYER

Heavenly Father, what a precious gift and responsibility it is that Your Spirit dwells within me. Help me to remember that I am worshipping You as I go about my day, making one choice after another that affects my body, Your temple. In Jesus' name, amen.

## SUFFICIENT STRENGTH

*No temptation has seized you except what is common to man. And God is faithful; he will not let you be tempted beyond what you can bear. But when you are tempted, he will also provide a way out so that you can stand up under it.*

### 1 CORINTHIANS 10:13

The word for "temptation" here can also be translated "trial." Trials and temptations come to all of us. None of us escape—everyone's lives are filled with difficulties, and sometimes they feel like they are almost more than we can bear. This promise, that His strength is sufficient to enable us to endure anything that comes to our lives, is amazing. But believing it will not be the majority response. If you survey everybody in your sphere of influence, probably not all of them will pat you on the back and say, "I agree. God will provide a way." But God's Word says He will provide a way, and you and I have to decide what we will believe. Belief in God's power is a minority response, but it is the right one.

## PRAYER

Heavenly Father, thank You for Your faithfulness to every generation. I believe in the power of Your strength to help me. If there is any doubt in me, I ask for a new portion of belief. I trust Your Word is true and trust You to provide all I need to endure. In Jesus' powerful name, amen.

# DAY 218

## KINGDOM AWARENESS

*Then King David went in and sat before the LORD, and he said: "Who am I, O Sovereign LORD, and what is my family, that You have brought me this far?"*

### 2 SAMUEL 7:18

Church folks are too often coached to come in on the weekend, take our place, stand up and sit down when we're supposed to, then go out and live our lives. That's awful! The greatest power for the transformation and satisfaction of our lives comes from interacting with Almighty God. David knew this. He's the king, with all the power that entails, and he goes in and sits in the presence of the Lord and asks, "Who am I before You, God, and why would You bless me this way?" That same awareness should be growing in us. We should not be people who endure worship and separate it from our daily lives; we should strive to understand the power of God and the possibilities of life with God in the midst of it. A growing awareness of the Kingdom of God will change not only every aspect of our lives, it will impact our communities and our world.

## PRAYER

Heavenly Father, thank You for a community of faith—men and women to encourage me as I seek You. Thank You for the privilege of worshipping You freely. I am grateful for Your presence, Your invitations, and Your power at work on my behalf. Strengthen me, Lord, so I may be faithful to You in all that I do. I ask this in Jesus' name, amen.

# DAY 219

## GOOD INFLUENCES

*Do not be misled: "Bad company corrupts good character." Come back to your senses as you ought, and stop sinning.*

1 CORINTHIANS 15:33-34

I have observed that when someone makes a conscious decision to do wrong, they'll do their best to get others involved with them. The more people they can recruit, the more momentum they will gain. This starts in childhood when we join someone throwing rocks or calling names. The process becomes a little more sophisticated as we grow older. As adults, it's easy to justify sin if you can find somebody who's written a book on the particular evil you're considering. And if they have a blog or podcast that's even better. There's a strategy to counter this kind of thinking and behavior, and that's to recruit friends to hold you accountable. We will never find maturity as Christ-followers if we huddle alone and isolated, with a "my life and my business" attitude. You should have people in your life who will ask you the questions you hope no one ever needs to ask you. We need that. Show me your friends, and I'll show you your future.

## PRAYER

Heavenly Father, give me wisdom to follow You and only You. May Your approval be the only thing I desire and strive to achieve. Thank You for the people You have placed in my life who hold me accountable and ask me hard questions. Help me to continually mature in You, Lord, so my life will bring honor to Your name. In the name of Jesus, amen.

# DAY 220

## THE GOOD FIGHT OF THE FAITH

*But you, man of God, flee from all this, and pursue righteousness, godliness, faith, love, endurance and gentleness. Fight the good fight of the faith. Take hold of the eternal life to which you were called when you made your good confession in the presence of many witnesses.*

### 1 TIMOTHY 6:11-12

Flee . . . pursue . . . fight . . . Where did we get the notion that the primary demonstration of being a Christ-follower is filing into church, singing songs, and sitting on our good intentions until we get to Heaven? That couldn't be more wrong. Maturing in the Lord is not a passive process, and it will require of us a willingness to engage in conflict. (Think about the lives of Jesus, Moses, Noah, David, Peter, Paul, or any of the other characters you want to pick from the Bible.) And the biggest battle of our lives is within ourselves. If we will allow the Spirit of God to bring transformation to us from the inside out, the external conflicts begin to reposition themselves. We can say with David, "Yeah, I know he's a giant, but God can handle this!"

## PRAYER

Heavenly Father, I acknowledge that there is a part of me that wants my own way and does not want to yield to You. Help me to flee from my carnal nature, pursue the things of Your Kingdom, and fight for the life of maturity You want for me. I long for the eternal life You have promised. Help me to fulfill Your purposes in the earth until that day. In the name of Jesus, our conquering King, amen.

## IMPROVED VISION

*And Elisha prayed, "O LORD, open his eyes so he may see." Then the LORD opened the servant's eyes, and he looked and saw the hills full of horses and chariots of fire all around Elisha.*

2 KINGS 6:17

For months, Elisha the prophet told the king of Israel where the foreign armies were deployed so the Israelites could avoid their ambushes. The foreign king finally heard that Elisha was the problem and sent his men to capture him. In the morning Elisha's servant saw the foreign army and knew they'd come for Elisha. Elisha prayed, asking the Lord to open his servant's eyes, and the man suddenly saw the Lord's horses and chariots of fire surrounding Elisha. Elisha didn't need his eyes opened; he saw the chariots of the Lord. He wanted his servant to see them and be reassured by them too. We can't afford to live in the darkness, where we stumble and lose our sense of perspective. God gives us eyes to see if we ask, and our improved vision has a ripple effect. We can see and believe God in a way that transforms us, our families, and others as well.

## PRAYER

Heavenly Father, thank You for this example of Your power through Elisha, a man who believed You. I believe this same power is available in my life. Give me eyes to see, Lord, so I may not walk in the darkness but in Your light. In Jesus' name, amen.

## MUST GO MOMENTS

*From that time on Jesus began to explain to his disciples that he must go to Jerusalem and suffer many things at the hands of the elders, chief priests and teachers of the law, and that he must be killed and on the third day be raised to life.*

MATTHEW 16:21

Jesus understood that to complete God's purposes for His life, He must go. It was a difficult path, yet it was a part of God's invitation before Him. The Scripture says that we were created in Christ Jesus to do good works, which God prepared in advance for us to do (Ephesians 2:10). God has a plan for your life and mine. Does your life with the Lord include an awareness that there are some things God has put before you that you must do? If we are going to find God's best for our lives and fulfill those things for which we were created, we need room in our imagination for the "must goes" of our journey. Sometimes they may not be "Yay, God" moments, but they will bear great fruit in both time and eternity.

## PRAYER

Heavenly Father, I choose to serve You, to give You first place in my life. How grateful I am that You have created me for a purpose in Your Kingdom. Help me to follow You daily, Lord, so I can fulfill the plans You have for me. Give me a willing spirit, even when facing the "must go" invitations You place before me. In the name of Jesus, amen.

## THE BATTLE

*And pray in the Spirit on all occasions with all kinds of prayers and requests. With this in mind, be alert and always keep on praying for all the saints.*

EPHESIANS 6:18

In Ephesians 6:10-17, there's a discussion about spiritual conflict and the spiritual armor necessary to "take your stand against the devil's schemes." The summary is in verse 18, which tells us that after we've got all the armor in place, we need to pray in the Spirit—directed by the Spirit, with all kinds of prayer. It doesn't say "practice self-discipline" or "withdraw from the battlefield." It says "pray in the Spirit," because that's the key to changing our thinking. Even a disciplined person who's withdrawn from many of the temptations of the world still faces those internal struggles that challenge the invitations of God. And prayer is given to us as that powerful tool for transformation. Prayer isn't part of the battle—it is the battle.

## PRAYER

Heavenly Father, thank You for the gift of Your Holy Spirit. I want to cooperate with Him in every way You would like. You have promised to hear my prayers, Lord, and I trust You to do that. Make me a more faithful prayer warrior, both for myself and others. In Jesus' name, amen.

## TOP PRIORITY

*Above all else, guard your heart, for it is the wellspring of life.*

PROVERBS 4:23

This verse is easy to read but hard to put into practice. Think of the things in your life that you're responsible to protect—your family, your house, your car, your finances, even your identity. All of those things are perfectly appropriate, and we put a lot of time and energy into them. But how many of us even think about including our heart's condition in that list, much less putting it at the top? It's tempting to spend more time on other things than on the state of our heart. Yet this verse tells us our spiritual condition should be our top priority because everything else flows out of that.

## PRAYER

Heavenly Father, let me always put You first in my life, and guard my heart above all else. Help me to align my priorities, as I take responsibility for those elements of daily life and family. In Jesus' name, amen.

# DAY 225

## REWARD FROM PAINFUL PLACES

*So do not throw away your confidence; it will be richly rewarded. You need to persevere so that when you have done the will of God, you will receive what he has promised.*

HEBREWS 10:35-36

If we're cautioned not to throw away our confidence, it's because many do. It's very plain language that if you cast away your confidence—if you throw it away, if you abandon the process early—you will forfeit your reward. And there's a phrase here—to me, the language is so gentle it's as if the Lord Himself put His hand on your shoulder and mine and said: "You need to persevere."

"I don't want to."

"I know. But you need to persevere."

"But I'm tired."

"You need to persevere."

"But it's not fair."

"You need to persevere."

Why? Because when struggles and disasters come, and they surely will, only an Almighty God can bring a reward from those painful places. Don't give up your confidence. Trust the Lord. Cry out to Him. He is faithful.

## PRAYER

Heavenly Father, strengthen me to persevere and not throw away my confidence in You. Thank You for caring about my well-being. Show me Your will for me, and help me to do it. I am trusting You to fulfill Your promises to me, Lord, because You are faithful in all things. In Jesus' name, amen.

# DAY 226

## NO LONGER OWNED

*What shall we say, then? Shall we go on sinning so that grace may increase? By no means! We died to sin; how can we live in it any longer? Or don't you know that all of us who were baptized into Christ Jesus were baptized into his death? We were therefore buried with him through baptism into death in order that, just as Christ was raised from the dead through the glory of the Father, we too may live a new life.*

ROMANS 6:1-4

Before we came to the cross of Jesus and chose Him as Lord, sin was our master. The good news of the Gospel is that the dominion of sin has been broken over our lives. We still face it and its invitations, but it does not own us. My motivation for living a godly life isn't so I can earn my way to heaven, because that's impossible. I lead my life in obedience and yield to Jesus out of appreciation and respect and honor for what He's done for me. Jesus didn't die on a cross for you and me to lead mediocre lives. He died on a cross so we could lead victorious lives.

## PRAYER

Heavenly Father, I come before You in thanksgiving and gratitude for the sacrifice Jesus made on the cross for me. I want to live in a way that shows honor and respect for that. Help me to make daily choices that show that sin is not my master, for I want to live a life that is victorious in You. In the name of Jesus, our victorious Savior, amen.

# DAY 227

## BEYOND BOUNDARIES

*The king said to me, "What is it you want?" Then I prayed to the God of heaven, and I answered the king, "If it pleases the king and if your servant has found favor in his sight, let him send me to the city in Judah where my fathers are buried so that I can rebuild it."*

### NEHEMIAH 2:4-5

Nehemiah was a Jewish cupbearer for the king of Persia. He ate and drank as well as the king and was living a very comfortable life. But when he heard that Jerusalem was destroyed, he was heartbroken. He asked for and received the king's permission and resources to rebuild the city. Nehemiah wasn't an engineer or a builder or even a stonecutter, but God gave him the assignment of rebuilding a city. God's plan for you and me isn't always about our plan for you and me. And it often doesn't matter what our background is. God stepped into Nehemiah's life and used him in a way that no one could have imagined to orchestrate a supernatural event. He will do the same for you and me if we are willing to say yes to His invitations.

## PRAYER

Heavenly Father, thank You that You are willing to use Your people to accomplish Your purposes. Thank You for allowing me to play a part in building Your Kingdom. Give me discernment to see beyond the boundaries I set for myself so that I might fulfill the plans You have for my life during my days in the earth. In Jesus' name, amen.

## GUARD THE MIND

*Each one is tempted when, by his own evil desire, he is dragged away and enticed. Then, after desire has conceived, it gives birth to sin; and sin, when it is full-grown, gives birth to death.*

JAMES 1:14-15

James just tells it like it is. In this passage he describes a downward progression that's launched by our own destructive desires. All of us have desires that are ungodly, and they need to be uprooted—not defended, not explained away, not blamed on circumstance or family or the injustice of something that happened in the past. When you have an ungodly desire, don't cultivate or even tolerate it. Eliminate it. I have learned I have to be careful. If we are Christ-followers, if we are people who say we love the Lord, we should be cultivating a different set of desires than ungodly people. What we dream about, what we do with our treasure, our talent, our time, our resources, should be different than the ungodly. Those things are a reflection of our desires. Be careful, because one little evil desire will grow a forest of friends and lead you toward an end that is death. And the opposite is also true: Desires that honor the Lord will multiply and lead to life and blessing.

## PRAYER

Heavenly Father, thank You for the truth of Your Word. Even when it seems to place limitations on me, I know it is because Your way leads to life and blessings beyond what I can see. Help me to guard my mind so that my desires will honor You. In Jesus' name, amen.

## APPOINTED ADVOCATE

*We are therefore Christ's ambassadors, as though God were making his appeal through us.*

### 2 CORINTHIANS 5:20

The best way to understand your life and mine is in the context of a Kingdom-assignment. God has something for us to do. People say to me, "Pastor, if I just knew what it was." I'll suggest that you begin with this notion of being an ambassador for the Kingdom of God, an advocate for Jesus of Nazareth. We've chosen Him as Lord, serve Him as King, and advocate for Him as the Messiah. And wherever God gives you influence, wherever people trust you, respect you, listen to you, He asks you to be an ambassador on His behalf. Not to be quiet about Him, lest you offend. Not to withdraw your advocacy for Him if someone might not want to hear it. He asks you to be an unrelenting, unyielding ambassador—an advocate—for Jesus of Nazareth. It is the highest privilege of our lives.

## PRAYER

Heavenly Father, thank You for the privilege of being Your ambassador in the earth. Thank You for the invitation to invest my strength and resources in pursuit of Your agenda in my generation. May my life bring glory to Jesus as Messiah and Lord. In His name, which is above all names, amen.

# DAY 230

## AWESOME PROMISES

*Blessed is the man who fears the LORD, who finds great delight in his commands . . . Surely he will never be shaken; a righteous man will be remembered forever. He will have no fear of bad news; his heart is steadfast, trusting in the LORD. His heart is secure, he will have no fear; in the end he will look in triumph on his foes.*

PSALM 112:1, 6-8

There are so many promises in this passage: We will be blessed if we fear the Lord and want to do what He says. This isn't fear of an angry father, but the respect we show toward a Father who loves us and wants the best for us. We will never be shaken. We can know a place of security and stability even as the world around us shakes and trembles. We will see with our own eyes the triumph God brings over our foes—our adversaries, those who oppose God's purposes. This is a marvelous passage for reflection. If you are in the habit of memorizing or meditating on Scripture, I commend it to you.  It will give you strength and reassurance when your world is shaking.

## PRAYER

Heavenly Father, thank You for Your Word. I pray this scripture over my own life. I am blessed because of my fear of the Lord. Surely I will never be shaken and will be remembered because of my righteousness. I will have no fear; my heart is steadfast, trusting in You. In Jesus' name, amen.

## GOOD HARVESTS

*The one who sows to please his sinful nature, from that nature will reap destruction; the one who sows to please the Spirit, from the Spirit will reap eternal life.*

GALATIANS 6:8

This verse describes a very simple principle: Living to please your sinful nature results in destruction, and living to please the Spirit of God results in eternal life. It's described in an organic way—you sow and you reap. That organic process can be deceptive because it is not immediate. Sometimes when you participate in ungodly things and there is no immediate response from God, you think, "There was no consequence! I'm free!" Sometimes when you cooperate with the Spirit of God, but you don't see an immediate result, you think, "Why did I bother if there's no reward for good behavior?" The truth is that both harvests are coming. Sowing to please the Spirit will bring you blessings in your own heart, in your family, in your business, as brothers and sisters in Christ, as citizens—in every aspect of your life.

## PRAYER

Heavenly Father, I want to sow in a way that reaps a harvest that is pleasing to You. I pray that I will always choose You in my heart, my marriage, my resources and my time. I thank You for the harvest of life and blessing You have promised. In Jesus' name, amen.

# DAY 232

## BELIEVE IN THE POSSIBILITIES

*Coming to his hometown, he began teaching the people in their synagogue, and they were amazed. "Where did this man get this wisdom and these miraculous powers?" they asked. "Isn't this the carpenter's son? Isn't his mother's name Mary, and aren't his brothers James, Joseph, Simon and Judas? Aren't all his sisters with us? Where then did this man get all these things?" And they took offense at him . . . And he did not do many miracles there because of their lack of faith.*

MATTHEW 13:54-58

There's a sad, one-line commentary in verse 58: "And he did not do many miracles there because of their lack of faith." What was in their hearts inhibited what God would do. If they had been a group of people who believed the possibilities of what Jesus could have and would have done that day, the story would have a dramatically different ending. As we grow in our awareness of God and our belief in God, He will do things in our midst beyond what we've seen Him do in the past. There will be an increase in the God-stories you will hear and tell—miraculous things that only God can orchestrate.

## PRAYER

Heavenly Father, I choose to put my faith in You, my hope in You, my trust in You. I believe in Your power to perform miracles in my generation. Help me to see more fully the possibilities You place in my path and the power of God at work in my life. Thank You for Your faithfulness to me, Lord. In Jesus' name, amen.

# DAY 233

## DAILY PRESENCE

*Every day I will bless You, and I will praise Your name forever and ever.*

PSALM 145:2 • NASB®

I want to invite you to practice the presence of God on a daily basis. You can do it through prayer, or reading your Bible, or worship. A good example of the wisdom of interacting with God on a daily basis is when Jesus taught the disciples to pray. He could have instructed them to say, "Provide our daily bread forever," but He said, "Give us this day our daily bread." And when God provided nourishment for the Israelites in the wilderness, He provided just what they needed on a daily basis. God wants to do something in us, and in our midst, every day, so don't relegate God to a time slot on the weekend. Let God be a part of your daily routine.

## PRAYER

Heavenly Father, I will choose to bless You every day, and I will praise Your name forever and ever. Thank You for the privilege I have of coming into the presence Almighty God, Creator of the universe—every day, every moment of my life. May I never take that privilege for granted. In Jesus' name I pray and believe, amen.

# DAY 234

## DELIBERATE PRAYER

*"And lead us not into temptation."*

MATTHEW 6:13

You may have seen the bumper sticker that says "Lead me not into temptation; I'm perfectly capable of finding it on my own." Sounds like my story. The reality is that every one of us faces temptation. My observation is that we tend to underestimate our ability to handle adversity and overestimate our ability to handle temptation. I have sat with many people who have given in to temptation, and I hear this kind of reasoning: "I never imagined what those first steps would lead to." "No one faces the temptations I do." "It's hereditary. Everyone in my family is this way." When we think of temptation, we usually think of big things like adultery and stealing, but we face temptations over a whole spectrum of issues: spending too much, eating too much, overindulging our children, etc. When Jesus gave His disciples a template for prayer, I don't believe He wasted any words or just shared some casual thoughts. He very purposefully taught His disciples to pray that they would be delivered from temptation, so that's what we should also pray.

## PRAYER

Heavenly Father, give me the wisdom and courage and awareness to say no to temptation. Help me to banish ungodly thoughts before they take hold. Lord, lead us not into temptation, but deliver us from evil, that Your purposes might be worked out for the glory of Your Son, Jesus. It's in His name I pray, amen.

# DAY 235

## GOD'S STANDARDS

*Put off your old self, which is being corrupted by its deceitful desires; to be made new in the attitude of your minds.*

EPHESIANS 4:22-23

I've been a Christ-follower for a while, but I still have to be careful about what I fill my mind with—the music I listen to, the things I read, the television and movies I watch. We have this ongoing cultural debate about what is profane or obscene and what the government will allow to be broadcast during certain times of the day. May I be honest with you? If you're looking to the government to set the standards for what you will listen to and what you'll watch, you're in trouble. I'm very grateful for our freedom of speech, but that same liberty should be a warning that the government does not set the standards for righteousness and holiness and purity—God does. As Christ-followers, our boundaries should be different than those who are not Christ-followers. Don't follow your feelings, because your feelings can be wrong. Don't make yourself vulnerable to things that will force you to spend enormous effort weeding your heart and mind. Make a habit of filtering what goes into your mind. Choose things that you know will please the Lord.

## PRAYER

Heavenly Father, thank You for the discernment the Holy Spirit gives to me. Help me to vigilantly guard my mind, seeking to honor You with all that enters it. Continue to purify my thoughts, and help me to put off my old self. May the words of mouth and the meditation of my heart be pleasing to You, Lord. In the powerful name of Jesus, amen.

# DAY 236

## STRONG FORTRESS

*I will say of the LORD, "He is my refuge and my fortress, my God, in whom I trust."*

PSALM 91:2

When we're tempted, we need to know where we can go for refuge. It's worth noting that if the psalmist says we need a refuge and a fortress, there must be an adversary we need a refuge from and a fortress against. In our sophistication and intellectualism, and all the things that come with our twenty-first-century pride and arrogance, we like to imagine that we're just a bit too sophisticated to deal with the Devil and demons and spiritual conflict. But if we need Almighty God as our refuge and fortress, we should recognize that's because we will be facing spiritual warfare. The Bible describes a time when God's Kingdom will fully come to the earth—when Jesus will be acknowledged as Lord and King—but we're not there yet. So we need to understand that our refuge is not the force of our will or the power of our intellect. God is our refuge and fortress.

## PRAYER

Heavenly Father, we live in a sinful world where dark forces seek to pull us away from You. Until the day when Jesus returns and evil is banished, You are a shelter for the oppressed, a refuge in times of trouble. Thank You, Lord, for Your unfailing promise of protection. In Jesus' name, amen.

# DAY 237

## HIS PEACE

*"Peace I leave with you; my peace I give you. I do not give to you as the world gives. Do not let your hearts be troubled and do not be afraid."*

JOHN 14:27

There are very few times when Jesus specifically gave His followers something that was His. In this case He said, "You can have My peace." Jesus didn't say His peace would bring freedom from conflict. In fact, Jesus faced conflict from His infancy, when Joseph and Mary fled with Him to Egypt to protect Him from the murderous Herod. When He grew to maturity and began His public ministry, He faced hostility many times, mostly from religious leaders. In every circumstance Jesus faced, you never find Him frightened or intimidated or panicked. No matter what He encountered, whether it was a need, an angry politician, or someone with a trick question, Jesus had the calm assurance of God's abiding presence, and that's the gift He gives to us. "My peace I give to you." What an amazing promise for our lives.

## PRAYER

Heavenly Father, I put my trust in You and Your loving care over my life. Thank You for Your protection, provision, and plans for me. I choose to live in the peace You give, the assurance of Your abiding presence in my life. When I am afraid, I will trust in You and wait for Your deliverance. In Jesus' name, amen.

# DAY 238

## A GOD-PERSPECTIVE

*Without faith it is impossible to please God.*

HEBREWS 11:6

That's about as straightforward as it can be. Without faith, you will not please God! You can't be kind enough, good enough, moral enough, generous enough. You can't serve enough, volunteer enough. You can't sit in church enough, teach enough classes, or read your Bible enough. Faith is not in the optional category; it is in the necessary category. So what does it mean to have faith? People of faith make life choices based on a God-perspective. We do business with a God-perspective. We conduct our relationships with a God-perspective. We interact in our marriage with a God-perspective. And faith is not a static thing. We want to grow in faith every day of our journey as Christ-followers, increasingly making life choices that reflect a God-perspective.

## PRAYER

Heavenly Father, I want to please You. Give me increasing faith, Lord, which always puts Your perspective ahead of my own. May my faith in You be obvious, so that all who know me will see that pleasing You is my greatest aim. In Jesus' name, amen.

# DAY 239

## INVEST IN GOD'S PURPOSES

*Meanwhile, the people in Judah said, "The strength of the laborers is giving out, and there is so much rubble that we cannot rebuild the wall."*

NEHEMIAH 4:10

Nehemiah was cupbearer to the king of Persia. When he heard that Jerusalem was in ruins and the people were suffering, Nehemiah got permission from the king to go to the city and rebuild it. He recruited workers to reconstruct the massive walls, and the work was hard! The people were tired and discouraged and faced opposition—they wondered if their efforts were in vain. I don't think things have changed much since Nehemiah's day. If you and I are going to successfully fulfill the purposes of the Lord, it's going to come down to our willingness to work and persevere when the going gets tough. When we are willing to invest our strength and our energy on behalf of the Kingdom of God, two things will happen: God will change us, and He will change things through us.

## PRAYER

Heavenly Father, thank You for the faith of Nehemiah that spurred him on to rebuild Jerusalem all those centuries ago. I am grateful for his willingness to leave his position of comfort and accept Your invitation. Lord, grant me that same willingness, and perseverance when the tasks You have placed before me seem too hard or I face opposition. In Jesus' name, amen.

# DAY 240

## FEAR OR FAITH

*"There will be signs in the sun, moon and stars. On the earth, nations will be in anguish and perplexity at the roaring and tossing of the sea. Men will faint from terror, apprehensive of what is coming on the world, for the heavenly bodies will be shaken."*

LUKE 21:25-26

Jesus is describing the season prior to His return to the earth. He says fearsome things will be happening—signs in the heavens and roaring seas. Events will be so intense and frightening that men will faint in fear of what is coming. He's giving us this information so that our lives won't be dominated by fear. The Bible says there should be a difference between the people who choose to serve God and the people who don't choose to serve God—a difference in the way we live, and the peace that accompanies us. I believe one of the great opportunities in this season is for us to align ourselves and cooperate with Him to find the security and peace and confidence that comes with being the people of God. Fear or faith: This is our choice to make.

## PRAYER

Heavenly Father, I want to do my part in aligning myself to cooperate with You. I need Your security, peace, and confidence. I want to be a student of Your Word so I understand and do not become fearful of the times I'm living in. In Jesus' name, amen.

# DAY 241

## UNEXPECTED DESTINATIONS

*So do not fear, for I am with you; do not be dismayed, for I am your God. I will strengthen you and help you; I will uphold you with my righteous right hand.*

### ISAIAH 41:10

Deep in your heart, what do you believe about the power of God? Do you believe He hears our prayers? Do you believe He can heal our physical bodies? Do you believe He can restore a broken marriage? Do you believe He can _____ (fill in the blank)? God can do all of those things and more. Our journey with Him may take us to some unexpected places, but His plan is for our good.

## PRAYER

Heavenly Father, I am thankful that You allow us to make requests of You. I believe You hear and answer our prayers. I believe You can heal bodies. I believe You can restore marriages and families. Your power and possibilities are beyond what I can imagine, so help me to seek Your will and purposes in all things. In the powerful name of Jesus, amen.

# DAY 242

## LIFT THEM UP

*I urge, then, first of all, that requests, prayers, intercession and thanksgiving be made for everyone.*

### 1 TIMOTHY 2:1

Our world has shrunk, and the 24-hour news cycle brings it into our homes. We can have morning coffee and watch in real time the devastation of a weather event in Asia. We can pause at lunchtime and hear about conflict in the Middle East. The evening news will report on parents somewhere in the US who lost a child to gang violence. Our world is a stressed place. The best thing for us to do is pray for those people who are living through such troubling times. They began their day thinking they were relatively secure, but circumstances have turned their lives inside out. I believe prayer makes a difference, so let's pray for them right now.

## PRAYER

Heavenly Father, thank You for the privilege we have of lifting our hearts and voices in praise and petition to You. Lord, we pray today for people who are enduring hardship. We pray for Your intervention in their lives and circumstances. Be merciful to those people in Jesus' name. We pray for the Church in struggling places, that Your people will be faithful witnesses in times of trouble. May the Prince of Peace be revealed in all the earth. In the powerful name of Jesus we pray, amen.

# DAY 243

## APPOINTMENTS WITH OPPORTUNITIES

*All you have made will praise you, O LORD; your saints will extol you. They will tell of the glory of your kingdom and speak of your might, so that all men may know of your mighty acts and the glorious splendor of your kingdom.*

PSALM 145:10-12

Telling people about what Jesus has done for us is the highest privilege of our lives. God arranges divine appointments with people who will cross our paths, places of unique opportunity where our voice is the voice that makes a difference. I've discovered that I seldom recognize those moments at the time. Usually, the ones that I think are God-moments don't end up being so significant. And the times when I was simply trying to be obedient and do the right thing, as I knew it, God used to make a difference. God wants to use all of His people to build His Kingdom—even you.

## PRAYER

Heavenly Father, I am willing to use my energy and my effort and my voice for You. Prepare me so that when I am faced with an invitation to speak for You I will embrace the opportunity. Thank You for the presence of the Holy Spirit that empowers me to fulfill Your purposes in the earth. In Jesus' name, amen.

# DAY 244

## MORE...CONTENTMENT

*Godliness with contentment is great gain.*

1 TIMOTHY 6:6

We are a nation of people who are staggering with envy, and it's as real in the Church as without. I once read that no matter where we are on the socioeconomic scale, we think we'd be happier if we had 25 percent more. If there is a biblical word that captures God's desire for our thoughts regarding "things," I believe it would be "contentment." This verse says that a focus on godliness with an attitude of contentment is something Christ-followers will benefit from. And then it contrasts that with the thought life of those of "corrupt mind," "who think that godliness is a means to financial gain" (v. 5). I'm not advocating complacency or being satisfied with giving less than our best effort, but I am suggesting that contentment is possible. If envy is something that you struggle with, ask the Lord to give you a spirit of contentment.

## PRAYER

Heavenly Father, thank You for Your plans and provision for me. I put my trust in You and Your oversight of my life. When I am tempted to be envious or anxious about the circumstances of my life, give me a spirit of contentment. I will trust in You, my Lord and my Redeemer. In Jesus' name, amen.

# DAY 245

## A HEART COMMITTED

*"For the eyes of the LORD range throughout the earth to strengthen those whose hearts are fully committed to him."*

### 2 CHRONICLES 16:9

I love the imagery of that passage: the eyes of God roaming the earth, searching for men and women whose hearts are His. Many people want God to bless them, to deliver them, to heal them, to prosper them. But they're not particularly interested in meeting God's conditions; they simply want God to demonstrate His power on their behalf for their purposes. But this verse says that God searches for people whose hearts are turned toward Him. If you will begin to adjust your life and turn your heart toward the Lord, you will capture God's attention. What an amazing promise!

## PRAYER

Heavenly Father, thank You for Your people in the earth. Thank You, Holy Spirit, that You are in our midst to direct and guide and convict, to turn our hearts toward the Lord. May I always be fully committed to You, Your Kingdom, and Your purposes. In Jesus' name, amen.

# DAY 246

## INSIDE COMES FIRST

*And the child grew and became strong in spirit; and he lived in the desert until he appeared publicly to Israel.*

LUKE 1:80

Before John the Baptist was ever born, God said He was going to use him to prepare the way for Jesus. But this verse says that before John the Baptist ever had any public recognition, he grew and became strong in spirit. Personal growth, what happens within us, always precedes what happens outside us. As I look back over my years of ministry, I can say that has been consistently true: What happens beyond us is very much secondary to what's going on within us. Life happens to all of us, and how we respond determines the arc of our spiritual growth. For each one of us, what He's doing in us is preparing us for what He will do through us.

## PRAYER

Heavenly Father, thank You for the privilege of playing a part in Your plans for this generation. Continue to grow me up, Lord, and mature me in ways that will help me to fulfill Your purposes, even when they are not obvious to me. With a grateful heart, I pray. In Jesus' name, amen.

## NO LOSS OF HEART

*David said to Saul, "Let no one lose heart on account of this Philistine; your servant will go and fight him."*

### 1 SAMUEL 17:32

The story of David and Goliath is so familiar to us that we probably don't think about how bizarre it seems for a shepherd boy to take on a trained warrior (and a giant) and kill him with a stone launched from a sling while an army was cowering in their tents. Can you imagine the shame among those men? It is safe to say the Israelite army had lost heart. Sometimes we lose the imagination that God wants to do something in and through us because there are challenges that are so intimidating, and perhaps in place for so long, that we have lost any hope they can be overcome. Sometimes God's sense of timing and our sense of timing don't seem to coincide, and at other times we need a season of preparation before we engage the challenge, but Almighty God can do anything. My invitation to you is to dare to say to God, "I believe You can make a difference."

## PRAYER

Heavenly Father, give me a fresh filling of the kind of faith that David had—faith that believes You can do anything and trusts You to make a difference in our lives. May I never lose heart, Lord. Help me to depend on You as I face the big and small challenges before me. In Jesus' name, amen.

# DAY 248

## NEVER GIVE UP

*Let us not become weary in doing good, for at the proper time we will reap a harvest if we do not give up.*

GALATIANS 6:9

"If"—you should mentally circle that little word because it changes the meaning of the whole sentence: We will reap a harvest IF we don't give up. If you determine that God is the resolution to something in your life, and you begin to wait on Him, you'll be amazed at how it will give you a singleness of purpose. You'll be able to push things to the periphery that have been at the center of your life. Just as you gain physical strength when you reach the point of physical fatigue, you'll gain spiritual strength when you reach the point of spiritual fatigue. So if that's where you find yourself today, it's because God has chosen to strengthen you, not to punish you. So keep going! Don't give up!

## PRAYER

Heavenly Father, I want to receive the harvest You have promised to those who do not give up. Give me strength to persevere, patience to wait, and determination to continue looking for Your resolution to the challenges in my life. I praise You for Your faithfulness to me. In Jesus' name, amen.

## IMPACT GENERATIONS

*"I will defend this city and save it, for my sake and the sake of David my servant."*

### 2 KINGS 19:34

This is a very intriguing passage to me. God says to the inhabitants of Jerusalem, "I'm going to deliver your city out of respect for My servant David." God is speaking to His people hundreds of years after David's death, and He is still honoring the life of David. Do you know that the life you lead and the God-choices you make will impact the generations who follow you? Sometimes when you are standing in a hard place and thinking, "Making a God-choice is more difficult than I thought it would be," or "I wish my deliverance would come a little sooner," it's good to remember that your choices bear weight in both time and in the years to come.

## PRAYER

Heavenly Father, I want to be known, like David, as one who is devoted to You. Help me to live in such a way that my choices today will have an impact for good, both in time and in the years to come. In Jesus' name, amen.

# DAY 250

## THE GOOD FIGHT

*For I am already being poured out like a drink offering, and the time has come for my departure. I have fought the good fight, I have finished the race, I have kept the faith.*

### 2 TIMOTHY 4:6-7

This is one of the most remarkable, triumphant statements in all of Scripture. Paul is in a Roman prison, and he knows that he probably will be executed. Note that he does not say, "I have preached sermons, and I have volunteered appropriately." He says, "I have fought the fight of faith." We don't always think of our spiritual lives in terms of a fight. But if you have been a Jesus-follower for any length of time, you'll agree that you're engaged in a constant struggle to let the purposes of God emerge within you. There's no shame in that, so don't be discouraged or embarrassed by it. Be excited when the Spirit of God illuminates an aspect of your life and begins to invite you to change. Celebrate the gift of His involvement in your life. Say, "God, thank You for the privilege of repenting. Thank You that You love me enough to say, 'Don't go that way.'" If there's a spiritual struggle in your life, it's because God is refining you and bringing something good to you.

## PRAYER

Heavenly Father, thank You that You care enough about me to refine and shape me for Your purposes. I pray that at the end of my days in the earth I will be able to say, like Paul, "I have fought the good fight, I have finished the race, I have kept the faith." In Jesus' name, amen.

# DAY 251

## GOD-EXPERIENCE

*"Wisdom is with aged men, with long life is understanding."*

JOB 12:12 • NASB®

When I was a younger man it annoyed me when people said there were some things I'd have to learn by experience. I'd think, "My determination and effort will work you and your experience under the table!" Over the years I've come to value experience very highly, especially God-experience. One of the ways to gain God-experience is to spend time with people who have experienced God in a way you have not. Sometimes you will have to travel for it and even pay for it. Often there are people around us with God-experience we could benefit from. I'd invite you to make attaining God-experience a priority in your life.

## PRAYER

Heavenly Father, thank You for those with God-experience who have impacted my life. Thank You for those who have guided me away from unhelpful paths and toward paths of blessing. I invite You to send people across my path who will challenge me to grow in my walk with You. In Jesus' name, amen.

# DAY 252

## DO IT NOW

*Now is the time of God's favor, now is the day of salvation.*

2 CORINTHIANS 6:2

I know we've all heard the expression that "timing is everything." Time is something that was created for us while we have this brief season on the earth, and timing is certainly a critical component of dealing with the challenges of life. But if you want to know how to unleash a God-response and make a difference for the Kingdom of God, the consistent invitation of Scripture is now. And that would be my invitation to you: In whatever way God has been inviting you, respond to Him now. Stop debating, or looking for a book on the subject, or polling your friends to see what their opinion is. Just say yes to the Lord.

## PRAYER

Heavenly Father, thank You for inviting Your children to participate in Your purposes in the earth. May the first words on my lips always be, "Yes, Lord," and may I always say them with a willing heart. In Jesus' name, amen.

# DAY 253

## SIDE EFFECTS

*Humility and the fear of the LORD bring wealth and honor and life.*

### PROVERBS 22:4

This verse speaks of a delivery that can be made into your life: wealth and honor and life. And what will bring that wonderful package? It will come if you make a conscious decision to cultivate humility and the fear of the Lord. Many of us have reversed it and think we should seek after wealth and honor and a full life, and then we will show reverence and respect for God. But Scripture says that wealth and honor and life are not life objectives, but merely the side effects of fearing the Lord.

## PRAYER

Heavenly Father, forgive me for when my priorities have been reversed and I have sought after the things of the world. Renew in me a spirit of humility and reverence before You, that I may be blessed by Your hand. In Jesus' name, amen.

## DAY 254

## NO OTHERS

*And God spoke all these words: "I am the LORD your God, who brought you out of Egypt, out of the land of slavery. You shall have no other gods before me."*

### EXODUS 20:1-3

If you ask me which of the Ten Commandments the contemporary American church is most guilty of violating, I'd say the first one: "You shall have no other gods before me." It's happened gradually, like the frog in the kettle. In the 1960s, there was a cultural revolution on many levels, and one of the things that emerged was the idea of multiculturalism. Somewhere along the way multiculturalism changed from valuing the ethnic groups among us to suggesting and then demanding that the faith represented by every person or people group should be treated with equal significance. We're very reluctant to publicly suggest that Jesus is the only path to fulfillment in this life and the next, but God has never amended or rescinded His instruction. It's still binding on our lives today: "No other gods before me."

## PRAYER

Heavenly Father, I come before You in humility, acknowledging that You are the one and only God, the Creator of all and the Redeemer of mankind. Help me to speak in a way that all who hear will know that You are the only answer for this world's challenges. I worship You today, Lord. In Jesus' name, amen.

# DAY 255

## AN ATTITUDE OF GRATITUDE

*Let us continually offer to God a sacrifice of praise—the fruit of lips that confess his name.*

### HEBREWS 13:15

When we give thanks to God, we unleash the power of God to work on our behalf. Even Jesus showed gratitude toward His Father. Before He called Lazarus out of the tomb, He stopped to thank His Father for hearing His prayer. I would encourage you to guard your heart against ingratitude and become a person of thanksgiving. When you are more focused on being thankful for what you do have instead of harboring resentment about what you don't have, you will change the trajectory of your life.

## PRAYER

Heavenly Father, I will give thanks to You with the breath and the strength I have. You have delivered me from darkness and brought me into the Kingdom of Your Son. You have given life to me and blessed me beyond my imaginings. I entrust myself to You. In Jesus' name, amen.

# DAY 256

## ACTIVE FAITH

*O God, you are my God, earnestly I seek you; my soul thirsts for you,*
*my body longs for you.*

### PSALM 63:1

"Seek" is a word that shows action. It means "to search for" or "try to acquire." The psalmist is not sitting and waiting for God to come to him—he is seeking Him with his body and soul. I'm afraid that American Christians have developed such a consumer mentality toward faith that instead of actively seeking God we are looking to be entertained in a comfortable setting. I've been to places in the world where people sit on the floor all day long to hear someone teach the Bible because they don't have one of their own, or stand in line for hours to get an outline of the lesson because they have no material to study. Let's recognize our blessings and commit ourselves to seeking God with everything we have.

## PRAYER

Heavenly Father, thank You for the resources readily available to me. Give me a greater appreciation for the ease of practicing my faith. I ask that You pour rivers of blessing on my brothers and sisters around the world who worship You with whole hearts in spite of the obstacles they face. May their joy abound. In Jesus' name, amen.

## PERSISTENT PRAYER

*Then Jesus told his disciples a parable to show them that they should always pray and not give up.*

LUKE 18:1

In Luke 18:1-8, Jesus tells a story about an uncaring judge and the widow who kept coming to him with the plea, "Grant me justice." He refused and refused until he finally gave in so she would leave him alone! The teaching is rightfully known as the parable of the persistent widow. Luke thought the lesson to always pray and never give up was so important he gave it before the parable. I don't think we've learned how to be persistent. We pray occasionally and give up quite easily. Or perhaps we think we don't deserve an answer from God so we don't bother to ask. Perseverance and persistence are necessary for being an effective follower of Jesus, so let's pray—and not give up!

## PRAYER

Heavenly Father, thank You that You always hear me when I pray, and that You are not bothered by the persistence of Your children. Teach me perseverance when I am weary and tempted to give up. I have seen Your faithfulness in my life, Lord, and I praise You for it. In Jesus' name, amen.

# DAY 258

## STRONG AND COURAGEOUS

*"Be strong and courageous. Do not be terrified; do not be discouraged, for the LORD your God will be with you wherever you go."*

JOSHUA 1:9

Can you imagine the pressure Joshua felt when God recruited him to follow Moses? Moses spent so much time with God that he glowed in the dark! But Moses didn't get the people into the Promised Land, and God said, "You're up, Joshua. I want you to do what Moses couldn't." Why do you think God told him to be "strong and courageous"—seven times? I suspect it was because he was frightened and discouraged! God's message to Joshua is just as relevant to the Church today. We need to show the same courage for our faith that we show in the pursuit of our professions, in the protection of our families, even in the defense of our favorite sports teams. Don't let your greatest effort be directed at the secondary things of your life. Be strong and courageous for the Lord.

## PRAYER

Heavenly Father, I want to be strong and courageous for You. Give me strength when I am weak and courage when I am afraid or losing heart. Give me discernment so that my priorities will be aligned with Yours, Lord. In Jesus' name, amen.

# DAY 259

## OUR GOOD FATHER

*For this reason I kneel before the Father, from whom his whole family in heaven and on earth derives its name.*

### EPHESIANS 3:14-15

God chose to reveal Himself to human beings as Father. It was not accidental or arbitrary or the result of an ancient patriarchal culture that insisted upon it. This fact is not politically correct and is not always embraced, even within Christianity. But it was God's choice, and all fatherhood in the earth is based on this understanding. When we have a proper awareness of God as Father, it opens the door to understanding the whole story of Scripture and gives us insight into His role in our lives.

## PRAYER

Heavenly Father, may this be a season when I have a greater revelation of You. Give me the strength and courage to face the challenges of my life with the truth and encouragement of Your Word, for my desire is to honor You and live for Your glory. In Jesus' name, amen.

# DAY 260

## A PROMISE FOR HONOR

*"Honor your father and your mother, so that you may live long in the land the LORD your God is giving you."*

EXODUS 20:12

We all have parents, but the reality is that they parented us in varying degrees of effectiveness. Whether our parents did a great job or a terrible job, the Bible gives us a responsibility toward them. This instruction is one of the Ten Commandments that God gave to Moses on Mount Sinai. It's the first commandment that has a promise attached to it: Honor our fathers and mothers so that life will be better for us. It's worth noting that God did not say, "Honor your parents if they were good ones" or "Honor your parents if you are proud of them." We're simply given the commandment—not a suggestion, not a hint, not a nudge—to honor our parents. If your family life was less than ideal, that may require forgiveness on your part. God will be faithful to show you how to extend the same grace and mercy He has extended to you.

## PRAYER

Heavenly Father, thank You for my parents and the way they have shown me what it means to follow You. For those who have challenging relationships with their parents, I pray blessing and an extra measure of grace so that they will be able to obey this commandment with a whole heart. In Jesus' name, amen.

# DAY 261

## A BIG GOD

*"I am the Alpha and the Omega," says the Lord God, "who is, and who was, and who is to come, the Almighty."*

### REVELATION 1:8

We serve a God who is bigger than our imaginations, a God who works in the lives of men and women even as He speaks into history. The Bible is the story of God's interaction with humanity during the time He has allotted to us on the earth, a linear progression from "In the beginning God" to a vision of Jesus' return. It's easy to lose a sense of the majesty and magnitude of the God we serve in the midst of our everyday busyness. But He is a big God, and we need Him to help us meet the challenges that face humanity.

## PRAYER

Heavenly Father, You are the Alpha and the Omega—the Beginning and the End. Our imaginations of time cannot describe You or contain You. Thank You that You are at work in the earth, as You always have been and always will be. Help me to fulfill the purposes You have for me during my days in the earth, as I await Jesus' coming. In His name I pray, amen.

## DAY 262

## INVOLVED AND IN CONTROL

*Why do the nations conspire and the peoples plot in vain? The kings of the earth take their stand and the rulers gather together against the LORD and against his Anointed One. "Let us break their chains," they say, "and throw off their fetters." The One enthroned in heaven laughs; the Lord scoffs at them.*

PSALM 2:1-4

Do you hear what the psalmist is saying? The rulers of the earth gather together and say, "We don't want our plans and purposes to be inhibited by God's plans and purposes. Let's ignore what God wants and do it our way." It's not a new thing. It was true in the days of the psalmist, and it's true today. The rulers of the earth imagine that their power and their will and their determination solely direct the course of human history. And the Bible gives us God's response. He chuckles and says, "You think so?" It's very easy for us to get caught up in the news of world affairs and forget that Almighty God is not an absentee landlord. Yes, He sits enthroned in Heaven, but He is intimately involved in our world.

## PRAYER

Heavenly Father, thank You that You are not just aware of what is happening in the earth, but You are actively involved in bringing about Your purposes. Give us strength to look to You, Lord, as we look expectantly to that day when You will be revealed in all of Your glory. May we be found faithful until that day. In Jesus' name, amen.

# DAY 263

## NOT MY OWN

*It was about this time that King Herod arrested some who belonged to the church.*

### ACTS 12:1

Acts 12 is an amazing story of the unfolding purposes of God. The city of Jerusalem is being shaken. Thousands of people are responding to the God-story, and the apostles are being repeatedly threatened and arrested. In this one chapter, James is executed and Peter is released supernaturally from prison. God didn't love one more than the other, but we serve at the Lord's pleasure. We often imagine our lives are our own. We assume that being a Christ-follower is about God meeting our needs and making us happy. The Bible says we are to offer ourselves as living sacrifices, to literally offer our bodies to God. In our humanity we struggle to believe it, but honoring the Lord with our lives will bring us greater benefits in time and eternity than anything else we can do for ourselves.

## PRAYER

Heavenly Father, You have given life to me and placed the very breath in my lungs. My life is not my own, Lord. It is Yours to do with as You please. Show me how I may serve You and not myself today. In Jesus' name, amen.

## EVERLASTING COVENANT

*"I will establish my covenant as an everlasting covenant between me and you and your descendants after you for the generations to come, to be your God and the God of your descendants after you. The whole land of Canaan, where you now reside as a foreigner, I will give as an everlasting possession to you and your descendants after you; and I will be their God."*

GENESIS 17:7-8

God is a covenant-keeping God. In 1948, on a tiny sliver of land at the end of the Mediterranean, the United Nations gave credibility to the rebirth of the nation of Israel. Jewish people began to come from all over the globe, and today there are more than six million Jews living in the land—over 43% of the world's Jewish population. They are surrounded by millions of people who are committed to their annihilation, and it's impossible that they could survive apart from Almighty God. It's a testimony to the whole earth that God is a covenant-keeping God. If He'll keep His promise to the descendants of Abraham, He will keep His promises to you and to me.

## PRAYER

Heavenly Father, what a privilege it is to see You honor Your covenant with the descendants of Abraham and restore them to their land. You are faithful to keep Your promises, Lord. Thank You that I can trust in Your promises for my life as well. Thank You for Your faithfulness. In Jesus' name, amen.

# DAY 265

## TUG OF WAR

*Submit yourselves, then, to God. Resist the devil, and he will flee from you.*

JAMES 4:7

I attended Oral Roberts University many years ago. President Roberts used to say, "God is a good God, and the Devil is a bad devil." As a young man I thought that was an oversimplification, but I've come to appreciate the wisdom of those words. It comes down to this: God wants good for you, and Satan intends to destroy you. Most of us imagine we can manage the Devil. We think we can walk with him awhile and then say, "That's as far as I want to go. I'll head back now." But it just doesn't work out that way. Whenever I've entertained evil, it has brought tremendous destruction. And when I've walked with God, He's brought good things to my life. The tug-of-war of these two perspectives seems to be the dilemma of human existence. When you feel that tug, remember: God is a good God, and the Devil is a bad devil.

## PRAYER

Heavenly Father, You know every detail, every circumstance of my life. You know when I am weak and tempted. Yet I know that Your power is greater than every wicked spirit that has stood against Your purposes in my life, and that Your power is available to me. I submit to God and resist the Devil. In the authority of Jesus' name I pray, amen.

# DAY 266

## REFLECT GOD

*May those who hope in you not be disgraced because of me, O Lord, the LORD Almighty; may those who seek you not be put to shame because of me, O God of Israel.*

### PSALM 69:6

There's nothing wrong with making requests of God, asking Him for His intervention or His involvement. Those aren't childish prayers—they're normal, important prayers. But here is an expansion of that imagination of what it means to pray: May I never bring disgrace to You, God. May I live in such a way that I don't bring shame to Your cause. Often, our prayer agenda is, "God, I want You to honor me, promote me, lift me up, set me free, bring something to me—and could You hurry up, please?" And here we're being asked to imagine that our agenda in life is to honor God and never do anything that would cause Him embarrassment. In the context of your work, your marriage, your relationships, your discretionary time, live in a way that will honor God.

## PRAYER

Heavenly Father, I praise You for the great honor of bearing the name of Jesus. I repent for demanding my own way. May I live in such a way that my life reflects Your faithfulness. May I conduct myself in a way that people will know I am His friend. For it's in His name I pray, amen.

## DAY 267

### SEEK UNDERSTANDING

*We have the word of the prophets made more certain, and you will do well to pay attention to it, as to a light shining in a dark place.*

2 PETER 1:19

I hear people say, "I just don't pay much attention to that prophetic stuff. I can't even pronounce those Old Testament names. And in the New Testament, what about the book of Revelation? There are all kinds of scary creatures. It's confusing. So I'm going to focus on the main thing. I just want to know how to go to Heaven instead of Hell." I understand where those ideas come from, and I'll admit that understanding prophecy is challenging. But if God has given it to us, and He's told us to pay attention to it, I trust Him and the Holy Spirit to make it available to each and every one of us. I would invite you to not just ignore it, but to say to the Lord, "I would like to understand." And let's see what God will reveal to you.

### PRAYER

Heavenly Father, I know that every word of Scripture is true and given for my benefit. Give me insight and understanding of the parts that are not clear to me. Show me what You want me to know from Your Word, Lord, that I may apply it to my heart and life. In Jesus' name, amen.

# DAY 268

## REST FOR THE SOUL

*Be at rest once more, O my soul, for the LORD has been good to you.*

PSALM 116:7

Occasionally I'll lie down at night and my brain will engage. I'll start thinking about my "to do" list, projects that are upcoming, and other responsibilities. Those things are replaying in my head, and before long adrenaline kicks in. I'm tossing and turning and agitated because I know I'll not be at my best the next day. So I have developed a habit. If that process starts, I'll get up and begin to worship the Lord and thank Him for all the good things in my life. And if that doesn't turn my thoughts around, I'll open the Bible and read aloud from the Psalms. Nothing brings rest to my soul like focusing on the Lord's goodness. Give it a try the next time you can't sleep!

## PRAYER

Heavenly Father, thank You for all the blessings You have poured over my life—blessings that are too many to count. Thank You for the peace and rest that You bring when I focus on You, Lord. You are truly worthy of all my praise. In Jesus' name, amen.

# DAY 269

## CAST AWAY DISTRACTIONS

*When tempted, no one should say, "God is tempting me." For God cannot be tempted by evil, nor does he tempt anyone; but each one is tempted when, by his own evil desire, he is dragged away and enticed.*

### JAMES 1:13-14

You may have noticed that in spite of being a Christ-follower, you will occasionally give in to temptation and make an ungodly choice. This verse gives a different perspective on temptation and describes it as a force pulling us away from God's best. Sometimes the greatest temptations we face are the ones we don't even recognize. We get so caught up in the culture and the ungodliness around us that we lose our sense of distinctiveness and are swept along with the tide. We all have these internal, carnal desires that pull us away from godliness, and we must ask God for the courage to identify and cast away anything that would distract or draw us away from Him.

## PRAYER

Heavenly Father, thank You for the gift of the Holy Spirit, who gives me insight into the state of my heart and mind. Help me to follow His leading as I make choices big and small, because pleasing and honoring You is my highest aim. Show me anything in me that would pull me from Your best. In Jesus' name, amen.

# DAY 270

## A LONGING FULFILLED

*All these people were still living by faith when they died. They did not receive the things promised; they only saw them and welcomed them from a distance. And they admitted that they were aliens and strangers on earth. People who say such things show that they are looking for a country of their own. If they had been thinking of the country they had left, they would have had opportunity to return. Instead, they were longing for a better country—a heavenly one.*

HEBREWS 11:13-16

Would you call your life a victory if you led a life of faith but didn't receive the promise of that faith before you died? Hebrews 11 lists the Faith Hall of Fame, men and women who experienced miraculous interventions of God during their days on the earth but "did not receive the things promised." Like them, we see things that trouble us and long for a better country, a heavenly one. Our days on the earth are God-ordained, and He has a plan and purpose for each one of them. But when you are discouraged and troubled by the world around you, remember that this is not our final destination.

## PRAYER

Heavenly Father, thank You for Your promise of a better home, one that I will share with You for eternity. Help me to live with my heart and hands at work to fulfill Your purposes for me in the earth while my eyes are fixed on You. In Jesus' name, amen.

# DAY 271

## FEAR OR FAITH

*"As surely as the LORD your God lives," she replied, "I don't have any bread—only a handful of flour in a jar and a little oil in a jug. I am gathering a few sticks to take home and make a meal for myself and my son, that we may eat it—and die." Elijah said to her, "Don't be afraid. Go home and do as you have said. But first make a small cake of bread for me from what you have and bring it to me, and then make something for yourself and your son."*

### 1 KINGS 17:12-13

These verses sound a little strange to us. Why would God tell Elijah to go to the home of an impoverished widow and ask for the last bit of food she had for her and her child? God knew the greatest challenge this woman faced wasn't hunger or poverty—it was fear. And if Elijah could help her overcome her fear, the rest of her challenges could be resolved. Our circumstances may be different, but we all face the tension between fear and faith, between anxiety and having the courage to say, "I will trust the Lord."

## PRAYER

Heavenly Father, I know that the challenges of my days on the earth will change, but they will never go away. I choose to turn away from fear and my own weakness and trust You because of who You are and the provision and abundance You have promised. You are a mighty God and greatly to be praised! In Jesus' name, amen.

## SHARING THE MESSAGE

*"I am the Living One; I was dead, and behold I am alive for ever and ever! And I hold the keys of death and Hades."*

### REVELATION 1:18

Sometimes when we watch the news it's easy to forget that as Christ-followers we have the certainty that one day Jesus Christ will be proclaimed Lord of all the earth. All authority is His. And the only resolution, ultimately, to human conflict and suffering is a revelation of the Prince of Peace. We're not Jesus-followers just so we can show up on the weekends with other church folk to recite a creed or add a little bit of information to our doctrinal notebook. We are Jesus-followers so that we can worship and serve Jesus of Nazareth by sharing His message of freedom and deliverance in our homes, workplaces, communities, and around the world.

## PRAYER

Heavenly Father, it is my privilege as an ambassador of Your Kingdom to share the good news of Your Son, who is alive now and forever. May the name of Jesus be lifted up over all the earth, and may His disciples come forth from every nation. In the name of Jesus I pray, amen.

# DAY 273

## UNSEEN THINGS

*Now to the King eternal, immortal, invisible, the only God, be honor and glory for ever and ever.*

### 1 TIMOTHY 1:17

Prayer is not a religious formality or something that professional Christians do in public to fill a spot on a program or move a meal along. Prayer is an opportunity for each of us to interact with the unseen world, specifically, Almighty God. I think sometimes Christians are a bit apologetic because we pray to a God we can't see. But unseen things influence our lives every day—think about technology—and we don't apologize for our belief in them. God invites us to be people who make a difference, and the most effective way to do that is by recognizing the life-changing power of prayer and making it a regular part of our daily lives.

## PRAYER

Heavenly Father, thank You for the privilege of coming to You with my praises and requests and concerns. Thank You that I can talk to You one on one, without an intermediary. Open my eyes to see the unseen, invisible God at work on my behalf. Thank You for what You will do. In Jesus' name, amen.

# DAY 274

## LEANINGS

*Turn from evil and do good; then you will dwell in the land forever.*

### PSALM 37:27

God is a good God. He's brought benefits far beyond whatever we have invested or entrusted to Him. And yet we struggle with questions about which way we will lean. If we cooperate with God, we will thrive and flourish. If we cooperate with evil, we will struggle and wither. If we cooperate with God, He'll bring peace and contentment. If we resist Him, we'll experience turmoil and dissatisfaction. If we give first place to Jesus, we will mature and be more responsible. If we don't, we'll become increasingly self-absorbed. If we cooperate with God, we'll live abundantly. If we don't, we'll find destruction. When you're faced with a decision about which way to lean, think about the results of each response. It will give you a life-perspective that is very helpful.

## PRAYER

Heavenly Father, I want to cooperate with You. I want to please You and honor You with my life. Holy Spirit, guide me as I go through this day. Help me to make decisions that will give first place to Jesus, bring abundant life to myself and others, and profit the Kingdom of God. In Jesus' name, amen.

# DAY 275

## A LIFE-CHANGING BELIEF

*Who is it that overcomes the world? Only he who believes that Jesus is the Son of God.*

### 1 JOHN 5:5

What do you believe about Jesus? I believe that Jesus of Nazareth is the Christ. He was born in Bethlehem of the Virgin Mary. As an adult He traveled around Israel for about three years proclaiming the Kingdom of God. At the end of that period He so threatened the religious establishment in Jerusalem that they orchestrated His arrest and convicted Him in a sham of a trial. A Roman governor condemned Him to death, and on a hill outside the city He was crucified. He was buried in a borrowed tomb, and three days later God raised Him to life again. The resurrected Christ was seen by many of His followers and others, and He ascended back to Heaven while standing with a group of His disciples on the Mount of Olives. Angels told them that He would return in the same way that He had gone. I have chosen that same Jesus of Nazareth as Lord of my life. I yield to Him and serve Him as King. You can believe those things too and be a participant in the Kingdom of God. It will change your life in time, and it will change your life in eternity.

## PRAYER

Heavenly Father, I choose Jesus of Nazareth as Lord. Thank You for His example of love, compassion, and forgiveness. I will serve Him all of my days. In His name I pray, amen.

# DAY 276

## PURPOSEFUL CHOICES

*"I tell you, whoever acknowledges me before men, the Son of Man will also acknowledge him before the angels of God. But he who disowns me before men will be disowned before the angels of God."*

### LUKE 12:8-9

God created humans different from everything else in creation. We don't just respond from instinct; God has given us a free will, and we make purposeful choices. Sometimes we make them assertively, sometimes we make them passively, but our lives are defined by our choices. I want to encourage you to be conscious of that. When you hear the name of Jesus demeaned, and you hear people critical and hostile toward the Christian faith, how do you respond? Are you silent, or do you speak up? Do you think, "This is not my battle. I don't have to say anything"? Or do you think, "I will not be silent while they mock the name of my Lord"? Either way, you make a choice, and it has eternal consequences.

## PRAYER

Heavenly Father, You have called me and claimed me as Your child who bears Your name. I will acknowledge You and defend Your name before all people. May I always be found faithful to be called a Christian. In the precious name of Jesus, the name that is above all names, amen.

# DAY 277

## EXPERIENCE REQUIRED

*"The LORD who delivered me from the paw of the lion and the paw of the bear will deliver me from the hand of this Philistine."*

### 1 SAMUEL 17:37

Experience with God is a very powerful tool. David said, "I can take on Goliath because of the experiences I've had." As a shepherd, he could have lost part of his flock to the predators that were about. Predators weren't unique to the flock he was keeping; they were indigenous to the region and preyed on all the flocks.  All of the shepherds faced those problems, but David recognized a God-opportunity in them and honed his fighting skills. He said, "God has delivered predator after predator into my hand, and God will deliver **this** predator into my hand." He had experience that separated him from a whole army of trained warriors. God-experiences in your life make a difference.

## PRAYER

Heavenly Father, thank You for the example of David, who trusted You to deliver a giant into his hands. Give me courage, Lord, when I am faced with problems that seem to tower over me like giants. Remind me that Your faithfulness to me in the past will bring deliverance and victory over the problems of today. In Jesus' name, amen.

# DAY 278

## HIS FAITHFULNESS

*Be joyful in hope, patient in affliction, faithful in prayer.*

ROMANS 12:12

I have found that when I have been willing to rejoice it has allowed hope to begin to emerge in my heart. During the most challenging seasons of my life, I've often found myself walking and praying. Many times there has been nothing left to say except, "God, I don't have much to be happy about right now. But I know You're faithful, and I want to thank You for that." And somehow it has always been the spark that let hope begin to grow in me again. Choose to rejoice, not because your circumstances are the way you want them to be or because everything is going according to your plan. Rejoice and be willing to say, "Lord, thank You for Your faithfulness to me."

## PRAYER

Heavenly Father, thank You for Your faithfulness to me. When I have faced challenges even of my own making, You have never abandoned me. You have lifted me up and let me see that I still have hope and a future, with You, sharing in Your purposes. Your grace overwhelms me, Lord, and I thank You for it. In Jesus' name, amen.

# DAY 279

## TAKING REQUESTS

*This is the confidence we have in approaching God: that if we ask anything according to his will, he hears us.*

### 1 JOHN 5:14

We often imagine that it's selfish or childish if we do too much asking when we pray. Certainly there are other forms of prayer, but I think it is fundamentally about asking. We wonder, "Doesn't God get tired of us asking?" Apparently not. We certainly don't know what Jesus said in all of His prayers to His Father, but in the overwhelming majority of the ones recorded in the New Testament He is asking for something. On arguably the most significant night of His life, He asked, "God, I'd rather go some other way. Do you have any other plan?" People say, "Well, I don't want to bother God with trivial things." Do you think that God is operating on such a thin margin that if you slip in one more request it's going to bring down the system? God says He can handle it, so I'm willing to keep asking.

## PRAYER

Heavenly Father, thank You for Your constant attention to my life. Thank You for the privilege of approaching the God of the universe with my requests. Thank You that You are ever present to hear and respond to me. Thank You for loving me more than I can imagine. In Jesus' name, amen.

# DAY 280

## A POSITION OF STRENGTH

*Be still before the LORD and wait patiently for Him; do not fret when men succeed in their ways, when they carry out their wicked schemes. Refrain from anger and turn from wrath; do not fret—it leads only to evil. For evil men will be cut off, but those who hope in the LORD will inherit the land.*

### PSALM 37:7-9

Do you ever get agitated when ungodly people prosper? I do. The psalmist says we should not only wait patiently for our own inheritance, we should not be concerned about the wicked who are doing well right now. From a biblical perspective, waiting is a position of strength, not a position of defeat or failure or inadequacy. If you're in a season where you are waiting to see the evidence of God at work in your life, rejoice. Something is being formed in you that will make you useful in God's hand that would not come any other way.

## PRAYER

Heavenly Father, thank You for all that You have done on my behalf. You have delivered me, rescued me from an empty life, and welcomed me into the Kingdom of Your Son. I choose to rejoice today as I wait on You. My trust is in Your gracious love for me. I choose to rest in Your strength and faithfulness. Holy Spirit, help me to receive all that God intends. In Jesus' name, amen.

## THE BLESSING OF WORK

*Whatever you do, work at it with all your heart, as working for the Lord, not for men, since you know that you will receive an inheritance from the Lord as a reward. It is the Lord Christ you are serving.*

#### COLOSSIANS 3:23-24

There is an innate dignity in work, but we have put unrealistic expectations on it. We want a job that makes us happy and fulfilled and even excited, but no job will do that all the time. The reality is that this side of eternity, we work. It's a necessary part of life under the sun. So we need to find a way to let the majesty of Almighty God be a part of that process, even the parts we don't like, because in reality we are serving Him. Think of it as an opportunity to worship God with the strength He's given you, to let His dignity be expressed through your character—even during the unpleasant times, because they will come. Work is important. Work is good for us. It has value before God.

## PRAYER

Heavenly Father, thank You for giving me work to do and the strength to do it. Thank You for parents that taught me to work and see the value in it. Help me to keep my focus on serving You when I am tired, when work is hard, when I cannot see that my efforts are accomplishing what I expect. May Your character be seen through me. In Jesus' name, amen.

# DAY 282

## PRICE PAID

*In him we have redemption through his blood, the forgiveness of sins, in accordance with the riches of God's grace that he lavished on us with all wisdom and understanding.*

### EPHESIANS 1:7-8

Jesus of Nazareth changed everything. We have chosen Him to be Lord of our lives because we believe He's the Christ, the Messiah. He redeemed us and restored us. In Him we have found grace and mercy and hope. There were charges against us that were true, and the penalty for those charges was death. Jesus said, "I'll pay that debt." He paid a price so that you and I might know freedom, and I gladly and gratefully bear His name and call Him Lord.

## PRAYER

Heavenly Father, thank You for sending Your Son Jesus to pay a price that I could not pay. Thank You that He purchased my freedom and restored me and gave me hope for this life and for eternity. I gratefully bear the name of Jesus, my Redeemer. In His name I pray, amen.

# DAY 283

## A HEALTHY IMMUNE SYSTEM

*What does the LORD your God ask of you but to fear the LORD your God, to walk in all his ways, to love him, to serve the LORD your God with all your heart and with all your soul, and to observe the LORD's commands and decrees that I am giving you today for your own good?*

### DEUTERONOMY 10:12-13

Respect and reverence for God are unmistakable characteristics of the people of God. When I look at the American church today, it seems we need an infusion of a sense of awe with regard to Him. The fear of the Lord functions as our spiritual immune system, keeping us from all kinds of trouble. Scripture is written to help us fear God, to know how to relate to Him, how to please Him, so that we can live in such a way that His blessings come upon us in both time and eternity. The Bible is a book of tremendous hope, and it shows us the benefits of giving Him the respect and reverence He deserves.

## PRAYER

Heavenly Father, forgive me for any place I've held a lack of respect for You. Open my heart to Your Word, fill me with awe and reverence for who You are, and show me new ways to know Your character better so that I can receive Your blessings. In Jesus' name, amen.

# DAY 284

## CONTENT UNDER HIS WINGS

*I know what it is to be in need, and I know what it is to have plenty. I have learned the secret of being content in any and every situation, whether well fed or hungry, whether living in plenty or in want. I can do everything through him who gives me strength.*

### PHILIPPIANS 4:12-13

Paul says he has learned "the secret" of being content in every situation, whether in need or in abundance. This doesn't make much sense to us. Abundance, yes, but how can we be content when we are in need? It's because we can be dwelling under the shadow of the wing of Almighty God in both places, living in the strength that God provides for us. Is one place easier? Yes! But both places can be God-directed. We need faith to understand that whether our comfort and convenience are being served in the moment or not, God is still in control.

## PRAYER

Heavenly Father, teach me satisfaction and gratitude for Your provision for me in all things. I choose to be content in every situation, for I can do everything through the strength You give me. In Jesus' name, amen.

# DAY 285

## ANCHORED

*May the God of hope fill you with all joy and peace as you trust in him, so that you may overflow with hope by the power of the Holy Spirit.*

ROMANS 15:13

I think one of the reasons the church struggles in our culture is that we are not the influence God created us to be. We have put our hope in the same things that the world has put its hope in. We're rattled and shaken, and we see our dreams breaking apart when the things that shake the world touch our lives. The invitation of God is to let our hope rest on something more certain, to put our hope in Him—in His Word, His name. As Christians, our future is anchored to something different than people who don't know the Lord. God is our hope, and He is faithful.

## PRAYER

Heavenly Father, thank You for the hope I find in You. Holy Spirit, fill me with joy and peace as I trust in the unshakeable Almighty God, the Creator of the universe who was before all things and who holds all things together. In Jesus' name, amen.

# DAY 286

## BETTER THAN NEW

*He prays to God and finds favor with him, he sees God's face and shouts for joy; he is restored by God to his righteous state.*

JOB 33:26

Kathy and I had friends who bought a really old home to restore, and they wanted us to see it. It was late in the afternoon when we arrived, and there was no electricity, no plumbing—it was awful. They were so excited, and all I thought was "money pit." Months later we went back to visit, and it was amazing, one of the most beautiful homes I had ever seen. It had central heat and air, indoor plumbing, cool gadgets, everything! When they restored it, it wasn't even the same house that was first built; it was much better. That's what God does through spiritual restoration: He makes you better than new. Instead of revisiting the opportunities of yesterday, He brings all the opportunities of today and makes them yours.

## PRAYER

Heavenly Father, thank You for Your promise of restoration. Thank You that You can make all things, even me, better than new. Lord, I seek Your favor as I live out my days in the earth. And when I see Your face, I will shout with joy! In Jesus' name, amen.

# DAY 287

## TENSION POINTS

*I keep asking that the God of our Lord Jesus Christ, the glorious Father, may give you the Spirit of wisdom and revelation, so that you may know him better.*

### EPHESIANS 1:17

When I was a young Christian, I thought there must be some mysterious point when you just knew how to live a Christian life. I knew I didn't know how to do it, but I looked at older people and they seemed to have it all together. "There's no tension in them," I thought. I was wrong. Even today, every time I walk up to those God-choices, I find that tension still persists. That's because every one of those is a growth point, a learning point, an experience point. I walk away from them with a better understanding of God and better equipped for the next opportunity. But I'd be untruthful if I said living the Christian life is not the same daily challenge for me as it is for any Jesus-follower. Like Paul, let's "keep asking" for "the Spirit of wisdom and revelation," so that we will know God better and make choices that honor Him.

## PRAYER

Heavenly Father, I want to make choices that You approve of. I want to honor You with my life. Give me the Spirit of wisdom and revelation, so that I may know You better. And I will give You praise for the victories in my life. In Jesus' name, amen.

# DAY 288

## QUICK TO BELIEVE

*The apostles said to the Lord, "Increase our faith!"*

LUKE 17:5

Like the earliest disciples, we too should aspire to be people of faith. I hear people say, "I'm not going to be one of those faith people. You almost got me, but no, you're not going to get me to believe that. I'm not going to get all worked up about my relationship with God." It's almost as if skepticism is held in high esteem in our culture—that the truly intellectual among us are unwilling to believe or trust. I have decided that I want to be quick to believe and willing to trust, because Scripture says that without faith, I can't please God.

## PRAYER

Heavenly Father, I repent for any skepticism I've held against Your Church. I want my faith and trust in You to increase every day of my life. I want to know You and love You more with each passing day. Lord, increase my faith, that I may become more like You. In Jesus' name, amen.

# DAY 289

## TODAY'S TO-DO LIST

*In his heart a man plans his course, but the LORD determines his steps.*

### PROVERBS 16:9

Very seldom do I feel like I'm doing something godly. Most of the time I'm doing the best I know to do in the midst of the opportunities that are before me, and God in His providence causes His purposes to go forward. I'm amazed to hear the God-stories that result when we say, "God, with all that's on my to-do list today, I'll keep turning my face toward You and let You do what I cannot." He'll do that for you. God has plans for each one of us, and He's going to use our lives in a powerful way.

## PRAYER

Heavenly Father, I give You this day. I ask You to take all the tasks and conversations, big things and little things, and use them for Your Kingdom purposes. Keep me faithful to Your plans, Lord, even when I cannot see an immediate result. Thank You for allowing me to have a part in Your work in the earth. In Jesus' name, amen.

# DAY 290

## PAYCHECK AND PRIVILEGE

*"Behold, I am coming soon! My reward is with me, and I will give to everyone according to what he has done."*

### REVELATION 22:12

How many of you would go to work if you didn't get paid? I wouldn't, and I don't imagine you would either. We go to work when we don't want to, we work harder than we're asked to, we keep working when we'd rather stop, and we do all of that with the expectation that someone will reward us for it. Serving God is a privilege, but it often looks and feels like work—sometimes very hard work. But God is very upfront with us. He said if we honor Him and serve Him during our days in the earth, we will be rewarded.

## PRAYER

Heavenly Father, sometimes working for You is easy and a pleasure and sometimes working for You is hard and uncomfortable. Jesus said that I will be rewarded for even giving a cup of cold water. Thank You for Your kindness and Your faithfulness and Your generosity toward me. Thank You for the privilege of serving You. In Jesus' name, amen.

# DAY 291

## TEMPORARY GIFTS

*So we fix our eyes not on what is seen, but on what is unseen. For what is seen is temporary, but what is unseen is eternal.*

### 2 CORINTHIANS 4:18

Some Christians limit their spiritual lives to trying to get God to do something for them in this earthly realm. The New Testament, however, continually invites us to participate in the spiritual, eternal world of God's Kingdom. Some throughout the history of the Church have abused this notion by suggesting that the world we live in is evil or that our physical bodies are ungodly. God created the world and everything in it for our pleasure. But He reminds us again and again that while these are gifts entrusted to us, and we are to exercise dominion and stewardship over them, they are only temporary and will pass away. We should not allow the desires of our earthly nature to overwhelm us. We should look for and receive our marching orders from another realm.

## PRAYER

Heavenly Father, You remind me again and again that this world is my home for just a short time, a mere blink of the eye compared to the totality of my existence. Give me a renewed vision of eternity, Lord, and help to keep it in view as I work to fulfill Your purposes for me during my days in the earth. In Jesus' name, amen.

# DAY 292

## WISDOM FOR THE ASKING

*My son, preserve sound judgment and discernment, do not let them out of your sight; they will be life for you.*

### PROVERBS 3:21-22

Perhaps, like many of us, you have chosen a pathway that, at the end of a lot of time and energy, did not lead to the happy outcome you had anticipated. We didn't see that when we first decided to walk that way. I don't think rational people think, "I'm going to do this. It will be painful and cost me lots of money, and in a few years I will be filled with regret. Let's go!" Sometimes it can be hard to distinguish between good and evil, and each of us will learn some lessons the hard way, by experience. But there are some things you can do to avoid mistakes. Work to obtain wisdom and understanding. Seek out friends who have more God-experience than you do, and listen to their advice. Read Scripture, and ask the Holy Spirit to open your heart and mind to its meaning and application to your life. Wisdom is there for the asking, so let's ask!

## PRAYER

Heavenly Father, I need Your help to distinguish between good and evil. Thank You for Your Word that gives light to my path. Unfold Your Word to me. Surround me with people who help me to make decisions that will honor You. In Jesus' name, amen.

# DAY 293

## TRAINING PLAN

*Have nothing to do with godless myths and old wives' tales; rather, train yourself to be godly.*

### 1 TIMOTHY 4:7

What immediately leaps out to me from this verse is that the responsibility for training in godliness is personal. Paul says we have to choose to train ourselves. Somebody else can't train for us. Just like someone else's workout at the gym isn't going to help you or me a bit, someone else's godliness won't make you or me a more faithful disciple of Jesus. Others can present you with opportunities, give you a little information, encourage you along the way, and tell you when you're heading in the wrong direction. But you and I have to be willing to train ourselves for godliness.

## PRAYER

Heavenly Father, I want to train for godliness. Give me perseverance to keep pushing ahead on the path toward godliness when I feel tired, or complacent, or good enough. Help me to keep this as a lifelong goal. In Jesus' name, amen.

## DAY 294

## CHURCH WITH A CAPITAL C

*He is the head of the body, the church; he is the beginning and the firstborn from among the dead, so that in everything he might have the supremacy.*

COLOSSIANS 1:18

Jesus is the Head of the Church. No matter what the sign says, no matter the doctrinal preference or the denominational affiliation, it's all Jesus' Church. Local churches are groups of people who have joined their hearts and lives together to seek the Lord, and all of our individual congregations are a part of His Church. We can have different styles of worship and use different translations of the Bible and sit in pews or chairs, but every church should have an awareness of the truth of Jesus and His redemptive work at the center of everything it is and does because, as He said, "I am the way and the truth and the life. No one comes to the Father except through me" (John 14:6).

## PRAYER

Heavenly Father, thank You for sending Your Son, Jesus, to live among us and die for our sins. Thank You that He established Your Church in the earth. Keep us faithful to Your purposes and free from the distractions of superficial things. May we be worthy of His calling, worthy of bearing His name, until the day of His return. In Jesus' name, amen.

## IT'S ABOUT THE OUTCOME

*O LORD, the God who saves me, day and night I cry out before you. May my prayer come before you; turn your ear to my cry.*

### PSALM 88:1-2

I exercise because I like the outcome. But I can't tell you that in the middle of a workout I'm thinking, "Oh, I'm having fun now." In my case there are messages coming from all over my body saying, "We've had enough of this foolishness. Park it!" I have a friend who coaches runners. When they're getting those internal messages he tells them, "Decide you're going to run to the next mailbox. And when you get there, run to the next mailbox. Just don't give up." When you are learning to persevere in prayer, not all of the messages you'll hear will be affirming. Everyone will not want to join you. Your prayers may not be answered in the way you expect or in your timing. Jesus coached His followers to pray and not give up. So let's pray, "day and night" . . . and not give up!

## PRAYER

Heavenly Father, day and night I will cry out to You. May my prayer come before You. Lord, turn Your ear to my cry. Apart from Your involvement, I would be without hope, desperate and alone. But with You, Father, I have great hope and I praise You for it today. Thank You for Your faithfulness to hear my prayers. In Jesus' name, amen.

## POWER BY YIELDING

*On the evening of that first day of the week, when the disciples were together, with the doors locked for fear of the Jews, Jesus came and stood among them and said, "Peace be with you!" After he said this, he showed them his hands and side. The disciples were overjoyed when they saw the Lord. Again Jesus said, "Peace be with you! As the Father has sent me, I am sending you."*

JOHN 20:19-21

Jesus' original followers were changed by the three years they spent with Him, but more importantly, they were changed by the cross and the resurrection. They started with willing hearts but knew very little about the Kingdom of God. They stood in amazement at what they saw Jesus do, and they were invited to participate in some miraculous things. Jesus told them He would be betrayed and killed, but they still were so unprepared that His death broke them and they lost their courage. Then, on the evening of Resurrection Day, Jesus stepped into the room, not a ravaged body but a whole man, and they saw the power of God. From that point they yielded their lives to His purposes with abandon and could not be deterred.

## PRAYER

Heavenly Father, what unimaginable joy Jesus' followers must have felt when He stepped into the room! Until the day I see Him face to face, may I know and share the power of His resurrection, so that many will choose to follow You. In the name of Jesus I pray, amen.

## DAY 297

### NO DO-OVERS

*"Now get up and stand on your feet. I have appeared to you to appoint you
as a servant and as a witness of what you have seen of me
and what I will show you."*

ACTS 26:16

God told Paul, "Today I've set you apart for My purposes." He did it again and again in Paul's life, and He will do it again and again in our lives. I don't want my relationship with God to be just about settling my whereabouts for eternity. I want my life to matter for Him—every day of my life, every season of my life. You only get one chance to be a young person for the glory of God. You only get one chance to be a senior adult for the glory of God. Whatever life stage you're in, there's no do-over, no reset button. You only get one pass through this life for the glory of God. There is good news, however: Whatever stage you are in, you can determine to set the rest of your life apart for the purposes of God. That's an amazing invitation.

### PRAYER

Heavenly Father, I choose to seek Your purposes today and for the rest of my days in the earth. I want my life to matter to You. Help me to honor You in every area—my family, finances, workplace, and in all my relationships. May I live today for Your glory. In Jesus' name, amen.

# DAY 298

## I DON'T KNOW

*Let the wise listen and add to their learning, and let the discerning get guidance.*

### PROVERBS 1:5

If I want to learn something, the best way for me to do that is to spend time with people who have expertise in that area—watching, listening, and asking questions. There's a challenge, though, with adult learning: it requires some humility. We don't like to admit that we don't know— especially in church. I want to give you permission to say without shame, "I don't know much about that." I want to encourage you to make the effort to find one or two people or a small group where there is no judgment or finger pointing. Ask questions and study the Scripture to find the answers. Invite someone who has been on the journey longer than you have to recommend good books or even join you. None of us knows enough, so let's be learners together.

## PRAYER

Heavenly Father, thank You for Your Word, my guidebook for life. Thank You for the Holy Spirit, who gives me wisdom and understanding. Thank You for surrounding me with people who are willing to teach me and mentor me. Give me humility, Lord, to say, "I don't know" and look for answers. In Jesus' name, amen.

# DAY 299

## THE WHOLE STORY

*All Scripture is God-breathed and is useful for teaching, rebuking, correcting and training in righteousness, so that the man of God may be thoroughly equipped for every good work.*

### 2 TIMOTHY 3:16-17

Some Christians seem to feel that the New Testament has more authority than the Old Testament. It's almost as if the New Testament is understood to be an amendment correcting the weaknesses of the earlier work. I meet Christians who have never really read the Old Testament, which is unfortunate, because the New Testament makes no sense without the context of the Old Testament. Jesus knew it well and quoted it often. His disciples, observant Jewish men, also knew the Old Testament writings. If God intended for us to put the Old Testament on the shelf and focus on the New Testament only, He would've told us so. In fact, the opposite is true, as Paul reminds Timothy that ALL Scripture is God-breathed and useful. Make a commitment to read your Bible. Reading the whole story of the Bible will bring good things to you.

## PRAYER

Heavenly Father, thank You for Your Word, ALL of Your Word, which is Your message to me. Thank You that You have not left me to wander through life, but You have shown me how to live through Your written Word, the example of Your Son, and the guidance of the Holy Spirit. I praise You for Your faithfulness to all generations. In Jesus' name, amen.

# DAY 300

## FAITHFUL LIVING

*"I will build my church, and the gates of Hades will not overcome it."*

MATTHEW 16:18

Empires rise and fall, and the social context changes, but the Church of Jesus Christ continues forward. Think of the empires that have come and gone while the Church has spread throughout the earth. Roman emperors sometimes illuminated their garden parties with Christians dipped in tar and set afire. Hitler's Third Reich executed Dietrich Bonhoeffer just two years after his book *The Cost of Discipleship* was published. And house churches meet in secret in many countries even today. There's something amazing in these stories. Whether on a river bank, or in a house, a prison cell, or a beautiful building, the message of redemption through Jesus Christ is shared, and believed, and the Church continues to grow. Every believer in Jesus of Nazareth carries the same assignment, no matter our generation, no matter our context.

## PRAYER

Heavenly Father, I am inspired by the stories of Your people living faithfully through the ages, even in the face of great persecution and death. I want to be known as a person who lived for You faithfully during my days in the earth. Show me what that means as I go through the activities of my days. Thank You for Your direction. In Jesus' name, amen.

# DAY 301

## IN SPITE OF

*David had done what was right in the eyes of the LORD and had not failed to keep any of the LORD's commands all the days of his life—except in the case of Uriah the Hittite.*

### 1 KINGS 15:5

David was a man of extremes: extreme passion, extreme cunning, extreme political astuteness, and extreme blunders. David's deceitful actions toward Uriah the Hittite in 2 Samuel 11 displeased the Lord, and he was punished severely for them. One of the remarkable aspects of Scripture, however, is that God commends David to us as a godly man—not because of his absolute consistency, but because of the passion with which he served the Lord. In spite of his imperfections, the Bible says David was a man after God's own heart. We too can serve God, in spite of our imperfections. Satan will tell you that you are not worthy of serving and worshiping the Lord, but do not let him convince you of that. Like David, you can be a person who loves the Lord with your whole heart.

## PRAYER

Heavenly Father, in spite of my many weaknesses and imperfections, I want to be a person after Your own heart, a person who worships and serves You all of my days. I ask for Your wisdom, Lord, so I will know how to do what is right in Your eyes. In Jesus' name, amen.

# DAY 302

## WE NEED JESUS

*Here is a trustworthy saying that deserves full acceptance: Christ Jesus came into the world to save sinners—of whom I am the worst.*

### 1 TIMOTHY 1:15

The Jesus-story is awkward and uncomfortable until you understand, like the Apostle Paul, that you're a sinner who needs a Savior: that you're not inherently good, that you can't earn your way to heaven, and that your best expressions of kindness and morality will leave you far short of the standards of Almighty God. The truth is that our wickedness put Jesus on the cross. We crucified Him just as surely as the Roman soldiers did. We have a desire for the power of God and the miraculous, but what precedes those is our recognition that we need a Savior. God's standards for righteousness are holiness and purity. And because God doesn't grade on a curve, we all, quite simply, need Jesus.

## PRAYER

Heavenly Father, I am a sinner and I need a Savior. Jesus, I ask You to be Lord of my life—my whole life. I thank You for the cross and all that it imparts to me. In Jesus' name, amen.

# DAY 303

## AN EXTRAORDINARY INVITATION

*"I confer on you a kingdom, just as my Father conferred one on me, so that you may eat and drink at my table in my kingdom and sit on thrones, judging the twelve tribes of Israel."*

LUKE 22:29-30

Do you imagine the disciples understood fully the implications of what Jesus was saying to them? No, they were struggling just to hang onto the moment. And I promise you they hadn't understood when Jesus met them on the shores of the Sea of Galilee and said, "Follow Me, and I will make you fishers of men." But for three years they've watched Jesus, and along the way they've learned what it means to yield their lives to serve the purposes of God. Jesus is making the extraordinary statement that just as the Father has shared His Kingdom with Jesus, Jesus will share that Kingdom with His followers. Being a Christ-follower is an invitation to an extraordinary life that will be experienced during our days in the earth and for eternity.

## PRAYER

Heavenly Father, thank You for the privilege of being known as a child of God, a Jesus-follower. Help me to live in a manner that is worthy of that name. I yield my life to Your Kingdom purposes. Lord, I want to live the extraordinary life that You have for me during my days in the earth, and I look forward to eternity in Your presence. In Jesus' name, amen.

# DAY 304

## GOD CHOICES

*I have chosen the way of truth; I have set my heart on your laws. . . . I run in the path of your commands, for you have set my heart free.*

PSALM 119:30, 32

Sometimes we make living as a Jesus-follower more complicated than it needs to be. One simple guideline is this: in order to please God, we need to make consistent choices that honor Him. That means we choose "the way of truth" and "run in the path" of His commands. Clearly, we sometimes lose focus and drift off the path. But our daily choices matter, and if we consistently choose to live in a way that honors Him, He will give us greater understanding of His laws and commands and His purposes for our lives. And that understanding in turn helps us make better choices.

## PRAYER

Heavenly Father, today I choose the way of faithfulness. Today I choose to run in the path of Your commands. Broaden my understanding, Lord, that I will honor You in the decisions I make today and be able to move forward in the purposes You have for me. In Jesus' name, amen.

# DAY 305

## AUTHORITY IN THE CROSS

*We know that our old self was crucified with him so that the body of sin might be done away with, that we should no longer be slaves to sin.*

ROMANS 6:6

We are hardwired toward ungodliness. Have you noticed? We don't need classes on how to be selfish or stubborn or impatient. We're just naturally good at those things! But this verse has great news: we have been given authority over our carnal nature. Many of us seem to live almost in ignorance of the authority that has been given to us. We think whatever authority we have is derived from the correctness of our doctrine, the group to which we belong, the sign on the building where we gather. Our authority is much greater than any of those things because it is anchored in the redemptive work of Jesus of Nazareth. When you are faced with your carnal nature, and you will be, remind yourself that you are no longer a slave to sin because your old self was crucified with Jesus. That's an amazing promise!

## PRAYER

Heavenly Father, I claim and rest in the authority You have given me through Your Son, Jesus of Nazareth, and His death and resurrection. Again today I place my ungodliness at the foot of the cross and remind myself that I am no longer a slave to my carnal nature. Thank You, Lord, for Your faithfulness to me. In Jesus' name, amen.

# DAY 306

## BE PREPARED

*Look, he is coming with the clouds, and every eye will see him.*

### REVELATION 1:7

When Jesus came to earth the first time, it was something of a covert mission. The religious leaders were clueless. The king wasn't paying attention. A few shepherds were given a heads-up and came to see the baby born in a barn. But for the most part, it was an overlooked event. When Jesus comes the second time, everyone on the planet will know it. He'll come as the ruler of the kings of the earth, "with the clouds, and every eye will see him." But the Bible seems to suggest that sadly, the majority of people will not be watching and waiting and will not be prepared for what is to come. Let's make sure we are prepared for that day. And let's help our families and friends and neighbors, here and around the world, be prepared as well.

## PRAYER

Heavenly Father, when I imagine Jesus returning to earth with the clouds it fills me with anticipation and joy! Until that day, give me strength to help all within my sphere of influence to be ready for His return. Come, Lord Jesus! In His name I pray, amen.

## ATTENTION TO INVITATIONS

*"The cry of the Israelites has reached me, and I have seen the way the Egyptians are oppressing them. So now, go. I am sending you to Pharaoh to bring my people the Israelites out of Egypt."*

EXODUS 3:9-10

God is ready to deliver the Israelites from slavery, and He says to Moses, "So now, go. I'm sending you." God was capable of removing His people from Egyptian control in any number of ways, but He chose to do it through a person. Moses doubted his abilities, but God assured him of His help. Moses was willing to have his plans interrupted, and the result was one of the most remarkable series of events in human history. God is still moving in the earth, and He is still doing it through people like us. One of the challenges we face is being too interested in our own plans to answer His invitations when He asks. God has a long and impressive track record of carrying the day, however, so I'd encourage you to do your best to cooperate with Him. You will be blessed as you have a part in advancing His Kingdom.

## PRAYER

Heavenly Father, I want to cooperate with Your plans and purposes in the earth. Give me a listening ear to hear Your invitations to me. Give me a willing heart to place Your agenda ahead of my agenda, for Your plans are far greater than my own. In Jesus' name, amen.

# DAY 308

## STOP AND THINK

*The wages of sin is death, but the gift of God is eternal life
in Christ Jesus our Lord.*

### ROMANS 6:23

Temptation is an invitation to something that entices you, especially something that leads to sin. The consequence for sin is destruction, while the "gift of God is eternal life." This isn't an issue just for the ungodly; temptation stalks all of us. So the next time you feel the pull of temptation, stop and think about the possible results. Could you lose your family? your reputation? your job? your health? I believe in the grace and the mercy of God, because that's how we got into His Kingdom. But it's equally true that God is a just and a Holy God. The Bible says God will not be mocked, that we will reap what we sow: death or eternal life. Let's live with that awareness. Let's reject the temptation and accept the gift.

## PRAYER

Heavenly Father, give me the wisdom and courage and awareness to say no to ungodliness and receive the gifts You have for me. Give me clarity of thought so that I will see the end before I take the first steps. Lead me not into temptation, Lord, but deliver me from evil, that Your purposes might be worked out for the glory of Your Son, Jesus. I ask it in His name, amen.

## BEYOND THE CIRCUMSTANCES

*Instruct those who are rich in this present world not to be conceited or to fix their hope on the uncertainty of riches, but on God, who richly supplies us with all things to enjoy.*

1 TIMOTHY 6:17 • NASB®

Like Christians the world over, we experience our faith through the lens of our own culture. As Americans, it's easy to let our lives of relative ease subvert our faith and imagine that the purpose of God is to make us comfortable. The truth is we are uniquely blessed, and the overwhelming majority of our brothers and sisters in the faith around the earth have no clue about the comforts and conveniences that fill our lives. God's objective—for all of us—is that we be holy, no matter our circumstances. While I'm grateful for the blessings I enjoy, I do not want my faith and my trust in God to be anchored to comfort and convenience. I want to fix my hope on God.

## PRAYER

Heavenly Father, thank You for the many blessings that fill my life. Forgive me for any places I've put my hope in things other than You. I choose to serve You, whether I am comfortable or uncomfortable and whether my circumstances seem convenient or inconvenient. I long to be holy, Lord, as You are holy, and serve You all my days. In Jesus' name, amen.

## HE HEARS OUR CRIES

*He has not despised or disdained the suffering of the afflicted one; he has not hidden his face from him but has listened to his cry for help.*

### PSALM 22:24

What are you crying about? More specifically, what is the cry of your heart in this season? We know of the unique ability of a mother to recognize her child's cry in a room full of others. But that instinct isn't limited to a mother and child; when you hear the cries of someone you love, it gets your attention, doesn't it? I think that is true with God and His children as well; He is moved when we cry out to Him in desperation and brokenness. Don't hesitate to cry out to God. He loves you and wants to hear the deepest pleas of your heart.

## PRAYER

Heavenly Father, thank You that You love and care for me even when I am feeling weak and desperate. Thank You that You are in control, even when I cannot see or understand what is happening to me or to those I care about. I trust You to listen to my cries for help. And I will give You all the praise when deliverance comes. In Jesus' name, amen.

## WALK SIMPLY

*Jesus replied: "'Love the Lord your God with all your heart and with all your soul and with all your mind.' This is the first and greatest commandment. And the second is like it: 'Love your neighbor as yourself.'"*

MATTHEW 22:37-39

Years ago I read a book called *Everything I Really Needed to Know I Learned in Kindergarten* by Robert Fulghum. The author said that wisdom isn't found at the top of the graduate school mountain, but in the simple lessons of childhood: Don't hit people. Wash your hands before you eat. Put things back where you got them. Cold milk and cookies do a body good. They are pretty fundamental things, but they make a lot of sense. We need to implement the spiritual equivalent of those simple notions in adulthood: Love God. Love your neighbors. Read your Bible. Pray. Let's make sure we get the simple things right. Our neighbors will be blessed, and we'll be happier and more productive citizens of God's Kingdom.

## PRAYER

Heavenly Father, I want to keep the simple things, the fundamental things, in the center of my walk with You. I put my trust in You and Your oversight of my life. Thank You for Your protection, Your provision, and Your plans for me. I choose Your way. In Jesus' name, amen.

## BUSYNESS ASIDE

*On another Sabbath he went into the synagogue and was teaching, and a man was there whose right hand was shriveled. The Pharisees and the teachers of the law were looking for a reason to accuse Jesus, so they watched him closely to see if he would heal on the Sabbath.*

LUKE 6:6-7

One of the challenges for God's people in every generation is to recognize God at work around us. Unfortunately, the most religious of us can be the least aware. That was certainly true in the New Testament. The people who were the best trained in the Scriptures, who orchestrated the religious feasts and festivals, who were responsible for temple worship and the sacrifices—they almost exclusively missed Jesus. They not only failed to recognize Him, they stood as His opponents. I would like to tell you that was a first-century phenomenon; but throughout the history of the Church, typically, the most religious people are the ones who have been the most resistant to what God is doing. Let's encourage each other to be aware of God's presence and activity, both in our personal lives and as we see Him working in the world, and praise Him for it.

## PRAYER

Heavenly Father, Your work has no beginning or end, and I know You are at work today—in me, through me, and around me. Holy Spirit, open my eyes to see. I don't want to be caught up in religious activity and miss the importance of my relationship with You. In Jesus' name, amen.

# DAY 313

## STREAMS IN THE DESERT

*"Forget the former things; do not dwell on the past. See, I am doing a new thing! Now it springs up; do you not perceive it? I am making a way in the desert and streams in the wasteland."*

ISAIAH 43:18-19

In the Bible the desert is a place where God gets people's attention. Yes, it's a place of isolation and danger and minimal resources. But it's also a place where God's people experience His deliverance, His provision, His revelation, His renewal, and His preparation for a new season. Sometimes there are desert seasons of our lives too. In fact, He may have led us there so that we can see Him more clearly. If you feel like you're walking through a desert and cannot see relief ahead, I want you to know that the Spirit of God is with you. Let's "not dwell on the past," but watch for the "new thing" He wants to do in our lives. "Can you see it?" He asks. "I am making a way!"

## PRAYER

Heavenly Father, thank You for the promise of Your presence and provision for me. Thank You that You are watching over my life even when I am not able to see You at work. Give me faith to watch and wait for You when You are preparing me for a new thing, because I always want to be in the center of Your plans and purposes for me. In Jesus' name, amen.

## DAY 314

## BE JESUS' CHURCH

*In Christ we who are many form one body, and each member belongs to all the others.*

ROMANS 12:5

One attitude that's unfortunately too common among groups of Christians is the notion that "We are more right than everybody else." We don't necessarily think everybody else is wrong; we just think we're more right. It's not a Kingdom-building use of our time to throw rocks at one another over Bible translations or musical instruments or what the preacher wears. The important thing is to be the Church, with Jesus of Nazareth as our head, and to welcome broken people into our midst and love them and communicate the Gospel message of His redemption. Let's pray for unity among Jesus-followers in our community and around the globe, that God's Kingdom purposes will be advanced.

## PRAYER

Heavenly Father, thank You for the Church in the earth. I pray You would send Your Holy Spirit to bring unity of heart and mind to Your people across every community. In Jesus' name, amen.

# DAY 315

## FOCUSED INTENT

*As the time approached for him to be taken up to heaven, Jesus resolutely set out for Jerusalem.*

LUKE 9:51

Jesus knew what awaited Him in Jerusalem, yet He "resolutely set out" in that direction. He knew He would be beaten almost to death. He knew He would be crucified. But He understands this is the assignment God has given Him, and He sets out with determination to complete the task. I'm intrigued by the way Luke chose to relay this information. He didn't say, "Jesus was going to Jerusalem to be crucified." Luke said before Jesus could be taken up to heaven, He would have to face these things. There's a key here for us. There are some seasons in our lives when God's assignments for us are not pleasant, but we have a choice: we can focus on the present difficulty, or we can keep our eyes on God's gracious invitation to us. We don't follow Christ just for the ease of the moment. We follow Christ because we recognize the great privilege of fulfilling our part in His plan. Jesus had a focused intent. You and I need a bit of that as well.

## PRAYER

Heavenly Father, thank You for the resolve of Jesus as He set out for Jerusalem, fully knowing what lay ahead of Him there. I want a heart to do Your will, no matter the cost. Keep my eyes on You, Lord, that I will fulfill Your purposes. In the precious name of Jesus, amen.

# DAY 316

## FULLY FOCUSED ON GOD

*Elijah went before the people and said, "How long will you waver between two opinions? If the LORD is God, follow him; but if Baal is God, follow him."*

### 1 KINGS 18:21

Mount Carmel is a mountain in Israel where Elijah summoned the leaders of the tribes of Israel and said, "Today you have to make a decision. Are you going to worship the God of Abraham, Isaac, and Jacob? Or are you going to worship the Canaanite gods?" The Israelites hadn't rejected God outright; they were still offering Him sacrifices. They were just offering sacrifices to the Canaanite gods as well. This is our time on Mount Carmel. We have to choose the object of our worship: Comfort? Convenience? Affluence? Or God? He is searching the earth, as He has done in every generation, for men and women whose hearts are fully devoted to Him. I desperately want to be one of those people, and I would encourage you to want that as well.

## PRAYER

Heavenly Father, You are the one and only God, and I choose to worship You and You alone. Keep me focused on You when I am distracted or tempted. Give me discernment to see the false gods of this age and turn from them. I will follow You, Lord, with all that I am. In Jesus' name, amen.

# DAY 317

## A NEW YOU

*And we, who with unveiled faces all reflect the Lord's glory, are being transformed into his likeness with ever-increasing glory, which comes from the Lord, who is the Spirit.*

2 CORINTHIANS 3:18

Some of us imagine that to be a Christ-follower means that God has picked us up, dusted us off, and given us a fresh coat of paint. That's not at all what the Bible teaches. It says to be in Christ—to accept Jesus of Nazareth as Lord, Christ, and King of your life—means you become a totally new creature. I know I look like the old Allen. I've still got a southern accent, and I still love junk food. But the truth is, in Christ, I have become a new person. Yes, my sins have been forgiven. But the Holy Spirit continues to transform me so that I better reflect the likeness and glory of Christ. When you follow Jesus, you will have a different set of desires and abilities than you had before Jesus. And you will have a far better future!

## PRAYER

Heavenly Father, I want to be like Jesus. I want to have His love for You, and His love and compassion for people. I want to have His priorities as I live and minister in this world. Holy Spirit, transform me so that I reflect the likeness and glory of Christ to everyone I encounter today. In His name I pray, amen.

# DAY 318

## NOT NEGOTIABLE

*"I love the Father and . . . I do exactly what my Father has commanded me."*

JOHN 14:31

Most of us don't like to be commanded. We'd rather be asked or invited or encouraged or persuaded. But here is Jesus—water-walking, dead-raising, blind-eye-opening Jesus—describing the purpose of His life as doing exactly what His Father has commanded Him. Are you willing to accept a commandment from the Lord, exactly, with no invitation to share your opinion and with no concern for your comfort or calendar? Or are you prone to negotiating? I have to admit much of my Christian experience has been a negotiation, but I'm trying to improve my thought processes in that area. When we say, "God, I love You and will serve You whether I get my way or not," we will be astounded by the things He will do in us and through us.

## PRAYER

Heavenly Father, I am humbled by the example of Jesus, who loved You and served You and obeyed You, even through His death on a cross. Give me a spirit of willingness to obey You without question and without reservation, even when Your plan doesn't seem clear to me. And I will praise You for the mighty things You will do. In Jesus' name, amen.

# DAY 319

## IN THIS SEASON

*There is a time for everything, and a season for every activity under heaven:*
*a time to be born and a time to die. . . .*

### ECCLESIASTES 3:1-2

I believe that God chooses specific persons to live during specific seasons. I believe that "in the beginning" God intended that a man named Noah would have the determination to build an ark. I believe that God knew David would be watching over his father's sheep long before anyone imagined there would be an Israel, and that Israel would need a king. I believe that God looked across time and called our names to stand today for His purposes, and that He has given us everything we need to lead godly lives in this season. We won't be held accountable for what we would have done had we been Noah's neighbors or David's advisors. Our responsibility is this season. What do we do with that? One, let's invite people to the cross of Jesus Christ, because it represents the power of God to transform a life. Two, let's be unrelenting, unapologetic ambassadors for Jesus, even when others are silent. There are no insignificant people in God's plans for humanity. This is our time. Let's not hide our reality or deny our truth. Let's stand up for Jesus during our season in the earth.

## PRAYER

Heavenly Father, my presence here is ordained by You, and I want to be faithful to You during all my days. Give me boldness to invite others to come to Jesus and kneel at the foot of the cross. Give me courage to speak for You, even when others remain silent. In Jesus' name, amen.

# DAY 320

## NO CONDEMNATION

*Therefore, there is now no condemnation for those who are in Christ Jesus, because through Christ Jesus the law of the Spirit of life set me free from the law of sin and death.*

ROMANS 8:1-2

Years ago a man told me he couldn't stay in a church where the pastor admits he struggles with sin. I said, "Well, we'll miss you." I don't boast in it, but sin is universal, and it's pointless to pretend we aren't challenged by it. And while religious environments are world class at distributing guilt, the redemptive story of Jesus means "there is now no condemnation" for us—now, in this moment. Yes, we will struggle with sin, but God made provision so that you and I do not have to lead lives defined by condemnation. Now that's remarkable!

## PRAYER

Heavenly Father, I am grateful that You are a God of forgiveness. You are holy and righteous in all Your ways, yet merciful toward all who call on You through the cleansing blood of Jesus. Thank You that I do not have to lead a life defined by condemnation. May I live for You and bring honor to Your name in my days under the sun. In Jesus' name, amen.

# DAY 321

## REMEMBER HIS PROMISE

*"I will not leave you as orphans."*

JOHN 14:18

Can you imagine the anxiety in the disciples' faces and the abandonment they felt as Jesus explained that He would soon leave them? They still had so much to learn from Him! None of them had commanded the wind to be still or the lame to walk, and they knew they were not equipped to carry on His work. Then Jesus made an amazing promise: "You will be OK. I'm not going to leave you alone or unprotected or without resources. I will send the Holy Spirit, and He will be your guide." That amazing promise is just as true for us today. But is there a little voice inside your head that starts whispering when you decide to trust the Lord? Like me, you may hear, "You'd better not take that step of faith. You don't want to push this trust thing too far. What if it's not true? You'd better protect yourself." When that happens I choose to remember Jesus' promise: "I will not leave you alone."

## PRAYER

Heavenly Father, thank You for this promise of help. Even when I feel alone, or unprotected, or without resources, the Holy Spirit is present to comfort and guide me. Thank You for this great gift! Lord, remind me to look to You, trust You, and depend on You at all times and in all things. In Jesus' name, amen.

# DAY 322

## INTERNAL WARNING SYSTEM

*He who conceals his sins does not prosper, but whoever confesses and renounces them finds mercy.*

PROVERBS 28:13

As we mature in the Lord, He creates in us an internal warning system that goes off when we engage in behaviors and thoughts and attitudes that displease Him. I've experienced that, and I imagine you have too. Sometimes we decide to ignore the warning and carry on with what we want to do. God gave us free choice, and if we decide often enough to ignore the warnings, we'll deplete the batteries and the system will fail. Our hearts will become so hardened that we will no longer recognize our sin for what it is. If you find yourself making a habit of ignoring the warning signs and heading away from God's best for you, take action. Confess your sins to God and turn away from them, and you will find mercy.

## PRAYER

Heavenly Father, thank You for giving me guidance for living my life in the earth. Your Word, Your Spirit, and godly people in my life remind me of who You are and who You want me to be. Give me the wisdom to recognize and respond quickly to Your warning signs. I want to please You above all things. In Jesus' name, amen.

# DAY 323

## THE HELPER

*"If you then, though you are evil, know how to give good gifts to your children, how much more will your Father in heaven give the Holy Spirit to those who ask him?"*

LUKE 11:13

Jesus' disciples had spent three years with Him, but they still were unprepared to carry on His ministry without Him. Jesus knew it, and they knew it. Even watching Him die on a cross and be raised to life again was not enough. That's why He told them not to begin ministering on their own until help came, and He would send it in the Person of the Holy Spirit—their counselor, teacher, comforter, guide. Jesus told them the Holy Spirit would remind them of the things He had said and show them the truth. If Peter and James and John and the other disciples needed to ask the Holy Spirit for help, I'm sure you and I need to do that as well.

## PRAYER

Heavenly Father, I know that I need the help and guidance of the Holy Spirit in every aspect of my life—at home, at work, in the community, and everywhere I go. I regret the times I have tried to do things my way and in the power of my will. I pray for a greater awareness of the Holy Spirit in my life, that I may accomplish greater things and do them in a way that pleases and honors You. In Jesus' name, amen.

# DAY 324

## NOT OPTIONAL

*Be kind and compassionate to one another, forgiving each other, just as in Christ God forgave you.*

EPHESIANS 4:32

It can be a real challenge to forgive when you suffer for something that wasn't your fault. Nobody makes it through life without some undeserved hurt, and it's easy to let that grow into an unforgiving spirit that touches your entire life. It can become a filter that colors everything. If you can't stop thinking about how much someone hurt you, if you can't wish the person well, or if you want them to suffer like you have, those are signs of an unforgiving spirit. If you find yourself harboring any of those feelings, remember that forgiveness is not optional, and it doesn't depend on your emotions. If you wait to feel like forgiving, you'll probably never do it. So we choose to forgive, just as in Christ God forgave us.

## PRAYER

Heavenly Father, thank You for the forgiveness You have shown to me. I choose to forgive just as You have forgiven me. Specifically, I forgive (insert person's name). I forgive them for _____ (tell the Lord what they did or did not do). I cancel the debt they owe me. Bless them in all they do. In Jesus' name, amen.

## BETTER THAN BEFORE

*"I will make the Egyptians favorably disposed toward this people, so that when you leave you will not go empty-handed. Every woman is to ask her neighbor and any woman living in her house for articles of silver and gold and for clothing, which you will put on your sons and daughters. And so you will plunder the Egyptians."*

### EXODUS 3:21-22

The Israelites had been slaves in Egypt for many generations when God spoke to Moses and told him it was time to set His people free. In order to make their captors happy for them to leave, God instructed Moses to "plunder the Egyptians." This wasn't just deliverance; the Egyptians would pay them to get out of town! That's a God-sized miracle. God's deliverance in your life is not just an escape. He will take you out of a difficult, oppressive place and put you in a position that is better than when you got in that place to begin with. God is powerful enough to make a difference in our lives, and that's why we worship Him.

## PRAYER

Heavenly Father, thank You that You are a mighty God, a loving God, a God who stands ready to deliver Your people. Thank You for the deliverance You have given to me, even when I've been in bondage of my own making and could see no future. Thank You for the good plans You have for me, Lord, and help me to fulfill them. In Jesus' name, amen.

# DAY 326

## BEYOND OUR INCONSISTENCY

*If we claim to be without sin, we deceive ourselves and the truth is not in us.*

1 JOHN 1:8

People say to me, "I can't be a Christian because so many of them are hypocrites." That's true, there is a lot of hypocrisy among Jesus-followers, but it's a lousy excuse not to follow Him. Sometimes we think that because someone is inconsistent in their practice, the truth they hold is irrelevant. If your doctor tells you to change your diet because your arteries are getting blocked and then you see him at Waffle House with a plate of scattered and smothered hash browns, his behavior has nothing to do with your heart health. Don't set the truth about God aside because the messenger has clay feet. Following the Lord is tough. And if you're a believer who struggles to get it right, welcome to the team!

## PRAYER

Heavenly Father, thank You that You see beyond my inconsistencies to love me and allow me to serve Your Kingdom purposes. Forgive me for the times when I have looked on other Jesus-followers with judgment. May I see people with Your eyes, Lord, and draw them closer to You. In Jesus' name, amen.

# DAY 327

## THE MOST IMPORTANT OPINION

*"I tell you, my friends, do not be afraid of those who kill the body and after that can do no more. But I will show you whom you should fear: Fear him who, after the killing of the body, has power to throw you into hell. Yes, I tell you, fear him."*

### LUKE 12:4-5

I know this is Jesus talking, but when He says, "Don't be afraid of people who can just kill your body," my response is, "Why not?" "Because," He says, "I'll tell you whom to fear." Now He really has my attention: "Fear the One who has the power to cast you into hell." No person, no devil has that authority. The Bible says that God the Father reserved the right to judge humanity. And, because of Jesus' obedience, He gave that privilege to Jesus. Jesus said that He was the only door to God's Kingdom, and there is only one alternative for our eternity if we choose not to go through it. In this context, fear is not terror and dread and hiding; fear is respect and reverence and awe. And Jesus is the one we should want to respect and revere above all else.

## PRAYER

Heavenly Father, I want to respect Jesus' opinions more than I respect the opinions of anyone else. I want to please Jesus more than anyone else. May my words and actions show to everyone I interact with today that I hold You above all people and things. Thank You that I will be a part of Your Kingdom for eternity. In Jesus' name, amen.

## THE GIFT OF WISDOM

*"I will give you a wise and discerning heart, so that there will never have been anyone like you, nor will there ever be."*

1 KINGS 3:12

At first glance the book of Proverbs may just look like a collection of wise and sometimes witty sayings. But it's more than the musings of one man or even the collected wisdom of the Jewish people. It is a response from God to Solomon's request for wisdom. God was so pleased by Solomon's humble request that He supernaturally inspired him with wisdom and insight greater than any who had come before or who would come after. So when we read the book of Proverbs, we are not just reading the good ideas of some smart guy; we are reaping the benefits of what God poured into Solomon's life. It's a remarkable privilege and a wonderful portrayal of how God can use a person across time.

## PRAYER

Heavenly Father, thank You for the heart and mind of Solomon, who sought You with humility and was given so much. Thank You for the wisdom of the book of Proverbs, simple but profound advice that stands the test of time. Thank You for Your Word, a steadfast and true guide for me. In Jesus' name, amen.

# DAY 329

## NOT OUR PROBLEM

*With God we will gain the victory, and he will trample down our enemies.*

### PSALM 108:13

The meaning of the redemptive work of Jesus on the cross is that God gave us victory over evil. For the most part I think we undervalue the work of the cross. We typically hear the cross described as the place where our sins were forgiven. That's true, but it's not the full truth. On the cross Jesus defeated Satan and all of his authority over your life and mine—body, soul, and spirit. Evil still touches our lives, but it doesn't have dominion over us. God not only gives us victory, He also sees that our enemies receive justice. They are not our problem. So let's not spend our time and energy focused on our adversaries. Let's spend our time and energy focused on pleasing and praising God for His deliverance.

## PRAYER

Heavenly Father, I thank You that through the blood of Jesus Christ I have been forgiven and been given victory over evil. Thank You for Your love and grace and mercy extended to me. Thank You for new beginnings. I praise You for the cleansing that washes over me day by day. In the name of Jesus I pray and believe, amen.

# DAY 330

## STAY IN TOUCH

*Pray continually; give thanks in all circumstances, for this is God's will for you in Christ Jesus.*

### 1 THESSALONIANS 5:17-18

What does it mean to pray continually? Are we supposed to spend the day with our eyes closed? I've come to understand it as inviting God into the breadth of my life. I don't want to relegate Him to a few minutes on the weekend or a special location where I sit for a while. When I wake up in the morning, I say, "Lord, thanks for the day. I'm grateful to have another one." On the way to the office, I'll tell Him, "Lord, I need Your help today." When I review my appointments for the day, sometimes I'll say, "God, please get there early for this one." Let's make it a habit to keep in touch with the Lord and invite Him into the activities of our days.

## PRAYER

Heavenly Father, thank You for the privilege of having a personal relationship with You. Thank You that You care for me and want to be involved in my life, and that none of my concerns is too insignificant for You. Help me to cultivate a continual communication with You. I invite You into this day. In Jesus' name, amen.

# DAY 331

## WARNED AWAY

*There is a way that seems right to a man, but in the end it leads to death.*

PROVERBS 14:12

We are often confused about how we think of sin. We think that God says "Don't do that" because He doesn't want us to have too much fun. But when God warns us away from something, it's because that behavior will destroy us. Sin is presented by evil, and evil will take advantage of any opportunity to wedge its way into our lives. Evil doesn't play fair; it promises something it can't deliver and delivers destruction instead. The destruction may be emotional or physical or financial—or all three. We must have the courage to lovingly tell people the truth about sin because it will destroy them. God warns us for our own good, and we must warn others for their own good. That's what true friends do.

## PRAYER

Heavenly Father, thank You for loving me enough to warn me away from things that lead to destruction. Holy Spirit, give me discernment to see evil for what it is, no matter how it is packaged and presented. May my actions bring honor to You and build up Your people and Your Kingdom. I ask this in Jesus' name, amen.

# DAY 332

## HIS GRAND DESIGN

*We are God's workmanship, created in Christ Jesus to do good works, which God prepared in advance for us to do.*

EPHESIANS 2:10

Almighty God, who formed the universe and hung the stars in space and keeps the earth on the exactness of its orbit, has a purpose for your life. You're not just a blob that happened to emerge from something that washed up on a primordial beach a few billion years ago. The Designer of the earth and everything that's in it imagined you at this point in human history and created you uniquely to complete the good works that He prepared in advance for you to do. This verse makes a phenomenal statement about God's love for us, and it should affect how each of us lives out our days in the earth.

## PRAYER

Heavenly Father, thank You that I am Your workmanship, created to fulfill the purposes You have for me during my days in the earth. What a privilege it is to be a part of Your grand design! Help me to see Your plan clearly, so that I may stay focused on the work You have for me. In Jesus' name, amen.

# DAY 333

## THROUGH GOD'S EYES

*Dear friends, let us love one another, for love comes from God.*

1 JOHN 4:7

One of the unfortunate characteristics of human beings is that we look for ways to elevate ourselves above one another. We use every possible reason—birthplace, language, education, income, hair color, length of nose—you name it, we'll use it to justify those thoughts. But one of the great revelations of Scripture is that God loves us all. He is our Creator, and He designed each one of us to be unique, special, one of a kind. I imagine that He looks at identical twins and sees not their similarities, but their differences. And He looks at each of us and sees His wonderful creation. Let's be intentional when we look at others. Let's strip away all those categories of "like me" and "not like me" and see people through the eyes of God, the eyes of love.

## PRAYER

Heavenly Father, Thank You that You have created each of us beautifully and uniquely to reflect Your image. Give me the ability to see others as You see them and love them as You love them. May the attitudes of my heart and the words of my mouth honor You and all of Your creation. In Jesus' name, amen.

## SPEAK THE GOOD

*They despised the pleasant land; they did not believe his promise. They grumbled in their tents and did not obey the LORD. So he swore to them with uplifted hand that he would make them fall in the desert.*

PSALM 106:24-26

The Hebrew people who had seen God deliver them from slavery and provide everything they needed had several responses: They despised the good things from God. They didn't believe His promises. They grumbled. And they were disobedient. As a consequence God said, "You can just die where you are." If we listed our top ten sins, I'll bet that we would not include ingratitude, unbelief, grumbling, and disobedience. The New Testament says the story of that generation was written down as a warning for us, so let's not presume upon the grace of God. Let's believe. Let's be obedient. Let's be grateful.

## PRAYER

Heavenly Father, I repent for grumbling. I know it does not accomplish anything, and it is a bad habit to allow in my life that not only affects me but those around me. I believe You love me and have good things in store for me. Give me a spirit of joy that I may see and speak the good in all circumstances. In Jesus' name, amen.

# DAY 335

## COURAGE TO STAND

*They arrested the apostles and put them in the public jail. But during the night an angel of the Lord opened the doors of the jail and brought them out. "Go, stand in the temple courts," he said, "and tell the people the full message of this new life." At daybreak they entered the temple courts, as they had been told, and began to teach the people.*

ACTS 5:18-21

Paul was stoned and left for dead, and he got up and kept preaching! They put Peter and some others in prison for preaching the Gospel, and the angel who let them out said, "Go back to the same place they arrested you and tell about Jesus again." What motivated these people? Many of them had been with Jesus and counted it a privilege to stand for Him no matter the cost. You and I have the entire record of Scripture and two thousand years of history and God-stories. Let us, like the early disciples, count it a privilege to stand for Jesus in our generation.

## PRAYER

Heavenly Father, the faith and courage of those early disciples amazes me. May I see Jesus with the clarity of Peter and Paul. Help me to put my complete trust in Him and rest in the assurance that He watches over me. Give me courage to stand for Jesus—no matter the opposition. In His name I pray, amen.

# DAY 336

## JUSTIFICATION AND GRACE

*We, too, have put our faith in Christ Jesus that we may be justified by faith in Christ and not by observing the law, because by observing the law no one will be justified.*

GALATIANS 2:16

To be justified before God means we are as pure as if we had never sinned. That's hard for us to believe because we are well acquainted with our flaws and shortcomings. But when you understand the gift of Jesus' righteousness—that you are "justified by faith in Christ and not by observing the law"—you'll be more aware of the grace that God has showered upon you than you are the less-than-perfect chapters of your life. God's love for you will ring louder in your ears than Satan's accusations. Recognize that he is the source of those accusations and do not allow him to take up residence in your mind. Focus on God's love for you and the gift of justification that is yours through the blood of Jesus Christ.

## PRAYER

Heavenly Father, I come before You in humility, acknowledging that I am completely powerless to save myself. Thank You for sending Your Son, whose righteousness is now my own. Thank You that through His shed blood I am justified and blameless in Your sight. In the cleansing name of Jesus, amen.

# DAY 337

## CULTIVATING FAITH

*"Sow for yourselves righteousness, reap the fruit of unfailing love, and break up your unplowed ground; for it is time to seek the LORD . . ."*

HOSEA 10:12

An effective Church is no more an accident than a productive garden is an accident. You can sit in your easy chair and look through the window and pray, "God, give me a garden." You can pray until your tongue blisters, but unless you go outside and get to work you won't have a garden. You can't make the plants grow—God does that—but when you do your part, God will do His. The same is true about the Church. We can say, "God, make me a mature believer. Reach our world with the Gospel. Help lost people get to know you. Grow Your Church." But if we are not intentional about doing our part to facilitate those things, they will not happen. Look for opportunities to grow in your faith. Keep telling your Jesus-story. Support the Church with your resources. God will honor those efforts and bring change to peoples' lives—and in the process His Church will grow.

## PRAYER

Heavenly Father, thank You for the opportunity to participate in Your purposes in the earth. Your desire is to grow Your Church. This is my time, my generation, and I want my life to make a difference for You. Lord, help me to grow in the knowledge of You and share my Jesus-story effectively where I have influence. In Jesus' name, amen.

# DAY 338

## HE KNOWS

*Since the children have flesh and blood, he too shared in their humanity so that by his death he might destroy him who holds the power of death—that is, the devil.*

HEBREWS 2:14

When we read about Jesus casting out demons and calming the sea and raising the dead, it's easy to think that because He was the Son of God He must have had a pretty easy life. If you have that imagination of Jesus—a spiritually powerful but privileged man who couldn't possibly know how to relate to you—that's not His story. He grew up in a little town in the northern part of Israel. His hands would have been calloused from working in Joseph's carpentry shop. He would have worn simple clothes and eaten simple food. Even after His deity was revealed, He experienced hunger, thirst, weariness, and temptation. Don't ever think that Jesus can't relate to you. He understands us in all of our weaknesses and willingly took our burdens on Himself because He loves us and wants us to share in the power of His resurrection.

## PRAYER

Heavenly Father, thank You for the gift of Jesus and the salvation provided for me through His work on the cross. Thank You that He knows and understands everything about me yet doesn't abandon me. Holy Spirit, give me a greater understanding of the power of His resurrection in my life. In the name of Jesus, amen.

# DAY 339

## INVEST WELL

*As Jesus started on his way, a man ran up to him and fell on his knees before him. "Good teacher," he asked, "what must I do to inherit eternal life?"*

MARK 10:17

In Mark 10, we meet a man known as the Rich Young Ruler. He's a good man, a religious man, and he recognizes something unique in Jesus. He humbles himself and asks Jesus what he needs to do to inherit eternal life. That is not a typical question for a wealthy young person; his heart is bent toward God. He tells Jesus he has kept the commandments, and Jesus says, "Then you're only lacking one thing. You need to sell your things and follow me." It's the same invitation that Peter, James, and John received. But the young man went away saddened, because he was wealthy and thought the invitation was too costly. Did Jesus need his wealth? No. He was giving him an invitation to a life far beyond what his earthly riches could provide. The man was thoroughly invested in time and had a small imagination of eternity.

## PRAYER

Heavenly Father, I offer myself as a living sacrifice to You. You know my every need and see all of my tomorrows. Holy Spirit, show me how to be effective for You today. Help me to invest in things that will matter for eternity. In Jesus' name, amen.

# DAY 340

## MUCH LOVED CHILD

*Know that the LORD is God. It is he who made us, and we are his; we are his people, the sheep of his pasture. Enter his gates with thanksgiving and his courts with praise; give thanks to him and praise his name. For the LORD is good and his love endures forever; his faithfulness continues through all generations.*

### PSALM 100:3-5

This passage is a simple but wonderful reminder of the nature of God and why He deserves our love, our loyalty, and our praise. It says that God not only created us, He knows us by name—we are not just random combinations of DNA. It says the access code for the gates of God is thankfulness—and we should be thankful, because His love and goodness will endure forever. He always has been and always will be faithful—it is His very nature, and He can be no other way. On days when you are doubting God's love for you or His purposes for your life, read Psalm 100. Take comfort in knowing that you are a much-loved child of the God of the universe.

## PRAYER

Heavenly Father, thank You that You are my God. Thank You that I am unique among all Your created beings, with purposes You designed just for me. I praise You for all the ways You have blessed me and used me. Thank You for Your faithfulness to me. Lord, use me to extend Your Kingdom in the earth. In Jesus' name, amen.

## WATCH FOR IT

*"This happened so that the work of God might be displayed in his life."*

JOHN 9:3

Jesus and His disciples were walking through Jerusalem when they saw a man blind from birth. The disciples asked Jesus, "Who sinned, this man or his parents, that he was born blind?" These folks have been following Jesus for a while, but their questions show they still have a lot to learn. Jesus doesn't berate them. He simply says, "That's not the point. This happened so that people could see God at work in his life." I hope you have space in your faith journey to experience the work of God. I hope you are watching for it in the lives of others. We learn how to come to church, and when to sit and stand and sing along. But I'm not sure we always have room in our hearts for Him to act. Let's ask God to do something more than just give us theological studies or fun song services. Let's look for the works of God in our lives and in the lives of people around us. And when we see them, let's give Him the praise and honor He is due.

## PRAYER

Heavenly Father, how mighty are Your works! How great is Your mercy and love toward me! Thank You that You bestow good things on me, even though I am undeserving. Lord, let me see You at work around me, and I will give You all the praise. In Jesus' name, amen.

# DAY 342

## GOD WINS

*We have been made holy through the sacrifice of the body of Jesus Christ once for all.*

### HEBREWS 10:10

The last words of this verse are important: We have been made holy by the sacrifice of Jesus, the Messiah, "once for all." One time . . . for everyone. God's involvement in our lives is not arbitrary. Jesus paid the ultimate price that we might be justified before Almighty God. The redemptive work of Jesus is complete, entire, and irrevocable. There is nothing we can do to add to it or detract from it. Through His death on the cross and His resurrection, Jesus defeated every spirit, every principality and power, every dark and demonic thing that stands opposed to the will of God. There is still trouble in the world because His kingdom is not fully come. And it's through His Church, you and me, that His victory is being demonstrated in these days.

## PRAYER

Heavenly Father, thank You for being involved in my life. Thank You that through the death and resurrection of Jesus, the power of sin has been defeated in my life and I have been made holy and free. May my life demonstrate Your mighty power to save. In the name of Jesus, the Savior of the world, amen.

# DAY 343

## INVITATION TO TRUTH

*Listen to advice and accept instruction, and in the end you will be wise.*

PROVERBS 19:20

Conviction is when the Spirit of God shines His light into some aspect of your life and invites you to yield to Him more fully. It happens to all of us. And if the message makes us uncomfortable, we'll try to discredit the source. If a person is involved, he or she is a busybody. If it's a Scripture passage, it doesn't really apply to me. If it's a book I'm reading, it's a dumb book. If it's a sermon, it was a bad one. But if conviction is in play in your life, it is God inviting you toward truth that will bring you freedom. Don't defend your shortcoming or excuse it or say it's the way your family is or the result of your parenting or the choice somebody else made. Repent. Cooperate. Look for opportunities to grow as a Jesus-follower. Conviction is a great gift of the Holy Spirit, and it will bring good things to you.

## PRAYER

Heavenly Father, thank You for the wisdom You give me through the Scriptures and other believers who speak into my life. Holy Spirit, thank You for the light of conviction You shine on me, even when it makes me uncomfortable. I yield my thoughts, my words, and my actions to You, for I want to bring honor to You in all that I do. In Jesus' name, amen.

# DAY 344

## LONG TERM INVESTMENTS

*I know whom I have believed, and am convinced that he is able to guard what I have entrusted to him for that day.*

2 TIMOTHY 1:12

I hope you are putting money aside and investing it toward your future. But even the most carefully tended investments are subject to some things you have no control over—wars, weather, even the wisdom of fund managers. It's good to know there is one completely trustworthy place where you can invest that will never give you a diminishing return. Nothing you invest in God's Kingdom can ever be lost or even lose its value. And I don't primarily mean your money, though God certainly deserves a portion of that. I mean your time, your talent, your thoughts, your dreams, your heart—what you give your life to. Like Paul, let's give careful thought to how we plan for our future—our spiritual future—and invest in the things of God.

## PRAYER

Heavenly Father, Your Kingdom is the very definition of security—strong, safe, and unshakeable. Holy Spirit, show me how to invest my time, my talent, my thoughts and dreams in ways that serve Kingdom purposes. Show me how to live today with eternity in mind. In the name of Jesus, amen.

## HE CHANGES EVERYTHING

*"For God so loved the world that he gave his one and only Son, that whoever believes in him shall not perish but have eternal life."*

JOHN 3:16

A brief glance at the headlines on any given day will show that much of the world's conflict is because of religious differences. While followers of Islam and Judaism and Christianity agree that there is a God, Jesus is the One who makes the difference. You see, Jesus makes God personal. He brings a sense of moral responsibility because He was required to die for the sins of human beings. Through His death and resurrection He gives us His own righteousness and authority, and we can never afford to step away from Him. The greatest gift God will ever give to you and me is Jesus. He changes everything.

## PRAYER

Heavenly Father, thank You for the gift of Your Son. Open my eyes to see Jesus, not just as a character in my Bible but as a living Person who watches over my life. Help me to walk closer to Him every day and turn to Him when I face challenges and fears. Thank You for the eternal life I have through Him. It's in the redeeming name of Jesus that I pray, amen.

# DAY 346

## ACCEPTABLE ANSWER

*I trust in you, O LORD; I say, "You are my God." My times are in your hands.*

### PSALM 31:14-15

I'm a rational guy, but I have given myself permission to say "I don't know" about some things of God. People say, "Explain this Jesus to me." I reply, "Well, I'll tell you what I do know, and I'll tell you what He's done in my life. But there are a lot of things about Him that I won't know in my days in the earth." Learning to follow God is a challenge for all of us, but the realization that "I don't know" is an acceptable answer is a very powerful place. No matter what circumstances are swirling around you, believe that God wants the best for you. Place your days in His hands. Say, "I trust You, Lord, and I will follow You."

## PRAYER

Heavenly Father, I trust in Your unfailing love, in Your deliverance, and in Your plan for my life. I trust that You want the best for me and that You will see me through whatever challenges life has for me. My times are in Your hands, Lord. In Jesus' name, amen.

## OWN HIM

*"If anyone is ashamed of me and my words in this adulterous and sinful generation, the Son of Man will be ashamed of him when he comes in his Father's glory with the holy angels."*

MARK 8:38

One sure way to kill a conversation is to say, "I'm a pastor." It will take all the air out of the room. I used to play a little golf. One day we picked up a foursome, and one of the guys was from out of town. He had a very colorful vocabulary. He knew God, because he used His name a lot. We got to about the third tee box, and he said, "What do you do?" I admit it: I'd been waiting. I said, "I'm a pastor." He hit the ball in the woods and never did get his shot back. We'd better own Jesus, because there's a day coming when we're going to want Him to own us. Don't be condescending or critical or self-righteous, but be an advocate for Jesus. Just say, "You know, I believe in Jesus. He's my Lord."

## PRAYER

Heavenly Father, You are the Almighty God, Creator of everything. You sent Your Son, Jesus, to live among us and die for our sins. It is an honor to be a child of God, a Jesus-follower. May I never be ashamed of that but stand firmly for You, even when it seems uncomfortable. May Your Kingdom come. In the name of Jesus, my Lord, amen.

# DAY 348

## STANDING HERE AND NOW

*"Because of the increase of wickedness, the love of most will grow cold, but he who stands firm to the end will be saved."*

MATTHEW 24:12-13

Jesus is describing the wickedness of the season before He returns. The only way to experience His salvation, He says, is to remain committed to Him until the end, in spite of the wickedness. People get heated up about the end times. They say, "People have always said they're living in the end times. Do you think we are? How do you know?" The increased wickedness in the world makes me think we are approaching the end of the ages, but I don't know whether that means a year or ten years or a hundred years. But I can tell you this: As far as you and I are concerned, these are our last days. And if we're going to finish our time in the earth living out the purposes of God, we will be required to stand firm.

## PRAYER

Heavenly Father, give me a greater awareness of Your eternal Kingdom and a greater boldness to stand for Jesus in the here and now. May all who know me be able to see that I belong to You. Come quickly, Lord Jesus. It's in Your name I pray, amen.

# DAY 349

## WELL-PLACED HOPE

You are my refuge and my shield; I have put my hope in your word.

PSALM 119:114

Our culture is good at telling us that hope can be found in things. Television commercials tell me that this investment will secure my future, and this computer will make me a whiz in the office, and this pair of running shoes will make me an athlete. Perhaps you've put your hope in a house that was a money pit or even a job that wasn't the perfect fit you had hoped for. We've all placed our hope in things that proved to be a disappointment. Let's follow the psalmist's example and place our hope where we will not be disappointed: in our unchanging God and His unchanging Word.

## PRAYER

Heavenly Father, You have invited me to place my hope in You and Your Word. I am grateful that You are unchanging when so much around me seems to be changing. Your Word says that You have a plan for my good and not for my harm, and I choose to place my hope in You. In Jesus' name, amen.

# DAY 350

## CLIMB OVER THE DOUBT

*Then he said to Thomas, "Put your finger here; see my hands. Reach out your hand and put it into my side. Stop doubting and believe."*

JOHN 20:27

This is after Jesus' resurrection, and Thomas is having a hard time believing what he is seeing. "Stop doubting and believe," Jesus says. Thomas is not the only one who has to grapple with that statement. Each one of us has to decide whether we think His hands were pierced and His side was opened. We have to decide if we believe He is our resurrected Lord. We have to decide if the salvation He offers is real. And belief is more than a once-in-a-lifetime decision. There will be many times when God's Word or the Holy Spirit will place you at a crossroads and you will have to choose to believe or not believe. My advice is to climb over the doubt and say, "I choose to believe." Your life will be changed for good beyond anything you can imagine, both in time and in eternity.

## PRAYER

Father, thank You for the gift of Jesus. Holy Spirit, help me see Him as more than a character in the pages of my Bible, but as a living reality. Today, I choose to believe. Help my unbelief. I choose to lay aside my doubt, worry, and anxiety and to trust in Him completely. It's in the mighty name of Jesus I pray, amen.

# DAY 351

## OUTSIDE THE LINES

*The apostles and the brothers throughout Judea heard that the Gentiles also had received the word of God. So when Peter went up to Jerusalem, the circumcised believers criticized him and said, "You went into the house of uncircumcised men and ate with them."*

ACTS 11:1-3

God had sent Peter to Caesarea, a pagan city with a temple to a Roman god at its center. The events from the day of Pentecost were duplicated there, and the story of the Church forever changed. When Peter went back to give a report, the folks who had been at the very core of Jesus' ministry were unhappy with him because he'd gone outside the lines they had drawn. Peter assured them that what happened in Caesarea was due to the supernatural involvement of God. Is it possible that we too might still have room to grow in our imagination of how and where and when God might be at work? The reality is that none of us is fully formed spiritually. But the story of Scripture is that God will increase our understanding of His purposes if we will open our hearts and minds to cooperating with Him.

## PRAYER

Heavenly Father, I yield the strength of my life to You. In this generation, may Your Kingdom be expanded, the name of Jesus be lifted up, and the Church strengthened. Holy Spirit, open my eyes to see and my heart to understand where you are working and Your purposes for me. In Jesus' name, amen.

## CRY OUT

*This is what the Sovereign LORD showed me: The Sovereign LORD was calling for judgment by fire; it dried up the great deep and devoured the land. Then I cried out, "Sovereign LORD, I beg you, stop! How can Jacob survive? He is so small!" So the LORD relented.*

AMOS 7:4-6

Amos was a prophet God used to speak to his generation. God had decided to pour out judgment on the Israelites because of the condition of their hearts, and He revealed His intentions to Amos in a vision. Amos, when he saw that happening, had a choice. He could have said, "I agree. Wicked people. They're idolaters, they offer their children as sacrifices, they're greedy, they're immoral. They deserve it." But that's not what he did. He cried out to God for mercy, and God relented. It is tempting to complain about the condition of our nation, but what if we channeled that energy into asking God to be merciful on us and heal our land? As we see in this passage, God hears the cries of ordinary people like us. And who else will cry out to God but the people of God?

## PRAYER

Heavenly Father, we are a people in great need. You are a God of mercy and compassion, a God who restores and renews. Forgive our pride and rebellion and pour a spirit of humility and repentance upon us. May the fear of God wash over our hearts and minds. Our hope is in the name of our Lord. In Jesus' name I pray, amen.

# DAY 353

## OUR STRONG FOUNDATION

*"I will show you what he is like who comes to me and hears my words and puts them into practice. He is like a man building a house, who dug down deep and laid the foundation on rock. When a flood came, the torrent struck that house but could not shake it, because it was well built. But the one who hears my words and does not put them into practice is like a man who built a house on the ground without a foundation. The moment the torrent struck that house, it collapsed and its destruction was complete."*

LUKE 6:47-49

The foundation in this parable is Jesus. And He says that to build a stable life that will withstand the storms, we must accept the salvation that He offers and then live in a way that honors Him. The most important thing is not how our lives look; we all know how to build a life with a pretty façade. The most important thing is that our lives be built on the strong foundation of Jesus.

## PRAYER

Heavenly Father, thank You for the stability You bring to my life. Forgive me for the times I have been more concerned about the façade of my life than its foundation. Help me to build my life on the solid rock of Jesus. May all who know me see that He is my foundation. In His name I pray, amen.

# DAY 354

## THE NARROW ROAD

*"Enter through the narrow gate. For wide is the gate and broad is the road that leads to destruction, and many enter through it."*

MATTHEW 7:13

As Jesus-followers we are called to walk a pathway that is a little less conventional because of the character choices it requires. The best way to do that is to make pleasing God the overarching goal of your life. Open your calendar for tomorrow and look at the things that will occupy your day. Ask, "In the midst of those things, how might I please God?" We must intentionally choose to make some counterintuitive responses to life in order to walk His pathway and not drift along in the cultural mainstream. When your objective no longer is to look like most others look and choose what most others choose, you'll be in a place where you can more clearly see God's will and purposes for your life. And you'll demonstrate to all who know you that following Jesus is the best way to live.

## PRAYER

Heavenly Father, more than any other goal in life, I desire to please You. Holy Spirit, keep me on the narrow road so that my words and actions will demonstrate my allegiance to Almighty God. Refine my dreams and aspirations so that You are at the center of all of them, and I will glorify Your name. In Jesus' name, amen.

# DAY 355

## REFUGE IN THE SHADOW

*How priceless is your unfailing love! Both high and low among men find refuge in the shadow of your wings.*

PSALM 36:7

One of the most startling aspects of Scripture to me is the degree to which people—all people—matter to God. Scripture offers no explanation for it, just states it as fact. Our lives are filled with people, and for the most part we're pretty indifferent to them. I don't stop to connect and pray with every stranger who looks troubled. It's not that I dislike people; I've just got my own things to do. But God is not like me. He is moved by people's every care and concern. It's hard for me to really comprehend it, but the Creator of the universe not only knows us by name, He cares about everything that is going on in our lives. And when we are troubled, He wants us to run to Him for comfort.

## PRAYER

Heavenly Father, thank You for loving me in ways I cannot comprehend and caring about my every concern. Thank You for giving me refuge in the shadow of Your wings. Open my eyes to see all the ways Your love manifests itself in my life, Lord, and give me a grateful heart. May my life bring glory to Jesus Christ. In His name I pray, amen.

# DAY 356

## CELEBRATE THE GOOD

*Rejoice with those who rejoice; mourn with those who mourn.*

ROMANS 12:15

After many years of observing Christians, I'd have to say most of us are better at mourning than we are at rejoicing, even though we all experience more victories than losses. If our neighbors are going through a rough patch, we'll sympathize with them and pray for them and take them food—and we should. But if our neighbors are rejoicing over a victory, they're probably celebrating alone. Let's be as present in the victories as we are in the losses. Celebrating with others gives you an opportunity to thank God for His loving watch care over your life and to rejoice over His blessings on them too.

## PRAYER

Heavenly Father, I lift my heart to You in praise and thanksgiving. I thank You for the places where You've intervened on my behalf, the victories You've won for me, and the blessings You've given me. I rejoice in Your faithfulness. I give You glory and honor, because You are a faithful God. In Jesus' name, amen.

## DAY 357

## THE PERFECT WORD

*The law of the LORD is perfect, reviving the soul. The statutes of the LORD are trustworthy, making wise the simple. The precepts of the LORD are right, giving joy to the heart. The commands of the LORD are radiant, giving light to the eyes.*

PSALM 19:7-8

I want to be known as an advocate for God's Word, don't you? No other book ever has been or ever will be written that will add as much to our lives. It is "perfect," "trustworthy," "right," and "radiant." There are some simple things you can do to show people that you think the Bible is important. You don't have to climb on a soapbox and start waving it around. Just take it with you and don't say a word about it. Walk into a restaurant and lay it on the table. Leave it on your desk at work. Put one in your car. When someone comments on it—and they will—just say, "The Bible is important to me. There are some things about it I don't understand, but I'm working on it with God's help."

## PRAYER

Heavenly Father, thank You for Your Word, which is a lamp for my feet and a light for my path. Thank You that it is true and trustworthy for all people for all time. Give me a greater understanding of it, Lord, so I may walk closer to You every day. In Jesus' name, amen.

# DAY 358

## POWERLESS

*At just the right time, when we were still powerless,*
*Christ died for the ungodly.*

ROMANS 5:6

We don't like to think of ourselves as powerless. After all, humans can do some remarkable things. But we are the descendants of Adam, a race of rebels who are powerless to bridge the gap between ourselves and God. You don't have to teach us to be selfish or envious or critical because we're all hardwired that way. The prideful audacity of humanism suggests that if you give us enough education and time and cooperation, we'll solve the ills of humanity. It takes tremendous arrogance to think that after several millennia of civilization, when we still treat one another with unbelievable violence and hatred and cruelty, we can work this out. There are loud voices that deny our need for God, because it threatens their assertion that humans are innately good. The Church of Jesus Christ is the agency in the earth that holds the truth that we are powerless without Him. That's why you, with your voice for Jesus, are so valuable.

## PRAYER

Heavenly Father, I rejoice in Your great love for me. You have been patient and gentle, even when I have been selfish and rebellious. Today I choose to humble myself before You, to acknowledge my sin and to ask Your forgiveness. Jesus, I yield to You as Lord of my attitudes and actions. May Your Kingdom be lifted up in the earth. In Jesus' name, amen.

# DAY 359

## TAILOR-MADE GIFTS

*Do not be ashamed to testify about our Lord, or ashamed of me his prisoner. But join with me in suffering for the gospel, by the power of God.*

### 2 TIMOTHY 1:8

Would you want to go on a mission trip with Paul? Probably not—he caused riots and was beaten and spent a lot of time in jail. Yet we recognize that Paul was a tremendously effective advocate for Jesus, and his influence endures today. Paul recognized that God had given him unique gifts and abilities and opportunities. He knew that living out God's purposes for his life would not be easy, yet he never stopped going and never stopped talking about Jesus. God has purposes for your life too. He says, "Come! You are valuable to Me! I want to make your days under the sun meaningful and significant for all eternity." Keep honoring the Lord. His invitations to you are great gifts, tailor-made perfectly for you, and you will be blessed when you say yes to Him.

## PRAYER

Heavenly Father, I know that You have created me to accomplish the purposes You have for me during my days in the earth. Give me the passion and persistence of Paul, that I might say yes to You and push ahead even when I face obstacles. In the name of Jesus I pray, amen.

# DAY 360

## EXACT REPRESENTATION

*In the past God spoke to our forefathers through the prophets at many times and in various ways, but in these last days he has spoken to us by his Son. . . . The Son is the radiance of God's glory and the exact representation of his being, sustaining all things by his powerful word.*

HEBREWS 1:1-3

Because Jesus is the exact representation of His Father, the gospel narratives give us insight into God's attitude toward people. Watch as the events of Jesus' life unfold. Jesus didn't look at people and say, "Get out of my way. I've got important things to do." He encountered people with great needs and was moved with compassion—for a rich young ruler, a poor widow, a blind beggar, a promiscuous woman, a demon-possessed man, and many others. There are some things about God that will remain a mystery to us in this lifetime. But if you want to know more about the character of God the Father, just look at Jesus.

## PRAYER

Heavenly Father, thank You for the prophets who were faithful to speak Your message at Your time and in Your way. Thank You for the revelation of Yourself for me through Your Word and Your Son and Your Holy Spirit. You have shown compassion for me and invited me toward Your best, and I want to live with Your purposes in view. In Jesus' name, amen.

# DAY 361

## STANDING STRONG

*Then I heard the voice of the Lord saying, "Whom shall I send? And who will go for us?" And I said, "Here am I. Send me!"*

ISAIAH 6:8

God's people make such a difference in the earth! Just as God called Isaiah to stand and speak for Him in his generation, we are called to stand together for Jesus around the world today. I want to thank you for the place you take in your churches, serving and building God's Kingdom. I am grateful for the ways you stand for Him in your homes and neighborhoods and communities. I am thankful that you are not ashamed of your Jesus-stories, that your families and friends and coworkers know that you identify with Him. You have brought strength to our nations and freedoms to our lives and opportunities to our children. Let's lift each other in prayer, that we will be strengthened and multiplied and that God's Kingdom will be expanded.

## PRAYER

Heavenly Father, I pray that Your people will be multiplied exponentially around the world—men and women yielded to Your authority, gratefully bearing the name of Jesus and reflecting the values of Your Kingdom. It is a privilege to be a part of Your family across time and distance, Lord. May we be strengthened to carry out Your purposes until all have heard the name of Jesus. In His name I pray, amen.

# DAY 362

## OUR TRUE NORTH

*"For the Son of Man came to seek and to save what was lost."*

LUKE 19:10

Jesus came to earth to accomplish some very specific things, and one of them was to initiate a search-and-rescue mission. When you are lost, you have some sense of where you would like to be, you just don't know how to get there. All of us begin our God-journey at that point; we know we want to be more like Jesus, but we don't know how to get there. Jesus helps us navigate the path toward spiritual maturity. If you've ever used a compass, you know that it tells you just one thing: where north is. And when you know where north is, you can figure out other directions in relation to that. Jesus is like "north" on a compass; He is our guide point. As long as we continue to choose Him and orient our lives around Him, we'll be headed in the right direction.

## PRAYER

Heavenly Father, thank You for coming to rescue me. Thank You that You have set my feet on a path that honors You. Keep my course steady, Lord, with my eyes fixed on Jesus. In His name I pray, amen.

# DAY 363

## ON THE GUEST LIST

*Levi held a great banquet for Jesus at his house, and a large crowd of tax collectors and others were eating with them. But the Pharisees and the teachers of the law who belonged to their sect complained to his disciples, "Why do you eat and drink with tax collectors and 'sinners'?" Jesus answered them, "It is not the healthy who need a doctor, but the sick. I have not come to call the righteous, but sinners to repentance."*

### LUKE 5:29-32

Imagine that Jesus is going to be at your house for Sunday lunch. He says, "By the way, invite some of your friends." Who are you going to invite for Sunday lunch with Jesus? I suspect you would invite your most godly friends, wouldn't you? I think it's unlikely that you'd invite your pagan friends, but that's exactly what Levi did. He said to the pagans, "Come to my house. I want you to meet Jesus." The religious people were beside themselves with anger at having to share a meal with unrepentant sinners, but Jesus made it very clear that He was there to interact with the people who needed Him most.

## PRAYER

Heavenly Father, thank You for sending Jesus to interact with us, love us, and bring us into a right relationship with You. I want Your priorities to be my priorities, Lord, so keep my eyes focused on the wanderers of the world. In Jesus' name, amen.

# DAY 364

## NOTHING FORFEITED

*A faithful man will be richly blessed.*

PROVERBS 28:20

God has a plan for our good. I don't know why, but I find that many of us have a perpetual struggle to believe this. We have this nagging sense that if we say yes to God without reservation we will forfeit something good—pleasure or freedom or opportunity or resources. We believe that we will be rewarded in eternity, but for now we worry that we will be denied something. This is not a biblical idea. In fact, the consistent message of Scripture is that God rewards our faithfulness and our trust in Him. This has certainly proven true in my life. When I've been willing to cooperate with God—even when I feel like I've sacrificed something to do it—He's always given me something better in return.

## PRAYER

Heavenly Father, Your faithfulness is promised to Your people over all generations. I recognize my frailty and my need for a savior. Holy Spirit, direct my steps, and Father, please forgive my sins. I forgive those who have brought pain to my life. I choose to keep my eyes on Jesus. I accept Your invitations and say no to selfish indulgence. Today, I choose to become an encourager of those who are pursuing Almighty God. I want to honor You with my life and my resources. In Jesus' name, amen.

# DAY 365

## NO PAIN, NO GAIN

*Endure hardship as discipline; God is treating you as sons. For what son is not disciplined by his father? . . . We have all had human fathers who disciplined us and we respected them for it.*

HEBREWS 12:7, 9

My father believed in discipline. When I was in the midst of some disciplinary process, I never remember saying, "This feels so just and so appropriate. I want you to know how much I respect what you're doing." I respected it as I looked back on it later in my life, but I didn't respect it at the time. Discipline is never fun, whether we are children learning how to behave or adults learning how to relate to God. But we'll either be disciplined by God or we will forfeit the opportunities that are ahead of us, because we will need to be spiritually mature to thrive in the season to come, both as individuals and as the Church.

## PRAYER

Heavenly Father, help me to see when You are disciplining me as a child of God. Teach me to be still and know that You are God. I know that when I submit to You that You will be exalted in all the earth. I confess I often lose sight of You and become defensive. Instead, I long to let Your Holy Spirit turn my focus back to You as my Father. I know You care about me, and everything comes from Your loving hand. In Jesus' name, amen.

# NOTES

# NOTES

# NOTES

# NOTES

# NOTES

# NOTES

# NOTES

# NOTES

# NOTES

# NOTES

For more resources from Intend Ministries
and Pastor G. Allen Jackson, visit:
intendresources.com


To watch or listen to sermons from Pastor G. Allen Jackson and learn
more about his home church in Murfreesboro, Tennessee, visit:
wochurch.org

## About The Author

G. Allen Jackson is passionate about helping people become more fully devoted followers of Jesus Christ who "respond to God's invitations for their life."

He has served World Outreach Church since 1981, becoming senior pastor in 1989. Under his leadership, WOC has grown to a congregation of over 15,000 through outreach activities, community events and worship services designed to share the Gospel.

Pastor Jackson's challenging messages are broadcast via television and streamed over the Internet across the globe. He has spoken at pastors' conferences in the U.S. and abroad, and has been a featured speaker at the International Christian Embassy Jerusalem's Feast of Tabernacles celebration. Through Intend Ministries, Jackson coaches pastors around the world, writing and publishing small-group curriculum used in 34 states as well as Israel, Guatemala, the Philippines, Bermuda, Mexico, the United Kingdom, and South Africa.

With degrees from Oral Roberts University and Vanderbilt University, and additional studies at Gordon-Conwell Theological Seminary and Hebrew University of Jerusalem, Jackson is uniquely equipped to help people develop a love and understanding of God's Word.

Pastor Jackson's wife, Kathy, is an active participant in ministry at World Outreach Church.